Deadly Reunion

by

Linda Hope Lee

The Nina Foster Mystery Series
Book Three

Deadly Reunion

Cover Art by *Kim Mendoza*

The Wild Rose Press, Inc.
PO Box 708
Adams Basin, NY 14410-0708
Visit us at www.thewildrosepress.com

Publishing History
First Crimson Rose Edition, 2021
Trade Paperback ISBN 978-1-5092-3520-9
Digital ISBN 978-1-5092-3521-6

The Nina Foster Mystery Series, Book Three
Published in the United States of America

Balancing her plate on one hand and gripping her cup with the other, Nina followed Stephen under the canopy and down the center aisle dividing the tables. The noise level was high, and the air rang with talk and laughter.

A scream pierced the air. "Help! Help!" a woman shouted.

"That's Gloria!" Depositing his food at the end of a nearby table, Stephen ran ahead.

Nina added her plate and cup to his and hurried after him, soon reaching the site of the commotion.

Mark McTeague slumped over the table, his face buried in his food plate.

Her pulse racing, Nina followed close behind Stephen as he pushed through the crowd to join Gloria and Oren, who stood over Mark.

Oren grasped Mark's shoulders and shook him. "Come on, buddy."

Mark remained limp.

"What happened?" Frowning, Stephen laid a hand on Gloria's arm.

Gloria turned to Stephen and Nina, her eyes wide. "I don't know. We were eating, and he just all of a sudden fell over." She bit her lip and gestured toward Mark, still bent over the table.

Dedication

To Ted,
for introducing me to the beautiful state of Idaho

Chapter One

Nina Foster sipped her wine, enjoying the sweet, fruity flavor, and gazed around the crowded room, full of Parkers Landing High School alumni. Tonight's Meet-and-Greet, held at the Greystone Inn and Casino, was the first event of the school's All Class Reunion. She turned to Stephen Kraslow, a graduate of the Idaho school and the man responsible for her attendance. "So many people. I'll never remember everyone's name."

"That's why we have name tags." Stephen patted the plastic-encased tag pinned to his blue shirt's breast pocket. "I don't know everyone, either, since alums from the last fifteen years have been added since my class graduated. But relax and have a good time." He put his arm around her shoulders and gave her a hug. "Keep in mind, this trip is also the vacation we've looked forward to."

She favored him with a smile. "You're right. Thanks for the reminder." She and Stephen lived in Richmond, Washington, a small town north of Seattle, and had been in a relationship for the past year. Stephen's high school reunion in Parkers Landing provided the perfect opportunity for their first trip together. She also looked forward to meeting some of his old friends.

Someone tapped Stephen on the shoulder. "Hey, buddy."

Stephen turned and his eyes lighted. "Mark! I hoped you'd be here." He shook the man's outstretched hand. "When did you get into town?"

"A couple days ago. Good to see you. It's been awhile."

Stephen nodded. "Three years, at least. Did you fly up from Sacramento? Of course, you did."

Mark grinned and took a drink of his wine. "Flying's the only way to travel." His gaze moved to Nina. "Hello."

"Nina, meet Mark McTeague." Stephen gestured toward his friend. "Best quarterback in Parkers High history and ace pilot for the Air Force."

"Aw, quit bragging about me." Mark flashed Nina a wide smile and offered his hand.

"If I don't, I know you will." Stephen chuckled.

While studying the newcomer, Nina accepted Mark's firm handshake. He wasn't quite as tall as Stephen's six feet, but he was sturdily built with broad shoulders and muscular arms. His black hair glistened with styling gel, and a neatly trimmed beard defined his square jaw. "Are you still with the Air Force?"

Mark stepped back. "Not anymore. I'm still flying, though. Another alum, Oren Brown, and I own FlyGuys, a charter service. We're based in Sacramento, California."

"Speaking of Oren, is he coming to the reunion?" Stephen looked around. "And what about your wife, Gloria? Is she here?"

"They're here somewhere. Oh, there they are." Mark waved at an approaching couple.

Nina turned toward the arrivals. Gloria's shoulder-length red hair brought the word "flaming" to mind, and her black, pencil skirt and white blouse with a ruffled neckline set her apart from the more informally dressed attendees.

Wearing jeans and a Hawaiian print shirt, Oren Brown carried informality to the extreme. Like Mark, he sported a beard, but rather than neat, his was scraggly. Instead of wine, the group's favored drink, he held a can of beer.

After greeting the two, Stephen introduced Nina.

Oren looked at Stephen. "Heard you're in the newspaper biz now."

"Right." Stephen grinned. "I'm the proud owner of *The Richmond Review*."

Mark chuckled. "Editing the school newspaper cinched your profession, didn't it?"

"That and working part-time for Len at the *Post*."

"What do you do in Richmond, Nina?" Gloria smoothed a lock of hair from her forehead. "Do you work for Stephen?"

Sensing only politeness rather than genuine interest, Nina kept her reply brief. "I'm a librarian."

"Make that *managing* librarian." Stephen tucked an arm around her shoulders. "She runs the town's Seaview Library."

"How interesting." Gloria sipped her wine while looking over the rim of the glass at the rest of the room. "Oh, there's Harry and Margie Malone. Harry! Margie!" Smiling, she stood on tiptoes and waved a hand.

The Malones joined their group, which led to yet another round of introductions. Although Nina was interested in knowing Stephen's classmates, the sounds of clinking glasses, laughter, and talk, plus the unfamiliar topics, made following the conversation difficult. Stephen included her with comments and questions, and although she appreciated his thoughtfulness, eventually, she wanted to take a break. "I need a snack," she whispered in his ear and gestured across the room to the buffet table.

"Sure. Go for it." He smiled and turned back to his friends.

Nina left the group and made her way through the noisy crowd to the buffet table, decorated with crepe paper in the school colors of navy blue and gold. The offerings included the usual cheese-and-crackers, chips and dips, plus miniature, pastry-wrapped hot dogs and barbecued ribs. She filled a small paper plate and sampled the food, enjoying the rich pastry and tangy barbecue sauce.

Finished with her snacks, she looked around and saw Stephen still part of a group. Gloria, Mark, and Oren had moved on, but others took their places. She could join them, but the urge to explore captured her attention. Surely, Stephen wouldn't mind her absence a bit longer. She could visit the various gambling rooms across the hall but decided to wait until she and Stephen went together. The party room had a wall of glass beyond which was a deck facing the Kokuskie River, sparkling in the late afternoon sunshine. Fresh air might be a pleasant change from the crowded party. She pushed open the door and stepped outside.

Even though the day was at an end, the July air was still warm. Having shut out the noise of the party, she found the silence refreshing. Beyond a short expanse of lawn, the river flowed peacefully. On the opposite shore, homes nestled amid the evergreen and maple trees. To the left, a concrete bridge spanned the water, connecting the town with the highway leading to Canada, thirty-five miles to the north. Nina's research prior to the trip revealed Parkers Landing had a population of two thousand five hundred, quite a bit smaller than her hometown of Richmond.

Several other reunion guests were on the deck, too, sitting under umbrellas at wrought iron tables or standing at the railing looking at the view. As Nina passed by, several nodded and smiled. Appreciating their friendliness, she returned the gestures.

After strolling the length of the deck, stopping here and there to admire a boat navigating the river or a flock of flying birds, she decided to rejoin Stephen, or he might worry and come looking for her. First, though, she would visit the ladies room. Recalling a restrooms sign from earlier, she exited the deck through a different door. She found herself in a dimly lighted hallway, made all the more dark due to the bright light she'd experienced outside. Removed from all the activity of the casino and the party room, the hallway had an eerie feel that prompted Nina to hug her arms. She crept along, waiting for her eyes to adjust. She'd gone only a few paces when she heard voices.

"...Just give me the rest of the stuff..."

"Not until you..." Mumble, mumble.

"I'm warning you...you're a dead man, Mark McTeague..."

Nina gasped and stopped in her tracks. Mark? Stephen's friend? The other speaker's angry tone indicated the seriousness of the threat. The voice sounded like a man's, but with the distance between them she couldn't be sure.

She continued on, and as she neared her destination, the arguing escalated, with both voices sharper and more strident. She hesitated to intrude, but the narrow hallway offered no escape. Plus, she was curious. She rounded a corner, primed to interrupt and nearly bumped into Mark headed in the opposite direction. A scowl twisted his handsome features, and his hands balled into fists.

He squinted and leaned toward her. "Nina? Stephen's friend?"

"Yes. Looking for the restroom."

"That way." He pointed over a shoulder then brushed past.

Nina stared after him, wanting to ask if he was all right, but he already disappeared into the hallway's gloom. She turned and continued on her way. Expecting to encounter the other person, she kept an eye out, but the hallway was empty.

Finally, she reached the restroom and, a few minutes later, was on her way back to the party. She'd almost reached the spot where she encountered Mark when the toe of her shoe hit something.

The object skittered across the floor and clattered against the wall.

Did Mark drop something? She stopped to investigate and saw a small, square, red stone. She picked up the stone between thumb and forefinger. Was it from a piece of jewelry—a ring or a tie tack or a cufflink? Did it belong to Mark or to the person he argued with? She lacked the knowledge to determine whether the piece was glass or a valuable gem. Thinking to examine it more later, she slipped the stone into her purse.

Back at the party, she looked around for Stephen, expecting to find him still part of a group. Instead, he was with only one person, a woman. Since she faced Nina's direction, Nina had a chance to study her. Long blonde hair framed her heart-shaped face. A white jersey top and blue slacks showed off her shapely figure. She and Stephen laughed and leaned toward each other, as though on intimate terms. Was she a former girlfriend? He'd never mentioned anyone special from his high school days. She made her way through the crowd to join them. When she reached the two, she caught Stephen's gaze.

His eyes lighted. "Here you are. I was beginning to worry." He put an arm around her waist and drew her close. "Nina, I want you to meet an old friend, Angie Delaney." He gestured toward Angie. "Nina's from Richmond, too."

"Hello, Nina." Angie smiled and extended a hand.

"Nice to meet you, Angie." Nina accepted the handshake, if it could be called that, since Angie's fingers only grazed Nina's before she withdrew.

Angie's brow wrinkled, and she turned back to Stephen. "You didn't mention you were married."

Stephen's eyebrows rose. "We aren't. We're—"

"—Good friends." Nina wanted to prevent Stephen from divulging anything too personal about their relationship. Then she wondered if her remark sounded as though he were fair game. Perhaps he was, since she was the one who kept their relationship from moving past dating to a more permanent arrangement. The problem troubled her, but she'd been unable to change.

"Angie and I worked together on the school newspaper." Stephen drank his wine. "I was editor, and she was a reporter."

Angie waved a hand. "I wrote all the social news, like who wore what outfit to the dance and who went with whom."

Nina smiled to herself. Angie's admission as chronicler of the school's social scene didn't surprise her.

"We both turned our experiences into lifetime careers." Stephen stepped aside to let a group pass by. "Angie writes for a magazine in Denver."

With a flick of a wrist, Angie sent an errant lock of hair over her shoulder. "You're still in the newspaper business. I never thought you'd return to small town living, though. You always had your sights set on the big city."

"I had a taste of the city when Carly and I lived in New York. But after she passed, I didn't want to be there anymore..." His voice faded, and he looked away.

Nina gave Stephen's free hand a squeeze. She knew the sad story of his wife. Carly was a pediatric nurse who loved children. They'd wanted their own but hadn't been able to have any before she fell ill with cancer.

Just then, Oren Brown appeared. "We're headed for the dining room." He thumbed over his shoulder. "Why don't you join us? Afterward, we'll hit the slots."

"Sounds good." Stephen's expression brightened, and he looked at Nina. "What do you think, hon? Ready for dinner?"

"I am." Despite the snacks she'd eaten, she needed something more substantial to carry her through the evening.

Stephen gestured toward Angie. "How about you,

Ang? Are you here with anyone?"

"Sort of." She shrugged. "But he didn't come to the party, so I'll skip dinner and join him at my aunt's, where we're staying."

Angie's coy smile made Nina wonder why she was being so mysterious.

Then Angie sobered and raised a forefinger. "Don't forget our meeting tomorrow afternoon, Stephen. Two o'clock, in the park."

"Right. I'll be there." Stephen nodded.

Angie and Stephen were meeting tomorrow? What was that get-together about? Nina didn't have time to inquire, though, as she and Stephen followed Oren to the casino's dining room.

Like the room where the Meet-and-Greet was held, the restaurant had a glass wall facing the river. Tiered seating allowed all diners to enjoy the view. Dusk was fast approaching, and lights in the houses across the river shone through the trees. Up on the highway, auto headlights reflected off the asphalt.

Looking around the room, Nina spotted Judy and George Barlow, Stephen's older sister and brother-in-law, with whom she and Stephen were staying. Judy was five years ahead of Stephen in school, and she and George sat with a group of her classmates.

They waved to Nina and Stephen.

Oren led Nina and Stephen to a table where Mark and Gloria sat with several other couples.

Listening to the conversation swirling around her and joining in when she deemed appropriate, Nina thoroughly enjoyed her meal. The filet mignon was medium, just as she'd requested, and the baked potato and sautéed green beans and almonds proved perfect complements.

When dinner was over, Oren stroked his beard and looked around the group. "Who's ready to win some money?"

Stephen leaned toward Nina. "Okay if we pass, hon? We'll have plenty of time this trip to try our luck."

"Fine with me." The day had been long, and although she would like to experience the ambiance of the game rooms, she viewed gambling as a potentially dangerous activity.

"I hope you two will have better luck than this guy." Mark pointed a forefinger toward Oren. "He's breaking the bank. Our bank."

"Aw, shut up." Oren frowned at Mark. "I'll get lucky again. You wait and see."

Mark stuck out his jaw. "Knowing when to quit works better than luck."

Sudden tension between the two partners thickened the air. The others shifted in their seats and exchanged uncomfortable glances.

The conflict brought to mind the conversation Nina overheard in the hallway. Was Oren the person who threatened Mark?

"Come on, you two." Sitting between her husband and Oren, Gloria looked from one to the other. "No fighting at the reunion. You promised me a good time."

Mark's fierce expression softened. "Sorry, Glo. Got a lot on my mind. Yeah, here's to good times in Parkers Landing." He picked up his wine glass and held it aloft.

"Good times." Along with the others, Nina raised her glass. Although she hoped Mark's toast came true, she couldn't help her misgivings. One concerned Mark and the disturbing conversation in the casino's hallway. The other was about Stephen and Angie's meeting tomorrow. Why did she want to see him away from the reunion?

****

Later that evening, Nina sat with Stephen in the swing on the Barlows' front porch. The two-story colonial was built on a hill above the town, in an area reserved for the more affluent population. The property included a detached, four-car garage, enough large maple and elm trees for a small forest, and a path that wound through a flower and a vegetable garden.

Relishing Stephen's arm around her, Nina nestled against his shoulder. The air was cooler now, and the darkening sky revealed a sprinkling of stars. From the bushes bordering the porch, crickets chirped, and owls hidden in nearby trees occasionally hooted. In the town below, lights twinkled, with the red and yellow neon Greystone Inn and Casino sign dominating the landscape. Across the river, the hills rose vague and shadowy, while the road north disappeared into the darkened distance.

Judy and George hadn't yet returned from the party. Their sixteen-year-old twin sons, Rick and Blaine, were attending their own high school function, and ten-year-old daughter, Katie, spent the night with a friend.

"What do you think of our trip, so far?" Stephen broke the silence.

A smile spread across Nina's lips. "Your family is wonderful. They've been welcoming and gracious hosts. I enjoyed meeting your classmates tonight. Mark and Gloria and Oren." She named a few others. "Your

11

old girlfriend, Angie, was a surprise." Interested in his response to the term "old girlfriend," she slanted him a glance. His frown indicated she'd hit a nerve.

Stephen cleared his throat. "Like she said, we worked together on the school newspaper. I suppose you could call some of our times together 'dates.' "

"Uh huh. Like *I* said, 'old girlfriend.' " Sarcasm edged her voice.

"Don't you have old boyfriends?" One eyebrow peaked.

"None that have popped up, thankfully." Darren Johnson, the man she'd dated just prior to meeting Stephen, moved to Palm Springs.

Withdrawing his arm, Stephen shifted to face her, taking both her hands in his. "Look, Angie and I were only saying hello tonight. Nothing more was discussed."

Although he sounded sincere, Nina suspected Angie had more in mind than just a casual hello. "But you two have a date tomorrow afternoon. After the picnic lunch."

Stephen frowned and shook his head. "I don't know why she wants to see me, but I wouldn't call our meeting a date. Besides, you'll be with me."

"I could find something else to do. I don't want to intrude." They'd probably be discussing their high school days, and she'd have nothing to contribute.

"You won't be an intrusion. You and I are a couple, and I want you to share everything that happens here." Stephen pressed a foot to the porch floor and set the swing in motion. "We have a busy agenda. Tomorrow is the all class picnic at the county fairgrounds then my class's dinner at the Rusty Spur.

Sunday morning has another all class event, breakfast at the airport. Sunday night, the reunion ends with a downtown street dance. After that, we're on our own. We have the remainder of our vacation to explore the countryside, just the two of us."

Just the two of us. She caught the excitement in his voice. The promise sounded heavenly, as her Grandmother Jessica would say. "I have looked forward to this trip."

"Me, too. The first of many." Letting go her hands, he drew her back into his arms and kissed her.

She melted into him, lost in the warmth of his embrace and the promise of their special time together.

After a while, the Barlows returned. Rick and Blaine watched TV in the living room, while Judy and George joined Stephen and Nina on the porch to chat about the party and the classmates they met.

Only later, when Nina lay in bed, did she recall the argument she witnessed in the casino hallway. She'd meant to share the details with Stephen, but their discussion about Angie made her forget Mark's strange encounter. Tomorrow, she'd tell Stephen. Mark was a good friend, and if something troubled him, she was sure Stephen would want to know.

Chapter Two

The following morning, Nina awoke, rubbed her eyes, and checked the bedside clock. Eight, already. She'd better get moving. Today promised to be busy.

Tossing back the covers, she rolled out of bed and headed for her private bathroom. At home in Richmond, she and Stephen spent the weekends together, alternating between his house and her condo, but here at the Barlows', for the sake of propriety, they each had a separate room. Hers contained antique-style maple furniture that included a dresser topped with a mirror, as well as a comfortable chair and reading lamp. The double bed displayed a colorful quilt that Judy, an accomplished quilter, created.

After showering, she chose beige cotton slacks and a short-sleeved, brown and orange print blouse, since the day would undoubtedly be hot. She pulled her brown, shoulder-length hair into a ponytail and applied mascara and eye shadow to emphasize her wide-set blue eyes, which she considered her best feature. Grandmother Jessica told Nina she had her father's eyes, but she had no proof. Since her father left the family when she was only five years old, she didn't remember the man.

Nina opened her bedroom door to the sounds of voices, along with the aromas of eggs and bacon drifting up from downstairs. Breakfast preparation must be well underway. She descended the stairs and walked the long, carpeted hallway to the bright, sunny kitchen at the back of the house.

Judy stood at the stove, flipping pancakes in a skillet.

She looked casual and comfortable in a blue T-shirt, jeans, and flip-flops. With the same sandy-brown hair color and wide smiles, she and Stephen were easily identified as brother and sister.

Stephen and George sat at a round oak table in one corner, drinking coffee and talking. George, who was five years older than Judy, worked as the loan officer at Parkers First National Bank. His black-framed eyeglasses matched his dark hair with only a hint of gray at the sideburns.

Rick opened a bottle of maple syrup, while his twin, Blaine, took plates from a cupboard and stacked them on the counter.

The boys were not identical twins, and their lifestyles were different enough to make them easy for Nina to tell them apart. Rick, who worked at a local garage and rode a motorcycle, wore his dark hair long enough to graze his shoulders. Blaine, who was part of the restaurant staff at Greystone, kept his hair in a crew cut. Like his father, he wore eyeglasses.

The last member of the family, ten-year-old Katie, back from her sleepover, transferred silverware from a drawer to a tray. She had her mother's delicate features and brown hair, worn this morning in a thick braid. Her blue sleeveless blouse and shorts showed a summer tan acquired at day camp.

Stephen looked up and smiled. "There she is."

"Good morning, everyone." Nina placed hands on

her hips and gazed around the room. "Anything I can do to help?"

"No, everything's almost ready." Judy scooped pancakes onto a large oval plate. "Go join the guys." She nodded toward the table where the two men sat.

George pulled out a chair and patted the cushion-covered seat. "Yes, you're on vacation, Nina."

"All right." Nina slipped into the chair, vowing to arise earlier in the future so that she could be useful. "What are you two talking about?" She looked from one to the other.

George sipped his coffee. "I'm bringing Stephen up to date on the happenings around town. Not much to share, though. We're a pretty quiet place."

Stephen laughed. "Until we alums arrived."

George added his laugh to Stephen's. "You folks do add some excitement."

Katie approached carrying a tray of silverware and napkins.

Seeing an opportunity to participate in the meal preparation after all, Nina helped her set the table. She and Katie had already developed a rapport when Katie, an avid reader, learned Nina was a librarian.

Soon, they all were seated enjoying their eggs, bacon, and pancakes.

Not surprisingly, the reunion continued as the topic of conversation. Nina let the talk swirl around her as she enjoyed her food. A special treat was the huckleberry jam Judy made from local berries.

"Are we leaving you out with all our reunion talk, Nina?"

Judy's voice broke into her thoughts. Nina finished a bite of pancake. "No, not at all. I'm enjoying breakfast and just being here." She spoke the truth. Despite her misgivings about meeting Stephen's family, from the beginning she had felt at home with the Barlows.

"We're glad to have you visit." Judy added a spoonful of sugar to her coffee.

The talk resumed. Plans for traveling to the picnic, what car to take, what time to set out, and so forth.

Nina was spreading huckleberry jam on a second piece of toast when the name Mark McTeague caught her attention.

"How's your old buddy doing?" George asked Stephen.

Stephen frowned. "I don't know. He seemed kinda preoccupied last night at the party. Maybe the flying business isn't working out as well as he'd hoped."

"Or maybe his partner is causing problems." Judy poured syrup on a second helping of pancakes. "When Oren's in town, he spends a lot of time at Greystone playing the slots."

"I saw Oren and Al arguing last night after the party." Blaine turned to Nina. "Al Montega manages the casino. He and Oren were leaving his office when I got off work."

"Something's going on." Stephen set down his coffee cup and folded his arms. "I'll see what I can find out today at the picnic."

Now might be a good time to add what she overheard last night. Or would Mark's argument be appropriate for Katie to hear?

Just then, the doorbell rang.

Rick put down his fork and jumped up. "That'll be Cassie. We're taking a ride to check out the bike repairs we made."

"Cassie is Rick's girlfriend," George said in an aside to Nina. "She's as much a biker as he is."

After Rick left, the subject moved from motorcycles to cars, with George describing the new electric car they planned to purchase. The friend Katie would spend the day with arrived to pick her up. Then Nina helped Judy clean up the kitchen while George took Stephen outside to see the Barlows' vegetable garden. Judy and Nina joined the two men for a pleasant walk through their wooded property, with George acting as tour guide, pointing out various landmarks visible from their elevated location.

Nina had no opportunity to share her story about Mark. Still, she couldn't shake the feeling the incident had an important significance. Soon, the time arrived to attend the reunion's picnic lunch, held at the county fairgrounds on the outskirts of town. Nina and Stephen took his car, leaving the Barlows to pick up several of Judy's classmates. At the fairgrounds, after parking in the assigned lot, Nina and Stephen walked across the field, past an arena with a covered grandstand.

"I attended many a rodeo here." Stephen gestured toward the arena. "I even rode in a few."

Nina slanted him an admiring glance. "Really? So you have a cowboy background I didn't know about?" She loved learning new facts about him.

He grinned. "Uh huh. Someday, I'll show you the belt buckle I won."

Nina and Stephen continued on past half a dozen long, white exhibit buildings until they finally reached an open-air pavilion. Some attendees already sat at the long metal tables enjoying their food, while others stood in the nearby buffet line. Smoke curled from a barbecue pit, and the aroma of spicy sauce floated through the air.

"Look for Mark, Gloria, and Oren." Stephen stretched his neck to scan the seated people. "They're saving us a place."

"I see them." Nina pointed toward the trio sitting at a table several rows ahead.

Stephen placed a hand on her arm. "We'll get our food and join them."

The line for the buffet wound into the field. Nina and Stephen passed the time chatting with others and finally reached the food.

Blaine, wearing a long white apron and a chef's hat, stood by the barbecued selections. His eyes lighted when Nina and Stephen approached. "Hey, guys, help yourself. We got ribs, chicken, pork, you name it." He pointed a spatula at the different trays of steaming food.

"Did you help cook?" Nina studied the choices.

Blaine shook his head. "I'm just a kitchen slave. But someday, I'll wear this for real." He pointed toward his chef's hat.

"You've chosen a noble profession." Holding a pair of tongs, Nina selected a chicken drumstick and placed it on her plate. The salads came next, and then fruit, and soon her plate was piled high. "I'd better slow down," she told Stephen.

He chuckled and pointed toward his equally loaded plate. "Yeah, you'd think we hadn't eaten breakfast."

Nina and Stephen moved on to the drinks, where Rick presided over dispensers of lemonade, cola, and several flavors of soda. His long hair was pushed back behind his ears and held in place by a baseball cap.

"What'll ya have?" Rick plucked two paper cups from a nearby stack.

Nina surveyed the choices. "I'll take lemonade."

Rick filled a cup and held it out. "How about you, Uncle Stephen?"

"Cola." Stephen juggled his plate from one hand to the other, ready to accept the cup Rick filled. "Thanks, buddy."

Balancing her plate on one hand and gripping her cup with the other, Nina followed Stephen under the canopy and down the center aisle dividing the tables. The noise level was high, and the air rang with talk and laughter.

A scream pierced the air. "Help! Help!" a woman shouted.

"That's Gloria!" Depositing his food at the end of a nearby table, Stephen ran ahead.

Nina added her plate and cup to his and hurried after him, soon reaching the site of the commotion.

Mark McTeague slumped over the table, his face buried in his food plate.

Her pulse racing, Nina followed close behind Stephen as he pushed through the crowd to join Gloria and Oren, who stood over Mark.

Oren grasped Mark's shoulders and shook him. "Come on, buddy."

Mark remained limp.

"What happened?" Frowning, Stephen laid a hand on Gloria's arm.

Gloria turned to Stephen and Nina, her eyes wide. "I don't know. We were eating, and he just all of a sudden fell over." She bit her lip and gestured toward Mark, still bent over the table.

Fortunately, an aid car was on standby for the occasion, and the attendants hurried to Mark's side.

Along with the others, Nina stepped aside and allowed the medics to take charge.

They lifted Mark off the table, laid him on the ground, wiped the food from his face, and checked his vitals. One of the attendants talked to Oren and Gloria and others who witnessed Mark's collapse. Finally, the medics placed Mark on a gurney and wheeled him to the ambulance They soon drove off, siren blaring.

Oren put an arm around Gloria's shoulders. "I'll drive us to the hospital."

"We'll follow you." Stephen's brow wrinkled as he grasped Gloria's hand. "I'm praying he'll be okay."

"I'll be praying, too." Sensing Gloria's anguish, Nina patted the woman's shoulder.

"Thank you." Gloria's voice was barely a whisper, and her eyes were bleak.

Hand in hand, Nina and Stephen hurried across the field, past the exhibit buildings and the arena, to Stephen's car. Once inside, Nina sat rigid in the passenger's seat, numb with shock. "What could have happened?"

His mouth a grim line, Stephen started the engine and bent over the steering wheel. "I don't know. He seemed okay last night. He didn't say he wasn't feeling well."

Nina recalled Mark's scowl and fisted hands when she encountered him in the casino hallway, but now wasn't the time to bring up that incident. As she'd promised Gloria, she concentrated on praying for Mark and his recovery.

At the hospital, Stephen parked in the visitors' lot

near the Emergency Room.

Inside the facility, Nina looked around for Gloria and Oren. Not seeing them, she assumed they were allowed to accompany Mark to a treatment room.

Stephen checked in at the desk and then led Nina to the rows of chairs facing a wall-mounted TV. The low volume blended with the sounds of people talking and the door opening and closing as new patients arrived. As she and Stephen waited, neither saying much, Nina's tension grew. She twisted her hands together and shifted in the hard plastic seat, unable to find a comfortable position. They waited for what seemed hours but, by the wall clock, was only thirty minutes.

Finally, Gloria and Oren pushed through the double doors leading to the treatment rooms.

Gloria's face was pale, a sharp contrast to her red hair. Tears streamed down her cheeks.

Oren's thin shoulders slumped, and his mouth was a tight line.

Oh, oh, this situation doesn't look good. Nina pressed a hand to her tense stomach. She glanced at Stephen and saw by his furrowed brow that he, too, feared for his friend.

Stephen jumped up and faced Gloria and Oren. "How is Mark?"

Oren shook his head. "Mark is dead."

"Dead…" Stephen's forehead wrinkled. "No, not Mark…"

Nina put an arm around him. "Oh, Stephen…your friend. I'm so sorry."

Later, when Nina and Stephen returned home to the Barlow house, they sat together on the front porch. After the trauma of Mark's death, the peaceful setting, with the Kokuskie River sparkling in the sunlight and framed by the distant mountains, offered solace to her troubled spirits.

Still, the events of the morning lingered, creating not only sadness but also questions. She hadn't learned much about Mark's death, only that he was alive when taken to the hospital. Once there, he lapsed into unconsciousness and subsequently died. An autopsy would reveal the cause, but Nina had no idea how long that would take or if the family would share the results.

Needing to give voice to her worries, she turned to Stephen. "What will Gloria and Oren do now?" She thought especially of Gloria. How tragic to lose one's mate.

Stephen shook his head. "I don't know what they'll decide about FlyGuys, but if they have a memorial for Mark, I want to be there." His phone buzzed. "This call might be from Gloria. I asked her to keep me informed." He pulled his phone from his shirt pocket and looked at the screen. "Oh, hell." His lips twisted.

Nina tensed. "What?"

Stephen tapped the phone's screen with a forefinger. "Angie. I forgot all about meeting her this afternoon."

Nina wrinkled her brow. The appointment had slipped her mind, too. "I can't imagine she'll insist on getting together under the circumstances—unless she doesn't know about Mark."

"She knows. Here's her text." He handed her the phone.

Nina read the message aloud. " 'Shocking about Mark but must see u. Very important.' " Wondering what could be so crucial, she handed back the phone.

"Are you planning to meet her?"

He shrugged. "I suppose I'd better."

She turned away and gazed absently at the view. "I don't have to go with you…" Uncertainty filled her. She truly didn't know what to do in this situation. While she wanted to support him, she also worried her presence would be intrusive.

"I hope you will." He reached for her hand and stroked a finger along her palm. "I've already told you I want you to come."

Nina bit her lip. "Well…all right." Still, misgivings kept her tense during the ride into town. What could this mysterious meeting possibly be about?

The park Angie chose was adjacent to the town's public library. Gazing at the white stone building shaded by towering maple trees calmed Nina. If she became too uncomfortable during Stephen and Angie's visit, she now had a place to escape.

Stephen parked the car and led them along a path that wound through the area.

Cement benches and wooden carvings of animals such as bear, deer, and fox decorated the landscape. Water from a fountain cooled the air. Nina scanned the people they passed but didn't see Angie.

"Over here, Stephen," someone called.

Nina spotted Angie sitting on a bench by a group of birch trees. But she wasn't alone. A teenaged boy sat beside her. Shaded by the trees, at first he hadn't been visible. Who was he? As she and Stephen approached, a burst of sunlight brought the boy's features into focus. He looked familiar. She glanced at Stephen and then again at the boy. They both had the same sandy brown shade of hair, the same straight nose and firm jaw…

Her heart flip-flopped.

Nina and Stephen reached the two. Nina held her breath and pressed a hand to her stomach, afraid of what would happen next, yet powerless to stop what she now feared was Angie's purpose.

"Hey, Angie..." Stephen's voice trailed off as he turned to the teen.

Angie stood and, a smile on her lips, gestured to her companion. "Stephen, meet your son, David."

Chapter Three

Although Nina sensed what was coming, now that her fears were confirmed, she froze. Then she turned to Stephen to learn his reaction.

Eyes wide, he stared at David.

Angie laid a hand on the boy's shoulder. "Stand up, David. Shake hands with your father."

David shuffled to his feet and extended a hand. "Hello, uh, sir."

"Hello, David." Stephen shook David's hand and then turned to Nina. "This is my friend, Nina Foster."

Impressed with Stephen's quick recovery, Nina forced a smile. "Hello, David."

"Pleased to meetcha." David matched her smile as they shook hands.

Angie gestured from David to Stephen. "I decided the all class reunion would be the perfect occasion for you two to meet."

The woman's disregard for the feelings of both David and Stephen churned Nina's stomach. Was a meeting in a public park really the best way to introduce a father and son for the first time? David didn't appear surprised, so he'd been prepared, but judging by Stephen's wide-eyed expression, he'd no clue he was the father of a teenager.

Stephen stepped back and eyed Angie. "We need to talk." He tipped his head toward David.

"Aw, I've heard all about you." David folded his arms and lifted his chin.

Not wanting to hear Angie's and Stephen's conversation, she turned to the teen. "David, have you been to the library?" She gestured over her shoulder toward the building.

David shifted his gaze to Nina and shrugged. "Uh huh. I went the other day."

"Well, I haven't had a chance yet. I'm a librarian."

"You are? Cool."

The faint smile and flicker of interest in his eyes encouraged her. "Yes, and libraries are always of special interest. Since you've been to this one, how about giving me a tour while your mom and Stephen catch up?"

"Okay."

Stephen held out a hand. "Nina—"

"We'll be back soon." Confident her idea to allow Stephen and Angie time alone was a good choice, Nina cut off what she guessed would be Stephen's protest and fell into step with David. "Have you been to Parkers Landing before?" Comfortable around teens from her work at the library, she hoped small talk would ease the situation, if not for him, at least for her. He appeared so calm, while her nerves still thrummed from Angie's shocking news.

"This trip is my first. I've heard a lot about the place, though. Seems like a nice town, if you like small towns."

"I do. Richmond, where Stephen and I live, is bigger in population than Parkers Landing." Nina kept pace with David as he rounded a curve in the path.

"Yeah, I know." David waved a hand. "I heard all

about that place, too."

As Nina guessed, David had been well prepared for today's meeting. Too bad Angie hadn't given Stephen the same opportunity. Perhaps she'd feared advance notice of such a surprising revelation would result in Stephen's refusal to participate. If so, then she didn't know Stephen very well. If he were David's father, he would never reject the boy.

Reaching the building, Nina and David climbed the steps and entered the plate glass front door. Once inside, Nina took a deep breath and shifted her focus to her surroundings. Already, her tension eased. Here, order reigned, and order always gave her comfort. Today's visit wasn't how she planned to experience the town's library, but she'd make the best of what turned out to be an awkward, not to say shocking, situation.

"That area's for kids." David pointed toward an alcove with low shelving, child-size tables and chairs, and posters of children's books decorating the walls. From there, he led Nina around the rest of the facility, stopping to explore each special area.

Along the way, she learned he was fifteen and a sophomore in high school. "Do you like to read fiction?"

David picked up a book on display and turned the pages. "I do. Sci-fi, mostly."

Nina leaned an elbow on the top of the shelf. "Have you read *Moon Madness* by John Darma? He writes about colonizing the moon. I just bought the book for our library at home."

David replaced the displayed book. "No, I haven't heard of it." He pulled his phone from a back pocket and tapped the screen. His thumbs flew over the keyboard. "Okay, the book's on my list. I'll take a look when I get a chance."

Nina and David explored the various areas, including the row of computers where patrons sat engaged in research. The tour ended near a window. She gazed out at the park, zeroing in on the bench where Stephen and Angie sat. They appeared deep in conversation, with Angie gesturing and Stephen leaning close. Nina turned toward David. "Meeting your birth father must be a shock."

He replaced his phone in his jeans pocket and shrugged. "Not really. Like I said, I've heard all about him."

Leaning on the windowsill, Nina shifted her gaze from Angie and Stephen to one of the paths, tracing its route until it disappeared around a bend. "Are you looking forward to knowing him?"

"Getting acquainted probably won't happen. Even if he hangs around, he'll eventually leave, just like Ernie and Bill left.

Having been abandoned by her father, Nina could relate. Still, knowing Stephen to be an honorable man, she needed to speak positively about him. "But Stephen's your birth father. I bet that relationship will make a difference."

He wrinkled his nose. "My friend Josie found her birth father through one of those DNA services. He wouldn't even talk to her on the phone."

"Stephen's different." Nina gestured toward where he and Angie still conversed. "You'll see." She hoped she spoke the truth. Already, in addition to feeling sorry for him, she liked David. But what would happen if she was wrong and, like her father had left her, Stephen rejected his son?

****

Returning to the Barlows' after meeting Angie and David, Nina and Stephen retreated to the front porch, which had already become a favorite spot.

Stephen stood at the railing.

Nina chose the swing. In the distance, the Kokuskie River sparkled under the afternoon sun, and a soft breeze cooled the air.

"What a day." Stephen slapped a hand to his forehead. "First, I lose a good friend, and then, I find out I'm a father. I feel like I've been hit by a truck."

"Today has been rough." Nina sighed and hugged her arms. She'd envisioned Stephen's high school reunion as a joyful experience, but already, after only two events, both tragedy and shock spoiled her expectations.

Stephen faced her. "I honestly hadn't a clue about David—well, I mean, in high school, Angie and I did, ah—"

"Never mind." She waved a hand to stop the rest of his explanation. "Spare me the details."

He planted both hands on his hips and paced the floor. "Okay, after graduation, I went off to college, and she moved to Denver to live with her aunt."

Nina wrinkled her brow. "Why didn't she tell you she was pregnant?"

"She kept quiet because she didn't want to tie me down. She knew I wanted to go to college. In Denver, she married a guy named Ernie. She met and dated him when she visited. But you know what I think?" Stephen stopped pacing and turned toward her. "She wanted to marry him instead of me all along. He was older and had money, and after the baby came, he put her through college."

Although Nina didn't know Angie well, from what she had seen so far, she couldn't discount Stephen's explanation. She folded her arms. "Did Ernie think he was David's biological father?"

"No, but he said he'd raise the child as his own. The marriage didn't last, though, and they divorced. Then she married another guy."

"Bill." Had Angie divorced because she still loved Stephen?

His eyebrows peaked. "Yeah. How'd you know?"

"David told me." At his frown, she shook her head. "I didn't press him for information. He volunteered. But as for you being David's biological father, shouldn't you two have a DNA test to confirm your paternity?"

Stephen rubbed his chin. "I suppose, but our relationship is obvious. Don't you agree?"

"You do resemble each other. I'd say, yes, you are father and son. But taking the test is still a good idea for legal reasons." She sat back and set the swing in motion while phrasing her next question. "What does Angie want from you now? Does she expect you two to get back together and finish raising David?" Having voiced her worst fear, Nina stiffened and held her breath.

"Doesn't matter what she wants." Stephen frowned. "Being with her again will not happen."

Although his firm tone reassured her, she recalled what he'd told her about his marriage. "You and Carly wanted a family."

"I know, and we tried, then she got sick… But now that I've met you…"

She looked away, her stomach again in knots.

Marriage and children were sore subjects between them. Her father's abandonment and her mother's preoccupation with her real estate career, which Nina considered abandonment as well, left her leery of both marriage and motherhood. She gripped the chain holding the swing. "Stephen, you know I can't—"

His brow wrinkled, and he held up a hand. "Never mind. We don't need to discuss our situation now."

Nina breathed a sigh of relief, but then, wondering how a teenage boy would fit in with their life in Richmond, she tensed again. "What will you do—about David?"

"I'll accept him as my son, spend time with him, and get to know him. I hope you'll join me?"

Hearing the uncertainty in his question, Nina made her tone firm. "You have my support, Stephen. You know that." Nina meant what she said, but she wasn't sure about trusting Angie. Did she only want father and son to get to know one another? Or did she see herself as an important part of the picture?

Silence fell. Stephen stopped pacing and again stood at the porch railing.

Nina, too, contemplated the view, settling her sights on the river, hoping the peacefully flowing water would calm her. But too much had happened, and her thoughts tumbled one over the other. The sudden appearance of David...the collapse and death of Mark...

Mark. She still hadn't told Stephen about the ominous conversation she overheard at the Meet-and-Greet. But was now the time? She bit her lip, considering. Stephen's voice broke into her thoughts, and she looked up to see him facing her.

"What's bothering you, Nina? Something else about David and me?"

"No, I was thinking about Mark and a conversation I overheard last night at the party. I've been meaning to tell you…but now probably isn't a good time. You have a lot to deal with."

"I do, but I've been thinking about Mark, too, so tell me." He crossed the porch and sat beside her.

She took a deep breath. "Okay, last night at the casino, when I went to the restroom…" Stephen kept his gaze on her while she repeated her experience.

"You didn't see either person while they were talking?" he asked when she'd finished.

"Both were out of sight, and I couldn't tell whether the second person was a man or a woman. The voice was deep, but some women have lower register voices."

He leaned closer. "But you heard the words clearly."

"Yes. The second person said, 'Just give me the rest of the stuff,' and then, 'You're a dead man, Mark McTeague.' "

Stephen frowned. "Could the person have been joking?"

"I don't think so. The voice sounded serious—and menacing." Nina hugged her arms. "When Mark appeared, he was upset and in a hurry. Oh, and after he left, I found something on the floor." Reaching into her jacket pocket, she pulled out the red stone. She'd kept it to have handy when she finally told Stephen about her experience. Placing the stone in her palm, she held it out.

He took the gem between thumb and forefinger and held it up to the sunlight. "You think this stone relates

33

to Mark and whoever?"

"I don't know. But it might be a clue."

"A clue." His eyes narrowed. "What are you thinking, Nina? Although I can probably guess."

Nina straightened, her heart pumping hard. "What if Mark didn't die from natural causes? What if the person who threatened him at the casino murdered him?"

Shaking his head, he returned the stone and placed a hand on her shoulder. "Aren't you jumping to conclusions before all the facts are known? I know you like a mystery, but—"

"I'm just saying, 'What if?' " She turned up both hands.

"Then the authorities need to pursue the crime." He made a dismissive wave. "You aren't involved, Nina."

"But I *am* involved. I overheard something that may be important." Nina set her jaw.

"*If* there was a crime."

Folding her arms, she looked away. "I shouldn't have told you."

"I'm glad you did. You know I would have done the same." He stretched an arm around her shoulders.

Encouraged by his gesture and gentle tone, she sighed and leaned into him. "What do you think?"

"I want to believe Mark died of natural causes, but as a reporter, I know better than to form conclusions before learning all the facts. But that reasoning doesn't mean I want you searching for a murderer."

Why? She'd had a good success rate. "I never said I'd become that involved."

He laughed. "You didn't have to. I know you, Nina. If a mystery's in the air, you won't rest until you solve it. True, you have helped to solve a couple crimes. But maybe in this case, you could—"

"Back off? Forget about what I overheard? I don't know if I can without at least telling the authorities."

Stephen slowly shook his head. "Somehow, I knew that step would be your next."

Nina let a few moments elapse while enjoying the breeze rustling the leaves of nearby maple trees. The sun sank lower in the sky, spreading a glow behind the distant mountains. "Do you know anyone on the police force? If not, I can contact them on my own."

Stephen looked away. Several moments passed before he spoke. "Okay, I have a plan. The police chief, Cal Donovan, was in my graduating class. If he's at our class dinner tonight, I'll introduce you. You'll make an appointment to go to the precinct and tell him your concerns."

"I'd appreciate an introduction. Oh, Stephen, I feel better already. Thank you." She planted a kiss on his cheek.

"You're welcome." He brushed a lock of hair from her forehead and trailed his fingers along her cheek. "But I hope a talk with Cal will be the end of your involvement."

Voices sounded from inside the house. Nina turned to see Judy and George step through the door. Judy appeared cool and casual in a sleeveless T-top, slacks, and flip-flops. George, who never seemed to lose his bank manager persona even when off the job, wore a white shirt and neatly pressed blue slacks.

"Here you are." Judy crossed the porch and sank into a wicker chair. "We heard the news about Mark. So sad." Her mouth turned down.

"Do you know what caused his death?" George eased into the chair next to his wife's.

Stephen's glance at Nina signaled caution. She gave a slight nod to indicate she understood and would keep their previous discussion to herself.

Stephen turned back toward Judy and George. "No official word, yet, but in the meantime, I have something else to tell you..." When he finished his story, he looked from one to the other. "You can imagine how shocked I was."

Judy clasped her hands and leaned forward. "Yes. We heard about Angie's marriage and baby, but no one ever thought the man she married in Denver might not be the child's father."

"Are you sure he's yours, Stephen?"

George's question told Nina she had an ally regarding Stephen's paternity.

Stephen nodded. "I'll find out for sure through DNA testing, but my gut feeling tells me, yes, he's my son. I plan to spend time with him while I'm here."

"If you like, we'll introduce him to the family." Judy looked at George and received a nod. "Rick and Blaine will accept him, I'm sure. Katie will, too."

"Having a new cousin will be a treat." George patted Judy's hand. "The nearest cousins are my sister's kids who live in Atlanta, and we don't see them often."

Stephen ran a hand across his brow. "Thanks, you two. I appreciate your support. I don't know what will happen in the future. We're in uncharted territory, as the saying goes, but with your help—and Nina's"—he gave her a hug—"David and I will get to know each other."

Despite her misgivings about the role Angie would

play in Stephen and David's relationship, Nina vowed to do her best where the young man was concerned. She liked working with teenagers. No reason she couldn't adapt to David. They'd gotten along well today while exploring the library. Still, what would happen in the days to come worried her.

Switching her thoughts to Mark didn't help. His sudden death plus the earlier conflict between him and his mysterious associate at the casino posed another dilemma. Would she voice her concerns to Cal Donovan and then forget the matter, as Stephen hoped? Or was she already involved in something that would grow to greater—and more dangerous—proportions?

Chapter Four

That evening, at the Rusty Spur Bar and Grill, Nina saw that tonight's party was to some extent a repeat of last night's Meet-and-Greet. Still, differences were apparent. This group, for just the members of Stephen's graduating class, of course was much smaller than the previous evening's assemblage. The venue was a contrast, as well. Instead of the glitzy casino with its view of the Kokuskie River, the Rusty Spur, located on the corner of First and Main in downtown Parkers Landing, offered dark walls decorated with spurs, coiled lariats, and cowboy hats.

Nor was Nina quite the stranger she'd been at the initial party. As she sipped her wine and gazed around, she saw several familiar faces. Gloria and Oren were absent, which was not surprising given what happened at the picnic lunch. Nina expected Angie to attend, but so far, she hadn't made an appearance. Although Nina wasn't particularly sorry, she hoped the woman hadn't stayed away on her account.

Uppermost on her mind was meeting Stephen's classmate and local police chief, Cal Donovan, and making an appointment. She had just decided to search him out when Stephen headed toward her with a man in tow.

"Nina, this is Cal Donovan." Stephen gestured toward his associate. "Cal, meet Nina Foster."

"Pleased to meet you, Nina." Cal nodded and held out his right hand.

Nina accepted the handshake. "Nice to meet you, too." Cal conformed to Nina's idea of a lawman. Sturdily built, he had chiseled features that included a prominent nose and a well-defined jaw. His short-sleeved shirt revealed a dragon tattoo curled around each muscular shoulder. Nina chatted with the two men for a few minutes about the reunion.

Then Cal leaned toward Nina. "Stephen says you want to tell me something about Mark."

Nina nodded. "Last night at the Meet-and-Greet, I overheard a disturbing conversation between him and someone whose voice I didn't recognize. I'd like to come to your office tomorrow and tell you what I witnessed."

Cal frowned. "I have a busy schedule tomorrow. Why don't you tell me now? At least, give me the basics."

"Well…" Nina glanced around, not sure a noisy party was the best place to share her experience. Then she looked toward Stephen.

He shrugged. "Why not?"

"All right." Nina launched into her story. Two interruptions occurred.

Both Cal and Stephen took time to exchange greetings and small talk with classmates.

Nina finally reached the main part of her narrative and took a deep breath. "Then I heard the second person say, 'You're a dead man, Mark McTeague.' I couldn't hear Mark's reply, but when he passed me, his face was contorted and his hands balled into fists."

"Are you saying you think he was murdered?" Cal

sipped his beer, gazing at Nina over the rim of the glass.

A woman appeared at Cal's side. "Murdered? Who?"

Another interruption. Nina heaved an inward sigh. Would the information she hoped to keep private now spread?

"Hey, honey." Cal smiled and put an arm around the woman's shoulders. "Nina, meet my wife, Becky."

Becky offered Nina her hand. "Hello, Nina."

"Hi, Becky." Nina shook the newcomer's hand. She stood barely as tall as her husband's shoulder, but she exuded energy and, like her husband, had sharp eyes Nina would guess didn't miss much.

Cal turned toward Stephen. "You remember this lady, don't you?"

"Sure do." Stephen nodded. "We had English Comp together. You still writing, Becky?"

Becky grimaced. "With three kids? Yeah, grocery lists and notes to teachers." She gave her husband a soft poke on the shoulder. "I want to hear about the murder."

Cal took another sip of his beer. "Nina overheard someone threaten Mark last night at the casino."

"Really? Who?" Becky's eyes widened as she focused again on Nina.

"I don't know." Nina raised a hand. "I don't want to start any rumors, but I wanted to let the authorities know, just in case…"

"Authorities." Becky's laughter rang out. "Is that what you are, Cal? An authority?"

"Darn right." Cal grinned and gave his wife a hug. Then he turned back to Nina. "You were sayin'—

before my lovely wife interrupted?"

"I never saw the other person. But—"

A loud clanging drowned out the rest of her sentence. A server dressed in a cowgirl outfit entered the room. She held a string dangling a piece of tin in one hand and a wooden baton in the other. "Soup's on! Come and get it!" Again, she hit the tin shield and then pointed her baton toward the buffet table where similarly attired servers placed dishes of food.

The aromas of barbecue and fried potatoes filled the air, making Nina's mouth water.

"C'mon, folks. Time to eat." Cal grasped Becky's elbow and led her toward the line quickly forming at the table.

"I could come to your office—" Disappointed in Cal's lack of interest in her news, Nina followed the retreating couple.

"Good idea." Cal glanced over his shoulder. "But not tomorrow."

Nina and Stephen followed Cal and Becky to the buffet line. Having missed the picnic lunch and only snacked during the afternoon, Nina was especially hungry. Barbecued ribs, baked beans, cornbread, vegetable trays, fresh fruit, and huckleberry pie beckoned. Plates filled, she and Stephen sat at the opposite end of a table from Cal and Becky, which prevented continuing their conversation. Not that Nina would, with so many others close by.

Midway through dinner, a man stepped to the microphone and welcomed all the classmates and their guests. "We are missing Mark McTeague tonight and extend our sympathy to Gloria and Oren, and to their families. I understand plans for a service are pending, and they will let us know when the information is available."

After dinner, the classmates gathered for a photo and then stood talking in small groups. Nina hoped to find Cal alone so that she might finish their discussion, but he appeared occupied with others, never casting a glance her way.

At last, she and Stephen were in his car heading back to the Barlows'. Nina gazed out the window at the moonlight beaming on the distant hills. As far as she was concerned, Stephen's plan to connect her with Cal Donovan fizzled. While he didn't give her a total brush-off, he didn't appear particularly interested in her information, either. Quite a contrast to the detectives back home that she assisted on two other murder cases.

Anxious to have his opinion, she turned to Stephen. "I don't think Cal took my experience seriously. What do you think?"

Stephen steered the car around a corner to the road leading up the hill. "He comes across as laid-back, but he's sharp. He'll give what you said serious thought. You can still make a formal statement at the station tomorrow, too."

"I don't know what good an appointment would do now." She made a dismissive wave. "I just hope I didn't start any rumors."

"Hmm, me, too. As I recall, Becky does like to talk."

Nina wrinkled her forehead. "But, Stephen, if Mark was murdered, you'd like to see his killer caught, wouldn't you?"

"Darn right, I would!" Stephen pounded a fist on the steering wheel. Then he cast her a frown. "But that doesn't mean I want you involved."

Biting her lip, Nina looked away. Although not wanting to contradict Stephen, she knew she already was involved. What she didn't know was where her involvement would lead.

****

"If I eat one more pancake, I'll explode." Nina put down her fork and sat back in her chair. She and Stephen attended the Sunday Pancake Breakfast, held at the county airport. Unlike the class dinner of the previous evening, this event involved all reunion attendees with long tables accommodating the crowd. One side of the building was open, exposing the airfield where dozens of planes were on display. Farther out on the runway, other small aircraft took off or landed, the sounds of their engines filling the air.

"I'm good for one more." Stephen helped himself to another pancake and then offered the plate to the man on the other side of the table. "Race, how about you?"

Race LaMott accepted the plate. "Sure, why not? Don't get pancakes at home very often." He gave a sidelong glance at his wife sitting beside him.

Tilda LaMott pursed her lips. "You oughta be thankful I'm watching out for your health. Weren't for me, you'd be on your way to a heart attack."

"You're the best, Tildy." Race grinned and scooped a pancake onto his plate.

Tilda owned Curly Locks Beauty Salon, Nina learned upon introductions. The woman's strawberry blonde hair reminded her of her grandmother, Jessica's, hair color.

Despite his penchant for pancakes, Race appeared trim and fit in gray slacks and matching shirt. His dark hair had patches of white above the ears, and the hint of a mustache covered his upper lip.

"Are you a Parkers alum?" Nina asked him.

Race shook his head. "I'm from the Midwest. I settled here a few years ago."

"Race owns Treasure Trove," Stephen put in. "Bet you get a lot of business during the reunion."

"I'm certainly busy at my shop." Tilda cut a dainty bite of her pancake, displaying manicured fingernails painted silver with gold sparkles. "Everybody wants a new 'do for the dance tonight." She tilted her head at Nina. "I could work you in, though. We had a cancellation for three-thirty."

Nina fingered a strand of hair hanging from her hastily tied ponytail. Did her "do" look that bad? "Thanks for your offer, Tilda, but Stephen and I are on a tight schedule this afternoon with so much to do before we leave town."

"Aren't you staying for Mark's memorial?" Race looked up from spreading butter on his pancake.

"We are." Stephen nodded. "Mark was a good friend."

"What a shock. Anybody know what caused his collapse? Heart attack?" Race put down his knife and picked up his fork.

"No official word yet." Stephen sipped his coffee.

Race frowned. "If he had heart problems, I wouldn't want to be flyin' with him."

"I don't fly in small planes, anyway." Tilda shook her head. "I'm claustrophobic. Oh, look, there's Flora Bane. How do you like her hair color, Nina? The shade is called Banana Blonde."

Nina studied the woman passing by their table.

"The color is…cheerful." Actually, Neon Blonde would have been more accurate, but Nina doubted Tilda would appreciate that description. Hoping to avoid more discussion about an appointment at Curly Locks, Nina turned to Race. "What kind of store is Treasure Trove?"

Race finished chewing a bite of pancake. "The definition of 'trove' will explain. The word means a store of valuable and delightful things. I call my inventory eclectic. We have some valuable antiques and some not so valuable. The same goes for the newer collectibles."

Tilda laughed. "In other words, Treasure Trove is a junk store."

Race's brows dipped into a frown. "Now, Tildy, the Trove is a popular place." He looked toward Nina again. "Customers often ask me to search for certain items, and I'm the first place they come when they want to sell a collectible."

"Treasure Trove sounds like an interesting store." Nina smiled at Race. "I look forward to a visit."

"Come any time. We open at ten, close at six."

After breakfast, the LaMotts joined other friends, while Nina and Stephen toured the airport field where pilots were on hand to answer questions and sign up reunion attendees for an afternoon of short flights.

"Look at that Cessna." Stephen pointed toward a red-and-white plane. "Isn't that a beauty? And what about the Beechcraft?" He indicated another plane. "I like the Icon, too."

Nina raised an eyebrow. "How do you know so much about small aircraft?"

"When I was in high school, I worked here part-time. Mark did, too. We helped wash the planes, scrub oil spots off the runway, and run errands."

"That job sounds perfect for a couple of high school kids." She liked knowing more about his hometown life.

Stephen caught her hand and drew her along the tarmac. "Yes, especially for Mark, because working here got him interested in flying. As soon as he graduated, he joined the Air Force. When he finished his time, he hired on as a pilot for a charter plane outfit, and then he and Oren established FlyGuys."

Nina gazed at the aircraft lining the field. "Is their plane here today? If so, I'd like to see it."

"Since they flew up from California, they're most likely in today's show." Stephen craned his neck. "Yeah, I see Oren by the white Cessna."

Nina spotted the plane and then Oren, who stood in the center of a group of people. By the time she and Stephen reached him, the others drifted away.

Oren looked up from making notes on a clipboard. "Hey, you two. Good to see you."

Although he smiled, his eyes looked tired and his shoulders drooped. Nina could only imagine the stress he'd been under since yesterday.

"Didn't know if you'd be in today's show." Stephen patted the side of the plane.

Oren nodded. "Mark would want me to keep our promise to join the tours. I've been busy filling our schedule." He pointed toward his clipboard.

Nina looked around, expecting to see Gloria, but she was nowhere in sight. She turned back to Oren. "How's Gloria?"

Oren's smile faded. "Not so good, but planning the memorial keeps her going. We're having a service here and another one later for family and friends in California."

"Burial here? Or there?" Stephen folded his arms and planted his feet apart.

"Nowhere." Oren shook his head. "In his will, Mark said he wanted to be cremated and his ashes spread over the mountains between here and California. Gloria and I are gonna make sure he gets his wish."

Stephen gave a solemn nod. "Those plans sound very appropriate."

"How about a ride for you two?" Oren tapped his pen on the clipboard. "I still have openings for this afternoon."

Stephen placed a hand on Nina's shoulder. "What do you say, hon? Would you like a plane ride?"

Nina gazed at the plane, not sure she'd be comfortable confined in such a small space, especially while airborne. Yet, hearing the enthusiasm in Stephen's voice prompted her to agree. "Ah, okay…a ride with FlyGuys sounds like fun."

Oren's eyes narrowed. "You sound kinda tentative. What's your flying experience?"

"Very limited, I must admit. I've had only two flights in a commercial plane, one to New York and the other to California. I've never been in a small plane such as yours. But, look, I'm game to go along today."

Oren's eyes brightened. "Good enough. I guarantee you'll enjoy our flight." He gestured toward the Cessna. "We have none of the hassle that goes with commercial flying."

"You mean we don't have to be searched to make sure we're not smuggling anything?" Stephen grinned.

"Nope. No searches. But anything you smuggled

today would end up right back here, so no point, is there?" Oren laughed.

Nina and Stephen chose two o'clock for their tour.

Oren had just finished his paperwork when two couples joined them. "Saw you at the casino last night," the taller of the two men said to Oren. "Looked like the slots were giving you a bad time."

Oren stuck out his chin. "Tonight'll be better. My luck's on top when the moon's full."

The other man's woman companion laughed and shook a forefinger. "Now, that's a new excuse." She turned toward him. "Don't you try that one on me, Harry."

Harry raised his hands. "Not to worry, dear. I gave up gambling when I won you in that poker game."

Nina joined in the ensuing laughter. Then she glanced at Oren and saw only a frown. For him, gambling was not a joke, and he'd been losing. Nina recalled the tension between him and Mark at dinner after the Meet-and-Greet. Did Oren's gambling involve company funds? Was he the person Mark argued with in the casino hallway? The person who threatened him with death?

****

Despite Oren's comment to the contrary, flying a small plane was quite involved, Nina learned, with all sorts of preparations. Finally, they settled in, with Nina sitting behind Oren and Stephen, buckling seatbelts and putting on headphones. She held her breath as they taxied down the runway. The moment the plane's wheels left the ground, she pressed a hand to her lurching stomach. Yet excitement filled her, too, as she gazed out the Cessna's window and watched the airfield and the buildings grow smaller and smaller.

Oren flew over the town, and then the Greystone Inn and Casino and the Kokuskie River, flowing peacefully in the sunlight.

Nina spotted several kayaks, representing another of the reunion activities offered that afternoon. The river disappeared, and the plane soared over forests and farmlands and hills. In the distance sat the Bitterroot Mountains, part of the Rockies.

Stephen turned to face her.

She saw his lips move and heard his voice in her headphones. "How are you doing?"

"Great." Nina made an okay sign with thumb and forefinger. "Flying is exciting." She meant the sentiment, too.

Just then, Oren made a turn, and the plane took a dive.

Feeling a bit lightheaded, Nina pressed a hand to her forehead. But then the plane leveled out, and the world was right again. In no time at all, it seemed, they returned to the airfield. The runway rushed to meet them. Waiting for the wheels to hit the ground, Nina held her breath. The moment arrived, along with a responding jolt of her stomach. Even though securely buckled in, she gripped the sides of her seat.

The plane rolled to a stop, and the propeller wound down.

Back on solid ground at last, Nina relaxed her tense shoulders.

Stephen helped her from the plane. "Was the ride fun?"

She gave him a sincere smile. "Yes, but I'm glad to have my feet on the ground again."

He laughed. "You are truly a down-to-earth person. If you want more excitement, though, we could always join the kayakers for a river run. I saw them from the plane."

"I noticed them, too. But I want my next exciting event to be dancing at the street dance tonight."

"I'm looking forward to the occasion, too." He planted a quick kiss on her cheek.

Knapsack slung over his shoulder, Oren exited the plane and joined them. "I have the next hour free, so I'll take a break."

Nina and the two men strolled the field bordering the runway, past planes taking off and landing. Along the way, they exchanged greetings with other reunion attendees.

Then Oren pointed ahead. "Here comes Gloria." He waved. "Hey, Glo! Over here."

Answering Oren's wave, Gloria turned in their direction and soon joined them.

Her pale face made a sharp contrast to her bright red hair, and her eyes were bleak. Sensing what she must be experiencing, Nina experienced a rush of sympathy.

"How're you doing, Glo?" Oren laid a hand on her shoulder. "Anything I can help with? I have a break between flights."

"Nina and I would be glad to help, too." Stephen stepped forward.

"Yes." Nina extended a hand. "Please, tell us what we can do."

Gloria's gaze slid over Oren and Stephen and landed on Nina. Her lips thinned. "I know how *you* can help, Nina. You can stop spreading rumors about Mark being murdered."

At the unexpected attack, Nina drew back. "But I—"

"What are you talking about, Glo?"

Oren's sharp tone drowned out Nina's plea.

Gloria pointed a finger toward Nina. "She blabbed her so-called suspicions at the class dinner last night at the Rusty Spur. The one we missed."

Stephen stepped between Gloria and Nina and held up his hands. "Now, wait a minute, Gloria. Nina wasn't spreading a rumor. She reported to Cal Donovan a conversation she overheard that might be important."

"Aren't reports to the police given in private?" Gloria planted her hands on her hips and stuck out her chin.

"What report?" Oren frowned and tugged his beard.

Regretting her report had spread to others, Nina stepped forward. "I'll explain." Just then a nearby plane started its engine, drowning out Nina's words. She raised her voice. "Can we go somewhere quiet and talk?"

"The terminal building has a lounge." Oren gestured toward the building ahead.

"All right." Gloria pursed her lips. "As long as we find a private corner."

Inside the terminal, Nina followed Oren, Gloria, and Stephen along a hallway to the lounge, a large, airy room with comfortable chairs and windows facing the runway. The aroma of freshly brewed coffee filled the air.

Oren and Stephen helped themselves at the urn, but Gloria waved away Oren's offer to pour her a cup.

Nina declined Stephen's gesture, also. Her stomach still churned from the plane ride, plus Gloria's sudden and angry confrontation.

Oren led them to a quiet corner with several vacant chairs and a sofa.

Choosing a chair, Gloria sat with her back rigid and her hands balled into fists.

Sitting next to her, Oren leaned back and sipped his coffee.

His gaze darted from Gloria to Nina, as though he expected war to break out any minute.

Stephen steered Nina to the sofa.

When they were settled, he laid a protective arm along the back. His gesture told her she had his support, for which she was grateful. Then, for the third time, she launched into her story. "At the Meet-and-Greet, when I went to the restroom…"

Except for an occasional flicker of her eyelids, Gloria's angry expression held.

Oren began with a frown, but when Nina finished, he smiled. "I know what that conversation was all about. Nothing serious." He waved a hand.

"You do?" Nina widened her eyes. "Tell us."

"Sure." Oren set his cup on an end table and leaned forward, resting his elbows on his knees. "Dead Man's Tag. A game we used to play. You remember, don'tcha, Stephen?"

Stephen rubbed his jaw. "Yeah, I remember. I didn't play much, though. Truthfully, I thought the game was kinda stupid."

Oren chuckled. "Probably was, but some of us kids thought tagging was fun." He turned toward Nina. "Here's how the game goes. You sneak up on a player, usually in the dark, tap him on the shoulder, and say, 'You're a dead man.' You get points for every person you hit, and at the end of a certain time period, the one with the most points gets to be King of the Dead."

Nina shrugged. "Okay, then what?"

"The game starts all over again." Oren looked at Gloria. "You knew about the game, didn't you, Glo?"

Her lips tight, Gloria nodded. "Mark told me. I have to agree, Stephen. I thought the game was dumb. But that explains what you heard, Nina."

Oren sat back. "Somebody was teasing Mark, reminding him of the old game."

"But the person also said Mark must give him something." Not satisfied with Oren's explanation, Nina frowned. "Did that request have to do with the game?"

"Who knows?" Oren shrugged.

"If I knew who the players were…" Nina looked from one to the other, hoping to glean more information.

"Oh, no." Gloria raised her hands. "This matter has gone far enough. Just back off, and let us have Mark's memorial without complications."

Gloria was right. Nina shouldn't interfere. "I'm really sorry about the rumors." She softened her tone. "I know you're going through a difficult time."

Gloria met Nina's gaze and then looked away. "I can't believe he's really gone."

"We'll set people straight about the rumor." Oren patted Gloria's arm. "Now, how about the memorial?"

A faint smile touched Gloria's lips. "I met with the people at Kline's Tribute Center. They have a lovely chapel…" She pulled a small notebook from her purse and flipped the pages.

Nina only half-listened. Instead, she mulled over what she'd learned about Dead Man's Tag. Were Mark and the mystery person engaged in a harmless kids' game? Or in an adults' pursuit with much more sinister consequences?

"You don't believe Mark, and whoever he was talking to, were playing a game, do you?" Stephen asked later when they drove to the Barlows'.

Nina turned from gazing out the window. "I have my doubts. Mark was really upset when I saw him. Attributing his distress to a child's game is difficult to accept." She wrinkled her brow. "But, oh, Stephen, I don't want to upset you, either."

He nodded. "I know. But if Mark did meet with foul play, then I want to see justice done, too. He was my friend. We experienced some rough times together."

"Then pursuing my suspicions is okay with you?"

He grinned. "Would my saying no make a difference?"

She narrowed her eyes but kept her tone light. "Hmmm, probably not."

"Just keep me informed, okay? I'll help as much as I can—when I'm not busy with David."

"Thanks for your support, Stephen." She patted his arm. "I'll let you know what I'm up to." Her thoughts spinning, Nina returned to gazing out the window. The mention of David made her think she should forget her suspicions concerning Mark and concentrate on helping Stephen get to know his son. Still, she couldn't forget Mark's look of desperation when he passed her in the hallway. The worry that Mark McTeague met with foul play lingered like a festering sore.

Chapter Five

Nina tapped a foot to the lively music played on the elevated stage at the end of Main Street. The Sunday night dance, the All Class Reunion's grand finale, was in full swing. Red, blue, and yellow lanterns cast a soft glow over the band members and the dancers, while in the distance a rosy twilight lingered behind the mountains. She'd looked forward to this event, but, so far, she and Stephen hadn't danced. Instead, they stood on the sidelines visiting with other reunion attendees.

Currently in their group were Tilda and Race LaMott, the couple Nina met at breakfast, and Mary Ellen Eckert, who owned Lovin's Bakery. In contrast to Tilda's tall, thin stature, Mary Ellen stood no more than five feet. Her plump figure filled out her pink blouse and gathered skirt, and her smile displayed a dimple in her left cheek.

"What's this rumor about poor Mark being murdered?" Tilda aimed her question at Stephen and then looked at Nina. "We had lunch at the casino, and people at the next table were talking."

"I want to know, too." Mary Ellen leaned forward. "I heard the word from Rilla, who heard it from Pansy's brother." She rolled her eyes. "If Mark *was* murdered, I'd look at Oren and Gloria."

"Those two are pretty thick." Tilda nodded and

patted her perfectly coifed hair.

Race's lips flattened. "Talk about rumors…"

"Oh, come on, Race." Tilda slapped his shoulder. "Everybody knows about Oren and Gloria."

Nina listened to the exchange with interest, hoping to learn new information about the rumors she, too, had heard.

"Gloria's the one with all the money." Mary Ellen aimed her comment at Nina. "Of course, Oren wanted to get on her good side, so she'd invest in FlyGuys."

Tilda's eyebrows peaked. "That's not *all* he wanted."

"I can't understand what she sees in him." Mary Ellen's nose wrinkled. "She's such a fashion maven, and he looks like something the cat dragged in, as my mother used to say."

Stephen cleared his throat. "How's business at Lovin's, Mary Ellen? Are you still making those great huckleberry doughnuts?" He placed a hand on Nina's shoulder. "You'll want to sample them before we leave town."

Mary Ellen's dimple flashed. "We've added several new goodies since you've been here, Stephen, but huckleberry doughnuts still rule. Come by Lovin's any time. Are you are staying for Mark's memorial?"

"We are, and I'd love to visit your bakery." Nina sent a silent thanks to Stephen for changing the subject before anyone asked her to explain her role in the rumor.

Others joined them. Mary Ellen broke away to talk to two women. Race shook hands with a man and then motioned to Stephen and Nina.

Nina couldn't catch the man's name over the

music, but she smiled and nodded politely. After a while, her attention wandered. Glancing around, she spotted the refreshment table and headed in that direction. Decorated with red, blue, and yellow crepe paper, the table held soft drinks embedded in tubs of ice, and coffee and water for tea dispensed from silver urns. Perusing the soft drink selections, Nina chose a strawberry soda. She opened the bottle and took a long swallow, enjoying the sweet, refreshing taste.

Nina was ready to return to Stephen and his group when she saw Angie join them. She wore a red T-top decorated with silver sequins, a knee-length black skirt, and high-heeled, red shoes. Nina's stomach tightened, and the soda suddenly tasted sour.

Angie greeted everyone but then leaned close to Stephen and nodded toward the dancers.

Stephen raised his head and gazed around.

Was he looking for her? Now would be a good time to return. However, without stopping to analyze her decision, instead of joining them, Nina remained where she stood.

Stephen shrugged and held out his hand to Angie.

She placed her hand in his and followed him into the crowd.

Nina closed her eyes to block out the sight. Tonight was supposed to be her and Stephen's special time to enjoy the reunion's last event. So, why had she backed off when Angie arrived? Because Angie and Stephen had a past relationship and shared a child? Was she afraid the three of them might have a future together? She didn't have the answer. She just stood there, knowing she was overreacting but unable to control her feelings.

Nina finished her soda and tossed the bottle in the recycle bin. Turning from the dance, she made her way along the sidewalk, weaving through knots of people. She'd take a longer break, and when she gained control of her emotions, she would return to Stephen and his group, Angie or no Angie.

Twilight had fallen, and the lanterns beamed brighter while shadows lengthened and deepened. A cool breeze drifted down from the mountains. Music from the dance faded into the background. Nina continued walking, stopping to gaze in store windows, noting the establishments she wanted to visit.

While staying for Mark's memorial was a sad occasion, the extra time also presented an opportunity to become better acquainted with the town. The Book Nook, Sparkles Jewelry, Tansy's Flowers, and several other stores caught her eye. She passed Treasure Trove and thought of Race LaMott. The brightly lighted window display showed an interesting array of objects, from carved wooden giraffes, kangaroos, and other exotic animals, to a table set with a lace cloth and colorful dishes, to metal sculptures of birds. She wondered idly if Race went on trips to select the items for his store. If so, he must be an experienced traveler.

At Lovin's Bakery, she stopped to look in the window where soft, interior lighting revealed trays of doughnuts, cookies, and cakes. A menu affixed to the inside of the window and the outlines of tables and booths indicated the bakery also served lunch. She added Lovin's to her must-visit list.

She reached the end of the business district. Beyond stretched the road leading up the hill to the Barlows' and the neighborhood's other elegant homes.

Here and there, lights peeked through the trees and swept down the hill from lampposts lining the road.

Looking around, Nina realized she was alone. No one else ventured this far from the dance. The darkness closed in, and the breeze drifting along the street turned cold. Nina hugged her arms. She'd meant only to take a quick break, not to be gone long enough to leave the area or to cause Stephen worry.

With back straight and arms swinging at her sides, she stepped up her pace. Shadows she hadn't noticed before loomed, and a skittering sound from an alley made her jump. Not even the glimpse of a cat scampering away calmed her. She hurried on, silently chastising herself for wandering so far from the others. Lost in her thoughts, she'd not paid attention.

Behind her, footsteps sounded. A shiver rattled down her spine. Who could that be? She hadn't seen anyone. Where could a person have come from? She shrugged off her nervous response. She was safe here in Parkers Landing. Still, she picked up her pace. The other footsteps kept up. Okay, she'd move aside and let the person pass. Then she could relax again.

The stranger closed the gap between them and gave her back a hard shove. "Get out of town!" a voice hissed in her ear.

Nina thrust out her arms, grasping at the air as she struggled to maintain her balance. Miraculously, she stayed on her feet. By the time she regained her equilibrium and turned to see who so brazenly attacked her, the person was only a shadowy form disappearing into the darkness. She couldn't tell whether the assailant was male or female, nor had the warning, deep and guttural, provided gender certainty.

Sucking in a breath, Nina took a moment to straighten her clothing and smooth her hair. Feeling competent enough to proceed, she headed back to the dance. Still, tension kept her shoulders tight and her breathing labored. She frequently glanced over her shoulder to make sure she traveled alone.

Fortunately, she soon encountered others strolling the sidewalk, and her shoulders relaxed and her breathing evened. No one paid her any attention, and she reached the dance without further incident. She spotted Stephen once again on the sidelines. No sign of Angie. He stood alone, searching the crowd. She hurried to his side. "Stephen…"

He turned and his gaze landed on her. "Nina!" Grasping her shoulders, he gazed into her eyes. "Where have you been? You disappeared, and I was worried."

Hearing his distress brought a rush of guilt. "Sorry. I went for a soda and then decided to take a short walk and get some fresh air. I didn't intend to be gone long."

"Well, I missed you. But you're here now, and we haven't had a dance." He drew back and held out his hand.

Should she tell him about the assault? Nina bit her lip. He should be informed. Probably the police needed a report, too. But, now, more than anything, she wanted to be in his arms dancing, enjoying what was left of the occasion she'd so looked forward to. She'd tell him later what happened. The danger was gone now. She slipped a hand into his and followed him to join the other dancers. The band played a slow tune, and Stephen drew her into his arms. Feeling warm inside, she placed her arms around his neck and laid her head against his shoulder. All thoughts and worries about the dark figure faded, and she concentrated on dancing and being close to Stephen again.

Later, though, as she lay in bed, worry kept her tossing and turning. Who had shoved her and warned her to get out of town? The mysterious person Mark argued with at the Meet-and-Greet, who now knew Nina overheard the conversation? Was he, or she, Mark's killer?

Her thoughts turned to Angie. What had she and Stephen talked about while they danced? Old times? The future? Did she want to reconnect with Stephen and finish raising their son together? Or was her intention only that father and son know one another? Nina hoped attending the reunion would give her and Stephen an opportunity to deepen their relationship, but unexpected events intruded on that goal. With a deep sigh, she settled back against the pillows, but worries about what else lay ahead led to a restless sleep.

****

Sitting with Stephen on the Barlows' front porch swing, Nina selected a lure from the tackle box between them, careful not to catch her fingers on the dangling hooks. Like a miniature fish, the lure was brightly colored in shades of red and blue.

"I wish you were coming with us." Stephen nodded toward the fishing rods propped against the porch railing. At breakfast, he announced he and David planned a trip to a stream he often fished while growing up. "Angie's not coming," he added, "so you don't need to worry about her." He shot Nina a sideways glance. "Not that you do...worry about her."

Nina chose to ignore the invitation to discuss her feelings toward Angie. She wasn't sure exactly what those emotions were, anyway. She replaced the lure in its slot and folded her hands in her lap. "I would join you, but I promised Judy I'd go to the Museum Mommas' meeting." True enough. Judy issued the invitation last night after they all returned from the dance.

Stephen nodded and sorted through the tackle box. "I suppose the museum will interest you more than fishing, but I hope you'll come with me and David next time we plan an activity."

"I will. I want to get to know him better, too."

Riding into town later with Judy, down streets aglow with sunshine, Nina struggled with her guilt feelings. She saw nothing wrong with her reasoning that David and Stephen would benefit from spending time together alone. But was she shying away for reasons of her own? Not because she didn't like David. During their exploration of the library, he proved to be quite personable, and she related to his interest in books and reading. Still, she held back where David was concerned. She only hoped her reticence didn't cause trouble between her and Stephen. Recalling the disappointment reflected on his face and in his voice, she feared perhaps her behavior already had. She made the right decision, hadn't she, in allowing Stephen and David to have their fishing trip without her?

Reaching the area where she was assaulted the night before interrupted Nina's worries. Even though in daylight the street appeared safe, a shiver rolled down her spine. She glanced at Judy. Should she tell her what occurred? No, she'd inform Stephen first. He probably would insist she report the incident. Considering Chief Cal's indifferent response to her concern about Mark, she doubted she wanted to talk to him again. Still, if her attacker might also threaten other citizens, the police should be alerted.

Farther downtown, cleanup from last night's dance was underway. Workers disassembled the bandstand, folded tables and chairs, and took down the lanterns. Shopkeepers swept the sidewalks in front of their stores. A noisy garbage truck made the rounds collecting refuse from trash barrels.

Located at the far end of the business district, the museum sat between a furniture store and a real estate office. From the outside, the establishment appeared too small to hold many exhibits. Yet, when Nina stepped inside, she saw the area was larger than she had thought. Glass cases, shelves, furniture, and pictures on the walls filled every available space. She was at once drawn to the exhibits and eager to explore. Perhaps after the meeting, she'd have time.

A woman appeared from the back of the building. In her forties, she had short, dark hair and a square-jawed face. Although she was small of stature, her brisk walk, with arms swinging at her sides, indicated a woman with a purpose. When she reached them, her face broke into a smile. "Hello, Judy." She turned to Nina. "You must be Nina Foster, Stephen's friend."

"Selene Thomas is our assistant director." Judy nodded toward Selene. "She's the one who really runs the place," she added behind her hand.

Selene straightened her shoulders. "Huh! Somebody has to be in charge while Hal is buried in his research. He's writing a book about our town." She glanced toward Nina. " 'The definitive history of Parkers Landing,' he calls his work. But, Nina, welcome to our museum. We're glad you joined us today."

"I've told her about the Mommas." Judy waved a hand. "She's ready to work, too. Aren't you, Nina?"

Appreciative of Judy's enthusiastic introduction, Nina nodded. "I love museums and am happy to help with any projects."

Selene gestured to the hallway. "Then let's get started. We're meeting in the Courtyard Room." Turning, she led the way.

In the Courtyard Room, several women sat at a table chatting over coffee and a plate of the fattest doughnuts Nina had ever seen. She greeted Tilda LaMott, owner of Curly Locks and wife of Race, and Mary Ellen Eckert, of Lovin's Bakery.

Selene nodded toward a woman wearing a bright orange print blouse. "Mona Truehorn is our Native American expert."

"Welcome, Nina." Mona smiled and waved fingers laden with turquoise rings. A turquoise squash blossom necklace and dangling earrings completed her matching jewelry accessories.

Selene pointed a forefinger toward the woman sitting next to Mona. "This is Della Comstock."

Della lifted her chin. "Of the *Harry* Comstocks. Our family was pioneers and very active in the development of the town." In her fifties, she wore a red T-top that matched the artificial rose tucked into a cloud of gray hair.

"...And this is Alexis Duggan." Selene rounded the table to stand beside the remaining woman. "Better known as Lexie. She works in the mayor's office."

Lexie finished a bite of doughnut. "I also do

genealogies. Ever had yours done?"

Lexie regarded Nina with large brown eyes set in an otherwise plain face. "No, I haven't." With the exception of Grandmother Jessica, Nina knew little about her mother's forebearers and nothing of her father's. After he left, her mother never spoke of him, as though he'd never existed. Although from time to time curious, Nina always pushed aside the feeling and dismissed him, as had her mother. She'd never given genealogy a thought.

Tilda waved a hand. "Don't believe her, Nina. She may hide behind her genealogy business, but in truth, she's a 'nosy busybody.' "

Lexie's gaze shifted to Tilda. "Someday, maybe you'll let me do yours, Tilda. Unless you're afraid of all the skeletons I'll find in your closet. Ha ha."

Nina looked from one woman to the other, not sure if their exchange was in fun or serious.

Mary Ellen picked up the plate of doughnuts and held it out. "Have a doughnut, Nina. I made them 'specially for our meeting. We have Chocolate Chirp, Vanilla Vanity, Mocha Moos, and Huckleberry Heaven." She pointed toward each one in turn.

"I will, thank you." Nina inhaled the sugary aromas. "They look delicious, and they're so—so big."

Mary Ellen giggled, flashing her dimple. "My secret ingredient."

Nina selected a huckleberry doughnut. She took a bite, savoring the sweet berry taste. "Ah, delicious."

No one seemed in a hurry to begin the meeting. While the others chatted, Nina wandered the room. Filing cabinets lined one wall, while shelves filled with books and cardboard boxes took up another. Reaching the door leading to the courtyard, she peeked out. Brick walls provided privacy from the adjacent furniture store and real estate office.

"All right, ladies, time to begin." Selene's voice reached Nina's ears. When everyone was seated, their leader tapped the table twice with her gavel. "The meeting of the Museum Mommas will come to order. Here's today's agenda." She picked up a stack of papers and handed them to Della. Once those were passed around, Selene turned to Mona. "Madame Secretary, please read the minutes of the last meeting."

Della raised a hand. "Do we have to hear the minutes? We all know what went on. We were there."

"We follow procedure." Selene frowned and tapped her gavel. "The minutes, please, Mona."

Mona picked up her tablet and, rings flashing, thumbed the keyboard. "Oops, I lost the file." More thumbing. "Oh, here it is…no, lost it again. Darn this thing."

Groans echoed around the table.

Selene briefly closed her eyes and pressed her lips together. "Never mind, Mona. We'll hear the minutes at our next meeting. In the meantime, have George give you another lesson on your tablet."

"Humpf." Mona frowned. "My son's a whiz at video games, but anything else goes over his head."

The door opened, and a man stepped into the room.

Jeans encased skinny legs, and a short-sleeved, tan shirt exposed bony elbows.

Pushing away sparse, gray hair hanging over his high forehead, he peered at the group through silver-framed eyeglasses perched on a long, thin nose. "Is this the group that works on museum projects?"

Selene nodded. "We're the Museum Mommas, if that's who you're looking for."

"I am." Grabbing a chair, he squeezed in between Mona and Lexie. "I'm here to join."

Frowning, Mona folded her arms. "But we're the Museum *Mommas.*"

The man's eyebrows peaked. "Okay, now the Mommas have a Papa."

"But—"

"Why would you—?"

"We can't—"

Curious as to how this situation would be resolved, Nina looked to the stranger for his reaction.

The newcomer stuck out his chin. "You can. Director Hal says so. He says you can't be gender exclusive, no matter what you call your group."

"Director Hal." Della turned up her nose. "He's not our boss."

Lexie pointed toward Selene. "She's our leader."

Mona nodded. "We have our own rules of membership."

Selene banged her gavel. "Quiet, everyone." She turned to the man. "Out of deference to Hal's title, I'll discuss the matter with him later. As long as you're here, stay for today's meeting. Please introduce yourself."

"I'm Oswald Farrington the Third." A frown wrinkling his brow, he gazed around the table. "But don't call me 'Ozzie.'"

"What about 'the Third'?" Mona leaned toward him.

Oswald shook his head. "Not that name, either. I am Oswald." He sat straight and stuck out his chin.

Selene laid her gavel on the table. "Tell us something about yourself."

Along with the others, Nina focused on the newcomer, interested to know more about him. Why did he want to join this group of women volunteers?

He nodded. "Of course. I'm from Montana. I learned my ancestors came from this area, and I want to find my roots."

"Roots—see Lexie for roots." Judy grinned and elbowed Lexie.

"Or Tilda, if your roots need a touch-up." Mona pressed fingers to her lips, suppressing a giggle.

Nina joined in the laughter rippling around the table. She admired the Museum Mommas for their sense of humor in this challenging situation. Then she turned her attention to Oswald Farrington, eager to see his reaction.

Oswald waved a hand. "I look forward to being a member of your esteemed group. Hal speaks highly of you all and praises you for the good work you do for the museum."

"Have a doughnut, Mr., ah, Oswald." Mary Ellen nudged the plate in his direction. "Coffee and tea are on the counter." She pointed over his shoulder.

Oswald looked down his long nose at the doughnuts. "I avoid sugar, and I've already had my daily coffee limit."

"No sugar, huh?" Mary Ellen whispered behind her hand. "I guess I won't be seeing him at Lovin's."

"His absence might be a good thing," Lexie whispered back. "He's kinda grumpy."

The sound of Selene's gavel snapped Nina and the others to attention. "We need to move on. First on the agenda is donations…"

Twenty minutes later, after discussing donations, fundraising, and the upcoming Pioneer Days open house, Selene again banged her gavel. "Our business is concluded. Now, on to the fun part of the program."

"We're working on a new exhibit," Lexie told Nina. "Recreating an early replica of Tilda's beauty shop."

"*Salon.*" Tilda leaned around Nina to glare at Lexie. "We are not a 'shop.' We are a 'salon.' 'Shop' sounds so—common." Her nose wrinkled.

"Now, ladies, no arguing." Selene shook a finger. "We are all friends here."

Nina sensed seriousness behind Tilda's and Lexie's sparring over the nomenclature of Tilda's business. Did something else cause their dissention?

Nina followed the others into the hallway, looking forward to the more active part of the meeting. What about the new, controversial member of their committee? How would he fit in? Did he think belonging to the Museum Mommas would aid his ancestry search? Or did his presence serve some other, hidden purpose?

Chapter Six

Moving from the Courtyard Room to the Curly Locks exhibit gave Nina a chance to see more of the museum. She passed a room that recreated a country store with a counter, shelves of dry goods, and a potbellied stove. Another displayed farm implements, including a horse-drawn plow, and a third showed a dining room complete with a sideboard and a table set with fine china.

The room reserved for Curly Locks was a work in progress, where vintage hair dryers, boxes full of hair products, and several mannequins waited to be arranged into an interesting display.

Tilda stood in the center of the room and clasped her hands. "I'm so excited my grandmother's Curly Locks will be part of our museum. As you know, she established the salon and, fortunately for us, she saved nearly *everything*. Now, her salon will be restored here in the museum for all to enjoy."

Della sidled up to Nina. "The Comstocks wanted this room to be a courtroom. My grandfather, Harry Comstock, was a famous judge. But Tilda's donation to the museum fund convinced Director Hal her salon would be more interesting."

Not wanting to take sides, Nina carefully phrased her reply. "Maybe you can find another space here at the museum."

"I hope so." Della stuck out her jaw. "I won't rest until the Comstocks are honored."

Selene put everyone to work unpacking boxes and arranging the furniture.

Nina's assignment was a box full of wigs and wooden heads. She'd barely begun to unpack them when Lexie approached, carrying a carton overflowing with pink and blue curlers.

"Nina, I heard you think Mark McTeague might have been murdered."

Nina sighed. "I didn't mean to start a rumor. I only wanted to tell the police what I overheard at the casino—in case he *had* been murdered."

Lexie dumped the curlers into a plastic tray on the counter. "Word spreads fast in a small town like Parkers, especially about something as shocking as murder. What did you overhear?"

"Oh, just Mark and another person talking." Nina wrinkled her brow. "Well, okay, the other person threatened Mark... Look, I don't want to start any more rumors."

Lexie waved a hand. "I understand. Just thought I might shed some light on what you heard. Mark might have appeared to be Mr. Nice Guy, but he had enemies."

"Really? Who?" Although Nina kept her tone casual, her heart beat faster. Was she about to learn something important about Mark that would lend credence to her suspicions?

Lexie glanced around and then leaned close. "His partner, for one. I heard Mark planned to dump Oren and run FlyGuys solo."

"Why would he split with Oren?"

"Because he found Oren with his hand in the company pot. Of course, Oren calls taking the money borrowing." Lexie made air quotes with her forefingers.

"I did hear something about Oren owing the casino." Nina pulled a blonde wig from the box and smoothed the tangled strands.

Lexie waved a hand. "Al Montega, the manager, allowed him to margin bet. Didn't work out and now Oren's in deep doodoo."

"And you know this how?" Nina placed the wig on a wooden head, adjusting the bangs over the forehead.

Lexie laughed. "Parkers is a small town, remember?"

"Okay, what else? Was Mark jealous of the attention Oren pays to Gloria?" Nina bit her lip. She probably shouldn't admit to having that knowledge.

Lexie fingered a curler from the tray. "I'm sure he was, but some think Oren's interest in Gloria is only for her money. She comes from a wealthy family. Mark met her when he was in the Air Force. He was in a parade where she was a float queen. They married, and she bankrolled FlyGuys."

"She must have loved Mark to use her money for his business."

Lexie sighed. "Love does funny things to a person." She pressed her lips together and looked away. Then she turned back to Nina. "Anyway, let's assume Mark was murdered. How, do you think?"

Nina had given the method of death some thought, but should she share a theory that might be spread around town? But, perhaps in turn, Lexie had information that would help her. "Judging from the way he died, I'd say poison."

Lexie's eyes widened. "Really? Any idea what *kind* of poison?"

"Not at the moment. I haven't had time to do research."

Selene joined them. "Lexie, put those curlers on that cart." She pointed toward a cart Della filled with hairbrushes and combs. "Nina, take a break from the wigs and run an errand. We need old magazines to display on the tables. The magazines are in the storeroom next to the office. Choose those published during the twenties and thirties. *Vogue* and *Life* would be appropriate."

"We'll talk more later." Lexie nodded to Nina and picked up the tray of curlers.

Mulling over her conversation with Lexie, Nina left the room and went down the hall toward the office. The woman gave Nina new information to consider. She hoped she hadn't blabbed too much herself and that her comments to Lexie wouldn't come back to haunt her. Framed photos hanging on the wall caught her eye, and she stopped to study them. Several were of the Kokuskie River. One showed a man standing on a raft while holding a long pole in the water. The photo's caption identified the man as Phineas Parker. From her research prior to the trip, she learned Phineas ferried people across the river, helping them to get settled. His important service resulted in the town being named after him.

Nina continued on, finally reaching the storeroom, which, as Selene had said, held stacks of old magazines. After perusing them and selecting an armful, she retraced her steps along the hallway. Passing one of the exhibit rooms, she heard a noise. She stopped and peered into the dimly lighted room.

A man bent over a display case.

He wasn't a visitor because the museum hadn't yet opened to the public. Director Hal?

The man closed the case and pulled the key from the lock. As he straightened and turned, his long, pointed nose caught the light from a nearby window.

Oswald Farrington.

"Mr. Farrington, what are you—?" She bit off the rest of the sentence. What he might be doing was really none of her business.

He lifted his chin and slipped the key into his jeans pocket. "Just familiarizing myself with the displays. What are *you* doing?"

His accusatory tone indicated she was the person out-of-bounds. What nerve. She pointed toward the magazines. "Selene sent me to the storeroom to collect these old magazines. What part of the exhibit are you working on?" She craned her neck, hoping to identify the display behind him.

He stepped closer, blocking her view. "I don't know." He sniffed. "I was taking a break when the assignments were given."

Taking a break? Or leaving the group so he could snoop? "Interesting place, isn't it?" She kept her tone casual.

"Yes, the past has always intrigued me."

"Well, I'd better get back to the Curly Locks exhibit." Nina turned and headed along the dark hallway, conscious of him following. She walked faster but was unable to shake the creepy feeling his presence created. At the exhibit, she found Lexie setting up a hair dryer.

She plugged the cord into the wall and flipped the switch on the dryer's metal hood. A whirring sound filled the air. "Look, the dryer actually works!" Lexie sent a beaming smile around the room.

Rushing to Lexie's side, Tilda turned off the switch. "This dryer is old, and the cord is worn." She pointed to the frayed cord. "Turning on the machine creates a fire hazard."

"Sorry." Lexie raised both hands and stepped back. "I wanted to hear what an old dryer sounded like."

Tilda propped both hands on her hips. "Well, now you know. But don't turn on any of the dryers again."

The two glared at each other.

Selene stepped between them. "Now, ladies, we're all friends here. Our time is up, anyway." She tapped her wristwatch with a forefinger. "Our meeting on Wednesday will be at Curly Locks, gathering more display items from the storeroom. Who can we count on?" Her gaze roved the group.

Judy raised a hand. "I'll help."

"I'll come with Judy." Nina stepped forward. "If I'm still in town." She might as well do something useful while waiting to attend Mark's memorial. Besides, working on the exhibit was fun.

Everyone else volunteered, too—except Oswald Farrington. When Nina looked around for him, she saw he'd disappeared again. His erratic behavior made her doubt his sincerity in joining their group. What was his agenda, anyway? Was he really searching for his ancestral roots? Or for something else?

A few minutes later, Nina and Judy were in the Barlows' car and on their way home.

Judy took her gaze off the road long enough to

glance at Nina. "What do you think of our group?"

Nina smiled. "I enjoyed meeting them. Everyone was friendly and congenial. I did sense tension between Lexie and Tilda, though."

Judy nodded. "Those two are often at odds with one another."

"Do you know why?" Nina shifted in her seat to give Judy her full attention. After witnessing several encounters between the two women, she was curious.

"As you might guess, a man is involved." Judy slowed to turn a corner. "Lexie met Race—Tilda's husband—when she was on a trip to Arizona. She brought him home to Parkers, and he ended up staying and opening his store."

"He told me about Treasure Trove at the Pancake Breakfast. I peeked in the store window yesterday. He sure has a lot of stuff."

"Uh huh. Some people call his place a junk shop, but he just laughs off the term."

"At the breakfast, he called his collection a trove of 'valuable and delightful things.' "

Judy laughed. "A definition straight from the dictionary. Anyway, Lexie expected to marry Race. She even bought a wedding dress from a store in Boise. But he married Tilda instead."

"Hmmm, what did he see in Tilda that he didn't find in Lexie?"

"Glamor, for one. Tilda always looks great, while Lexie's a Plain Jane. Tilda has money, too, inherited from her grandmother, who established Curly Locks. Whatever, as soon as he met Tilda, he dropped Lexie and pursued her."

"Were Lexie and Tilda friends before Tilda and

Race got together?" Perhaps Lexie had good reason to be resentful.

"They were. But Lexie blames Tilda for stealing Race. Lexie says she has another 'love interest,' as she calls the fellow, but no one's ever seen him. According to her, they get together in Sandpoint or Coeur d'Alene or Boise, but she's never brought him here to Parkers." Judy gripped the steering wheel to make another turn. "Anyway, I'm glad you could come today, and I appreciate your volunteering for more."

"I'm happy to help." Why not? Nina hoped learning more about the Museum Mommas would aid in her investigation. Or would she investigate? Should she honor her suspicions that Mark McTeague met with foul play, or not?

****

Later that afternoon, Stephen and David returned from their fishing trip, their ice chest full of fish. While they cleaned their catch and George fired up the barbecue, Nina helped Judy prepare mashed potatoes, fresh asparagus, and a tossed salad.

Soon, they all were seated at the outdoor picnic table.

George speared a piece of trout with his fork and popped it into his mouth. "Mmm, delicious."

Nina joined the murmurs of agreement circling the table.

"I didn't think we'd catch so many fish today." Stephen helped himself to another serving from the platter. "But the fish were just waiting for us. Right, David?" He turned to the teen sitting beside him.

David nodded. "We didn't even have to move around much. We just stood in the stream, and they came to us."

"I used to fish a lot." George straightened and sipped his coffee. "But then golf grabbed my attention. Which reminds me, David, do you play?"

David shook his head. "One of my dads did, but he never taught me."

The youth's unsuccessful experiences with fathers caught Nina's sympathy. Which would be worse, she wondered, having inadequate fathers or, as was her experience, none at all?

"Well, now's the time to learn." George's eyebrows peaked.

Judy groaned. "Watch out, David. If George gets ahold of you, you'll be chasing that hole in one along with the rest of the golf addicts."

"Wait a minute, Mom." Rick reached for the breadbasket. "You can't belong to this family without at least trying golf." He took a roll and passed the basket to his twin.

Blaine nodded and selected a roll. "Golf is a good game. Provides lots of exercise."

"Why, even Katie has her own golf clubs. Right, honey?" George leaned toward his daughter, sitting beside him.

She put down her fork and smiled. "I do, but I'd rather read."

"Reading's important." George patted her shoulder. "But like Blaine says, you need to keep physically active, too." He turned to Stephen and David. "I'll set up a time at the club when we can hit a few practice balls."

Stephen tilted his head toward David. "What do you say? Does golf sound like fun?"

"Sure. I'll give the sport a try." David shrugged.

George caught Nina's eye. "You're invited, too."

"I'd love to—if the time doesn't conflict with helping the Museum Mommas." Nina had enjoyed her time with the group and didn't want to miss a meeting.

George touched his napkin to his lips. "Don't worry; we'll make sure the outing is a family affair."

A family affair. Nina admired George's attempt to make both her and David feel part of the Barlow family. She looked forward to them all being together on the golf course.

After a kitchen cleanup with everyone pitching in, Rick and Blaine took David into the computer room.

Katie went to her room to get a book to read.

Nina followed Stephen, Judy, and George to the front porch to enjoy after dinner coffee. With the sun's disappearance behind the mountains, the heat of the day mellowed, and a cool breeze ruffled the leaves of nearby maple trees. Nina and Stephen settled on the swing.

Judy and George took matching wicker chairs. Judy brought her sewing basket, sharing with Nina a patchwork quilt she was making with another of her groups, the Quilting Queens.

George brought along the evening newspaper. "Here's an article on Mark." He pointed toward a page. "I read that after the Air Force, he flew for the Skyline Club." He handed the newspaper to Stephen. "Weren't they involved in a plane crash?"

Stephen accepted the paper and focused on the article. "The accident happened while I was in New York. Mark and I lost track of each other, but I heard about the crash. One of his passengers was killed. A guy named Harmon, who was Mary Ellen Eckert's fiancé."

Nina sorted the fabric patches Judy gave her to inspect, colorful prints of roses, tulips, and daffodils. "I met her at the dance and again today at the museum." She didn't know about her fiancé's death, though, which put Mary Ellen on her suspects' list.

As she threaded a needle, Judy squinted one eye. "Yes, Harmon and Mary Ellen were engaged, and when he died, she was heartbroken. She never married."

Nina finished examining the patches and handed them back to Judy. "Did she blame Mark for the accident?"

"She did." Judy nodded. "He wasn't cited, though. But as far as she was concerned, he was responsible."

"Strange the way Mark suddenly died at the picnic." George took the paper Stephen held out. "A rumor's going around that he was murdered."

Feeling they deserved to know her part in the rumor, Nina straightened and leaned forward. "My fault—sort of. I overheard something at the Meet-and-Greet…" She told Judy and George about the incident in the hallway, adding what she'd learned from Oren about Dead Man's Tag. "What do you two think?" She looked from one to the other.

Judy finished a stitch in her patchwork. "Oren's right about the game, but what you witnessed sounds more serious. But if Mark was murdered, I can't see Mary Ellen as the killer. Even if she blames Mark for Harmon's death, deep down, she's a kind soul. She donates her baked goods to the Food Bank. You had a sample of her pastry today, Nina."

"Yes, and the doughnuts were wonderful." Nina

recalled the delicious treat.

"I heard today that Mark died from kidney failure." George folded the newspaper and laid it on the wicker table.

Judy nodded. "Marcella at the Post Office told me the same. Her daughter works in the coroner's office."

"Does anyone know if he had a history of kidney problems? A disease?" As far as she knew, kidney disease was a deteriorating condition rather than a sudden development. Nina turned to Stephen. "Do you know?"

Stephen shook his head. "He'd have to be healthy to keep his pilot's license. I hear the test is a tough one."

David stepped onto the porch and approached Stephen. "Time for me to go. I told Mom I'd be back by nine."

"Sure. Don't want to be late." Stephen turned to Nina. "You're coming with us, aren't you?"

Nina hesitated. "Ah, no, thanks. I need to call Gran." True enough. She'd been so busy with the reunion she hadn't had much time to phone Jessica. She missed the daily calls and weekly visits they had at home.

Stephen's brows drew together. "All right. Tell her I said hello." He stood and placed a hand on David's shoulder. "Let's roll, buddy."

David bid goodnight to Judy, George, and Nina, and then he and Stephen descended the porch stairs and headed for the garage.

Struggling with her guilt, Nina waited to hear Stephen's car start. She would spend time with them, she promised herself. She really would. In her room a few minutes later, Nina took her cell phone and climbed onto the bed, propping pillows behind her back. She made the phone connection, and soon Jessica's smiling face filled the screen. Tonight, her grandmother wore a rust-colored blouse that complemented her strawberry blonde hair. Affection filled Nina at the sight of her beloved relative.

"Hello, honey." Jessica waved. "So good to see you."

"I sure miss you—and you, too, Joe," she added as Joe McGarrity's face appeared beside Jessica's. Joe was her grandmother's—what? Romantic interest? Special male friend? Nina was never sure exactly what to call him. He and Jessica had been dating—another term she stumbled over—for about six months. They both lived at Marley Manor, an elegant retirement home in Richmond.

"We miss you, too." Joe came more into view as he put his arm around Jessica's shoulders.

"Everyone here says 'hi.' " Jessica fluttered her fingers. "What did you do today?"

Nina told them about the meeting at the museum and about Stephen and David's fishing trip. On a previous call, she'd shared the news of David's appearance. "I was sorry I couldn't go with them today, but I'd already arranged to accompany Judy to her meeting. I do want to support Stephen, though."

"I know you do." Jessica nodded. "But I agree they need time alone together, too. What do you think, Joe?" She turned her head to look at him.

"Yes, but when you do get together, how about including Stephen's niece? Katie's her name, right? Another kid would round out the group."

"Good idea, Joe." Jessica clapped her hands.

Nina offered Joe an appreciative smile. "Thanks, Joe. Great suggestion."

Joe placed a hand on his chest and took a bow. "Glad to help."

"Any more news about Stephen's friend's death?" Jessica's brow wrinkled.

Nina sighed. "Not much. I've been dodging arrows for starting the rumor that he was murdered. I never meant to, but if he was, then shouldn't the murderer be caught and put to justice?"

"Of course, and you want to help make that happen."

"You know me and mysteries." Nina shrugged. "Besides, Mark and Stephen were good friends. I had a good friend who was murdered, too, and I know how Stephen must hurt." She referred to the death of Wildeen Bergman, a long-time friend who was brutally killed one night in her bookstore. Nina helped to discover and apprehend the killer.

"Stephen's okay with you getting involved?" Joe asked.

"Well…" Nina bit her lip. "Of course, he worries about the potential danger."

"So do we." Jessica pointed toward Joe and then herself.

"But he knows I can't let a murder happen without at least trying to help find the killer."

Jessica sighed. "All my fault."

Joe drew back and studied her. "Your fault? Why?"

"Because when she was growing up, I gave her a set of Nancy Drew mysteries, books I read when I was her age."

"Nancy Drew, the most famous teenage sleuth in literature." Nina smiled at the memory. "I still have those books, Joe. They were the start of my children's literature collection." She visualized the books with their colorful covers stored in glass-enclosed shelves in her home office.

Joe nodded. "I see where you're coming from, Nina."

"My wanting to help is not just because I like mysteries." Nina shifted to a more comfortable position. "I also have a strong desire to see justice done. If a killer is on the loose, he should be caught and punished. Then the world is right again."

"We understand." Jessica turned to Joe. "Don't we, Joe?"

Joe smiled at Jessica and then focused again on Nina. "I'll never forget how you helped bring Ellie's killer to justice."

Joe referred to another mystery Nina helped solve. Last winter, Ellie Larken, a Marley resident and Joe's long-time friend, drowned in nearby Lake Mead. The authorities decided her death was an accident, but Nina suspected foul play. Sure enough, she was right, and her investigation led to the killer's apprehension. Nina chatted with Jessica and Joe a few minutes longer before signing off.

"Love you, honey." Jessica blew her a kiss. "Our best to Stephen and his family. Maybe we'll all meet sometime."

"Love you, too." Nina waved. "Talk soon."

The couple's faces faded from the screen. A soft smile on her lips, Nina leaned back against the pillows. What would she do without Grandmother Jessica?

Okay, and Joe, too, who had become a friend. Talking to them tonight helped her to reach a decision about her involvement in Mark's death. She would follow her inclinations and treat his demise as murder. She'd keep a low profile, though—if that were possible in a small town such as Parkers Landing. Also, what would Stephen say? Would he approve? Or would he try to talk her out of her plan?

Chapter Seven

While she waited for Stephen to return from taking David home, Nina followed the next step in her investigation. She always thought more clearly when she organized her information. Settling herself again on her bed, this time with her tablet, she created a new file, dividing the blank page into two columns. One column she labeled *Suspect* and the other *Motive*.

The first suspect who came to mind was Oren Brown. She entered his name. Under Motive, she typed *Mark discovered Oren stealing company money to pay gambling debts.*

Next, she entered *Gloria McTeague.* The motive puzzled her. Were she and Oren having an affair? The two were so different that a liaison was hard to believe. Still, sometimes opposites did attract. For Motive, she wrote, *Wanted to be free of Mark and be with Oren.*

Next, Nina listed *Mary Ellen Eckert.* Even though Judy vouched for Mary Ellen's good character, the town baker might hate Mark and carry a grudge for his role in the plane crash that killed her fiancé.

Unknown Person in Hallway was her next suspect. Under Motive, she added, *Mark refused to turn over 'the stuff' he or she wanted.*

Another Unknown suspect was *Assailant at the Street Dance*, who didn't want Nina investigating the murder and exposing him or her. Both Unknowns could be Oren, Gloria, or Mary Ellen.

Nina sat back with a frown. The list provided little to work with. Mary Ellen was the only suspect with a solid motive. Nina needed to find out more about her. She'd see the woman again at the Museum Mommas. She could also visit Lovin's Bakery and, hopefully, glean more information there. Also, she'd keep her eyes and ears open to learn more about others who knew Mark. Hidden motives might come to light.

She glanced at her wristwatch. Stephen would return soon. Perhaps they could take a walk together in the Barlows' garden before going to bed. Nina put away her tablet and went into the living room, thinking to rejoin Judy and George while she waited. Instead of the couple, she found Katie sitting cross-legged on the floor with picture books spread out around her. "Hey, Katie. What're you up to?"

Katie's forehead wrinkled. "I belong to Story Mates, at the library. We're having a program telling stories with puppets."

"That sounds like fun."

Katie picked up a book and flipped through the pages. "I can't decide on a story, and I don't have any puppets."

Intrigued, Nina sat on the floor next to Katie. "Do all these books belong to you?" She gestured toward the array.

Katie nodded. "I like to read."

"I collect books, too." Nina picked up *The Blue-Eyed Fish*, pleased to have a topic in common with the child. "I've read this book at my library's story hour, and I've used puppets, too."

"Puppets on strings?"

"Yes, but also those made of socks to fit over your hand or out of felt to fit over your fingers."

Katie rested her chin in her cupped hand. "Do you buy them? Or make them?"

"Both." Nina paged through the book. "Making puppets is fun. I'd be glad to help you make yours."

Katie's eyes widened. "Wow. Really?"

Her enthusiasm brought a smile to Nina's lips. "Yes, really."

"Okay, but I still can't decide on a story." Katie gestured toward the books.

Nina leaned forward. "Here's an idea. Why don't you and I go to the library tomorrow? I want to visit again, anyway. David showed me around the other day, but we didn't stay long. Maybe together we can choose a story for your project."

Katie clapped her hands. "Going together would be fun."

Pleased they'd made a special connection, Nina helped Katie gather her books. She looked forward to spending more time with the child and sharing her own expertise. Recalling Joe's suggestion, she would invite Stephen and David to join them. She'd just stepped out to the porch to enjoy the view of the river and the shadowed mountains when Stephen's car pulled into the driveway.

A minute later, he climbed the stairs to the porch. "Hey, waiting for me?"

She returned his grin and matched his teasing tone. "Can't think of anyone I'd rather take an evening walk with."

Slipping his car keys into his slacks pocket, he held out a hand. "Let's do it."

Nina and Stephen left the porch and stepped onto a path that wound through the Barlows' property. Lights from nearby homes blinked through the trees, and the soft breeze carried the scent of wildflowers. She told him about her and Katie's planned trip to the library. "Why don't you and David come, too? David likes to read, and sharing books is another way for you to bond."

Stephen frowned and shook his head. "I wish we could, but David and Angie are spending the day with Angie's aunt who lives in Sandpoint, and I've scheduled an online video conference with my staff."

"Oh, too bad. Then Katie and I are on our own."

Stephen squeezed her hand and drew her onto a new section of the pathway. "So nice of you to help her. With the age difference between her and the twins and Judy's and George's busy lives, she's on her own a lot. But I promise the four of us will get together soon."

"All right, Katie and I will have a girls' day at the library. Maybe you and I can be together in the afternoon?"

"I was thinking the same. I have something I want to share."

His serious tone put her on alert. "What?"

He waved a hand. "I don't want to tell you ahead of time, but we'll need to take a car trip out of town. Not far, though."

Tilting her head, she studied him in the dim light. "Why are you being so mysterious? Does the trip have to do with Mark?"

"Yes, Mark is involved. But you'll have to wait to find out how."

Nina and Stephen walked on in silence. She wanted

to tell him about being assaulted at the street dance but hesitated, knowing he would be upset. He had a lot on his mind, and she didn't want to burden him with even more worries. Still, she should share the upsetting occurrence.

At the fence bordering the property, she and Stephen stopped to look at the view. The casino's red, gold, and green lights cast colorful reflections on the water. On the other side of the highway, except for a few neon signs, the downtown lay in darkness. Nina let a couple minutes elapse then cleared her throat. "Stephen, something happened at the dance last night that you should know about."

He faced her, his eyes solemn in the dim light.

"What? Tell me."

She took a deep breath. "Like I already shared, I went to get a bottle of soda and then decided to go for a walk…" She related the rest of the incident. "Luckily, I wasn't hurt, but no mistaking the person's anger." Recalling the vicious shove and the harsh, guttural threat, she shivered and hugged her arms. "The voice sounded similar to the person who threatened Mark at the Meet-and-Greet. I wonder if my assailant was the same?"

Stephen frowned. "Why didn't you tell me about this when you returned to the dance?"

"Because I looked forward to the evening, and when you said, 'Let's dance,' I didn't want to spoil our time together."

"The dance was a reunion highlight for me, too. But, seriously, you could have been hurt."

"Maybe the person was drunk." She made a dismissive wave. "Or joking. Or crazy. Maybe I had nothing to do with his anger."

"Okay. But we should report the incident to Cal. The person might've accosted others at the event."

Nina nodded. "You're right. The assault should be on record."

"We'll stop in the police station tomorrow afternoon on our way out of town." Stepping close, he put an arm around her shoulder. "For now, let's enjoy these moments we have alone."

Putting aside her concern, Nina leaned against him, inhaling his familiar scent.

Moments passed, and then he cupped her chin, tilted her head, and closed his warm lips over hers.

Nina returned the kiss with all her heart and soul. Oh, how she loved this man.

Later, when she lay alone in bed, doubts again nagged. Yes, she loved Stephen and believed he returned her affection. But could their relationship survive the tests they constantly faced? How much could any love take?

****

"You might as well use our spare car," George told Nina the following morning at breakfast. "We bought the car for Rick, but he prefers his cycle. Blaine has his car, and Judy and I each have our own, so Rick's sits in the garage."

Nina finished a bite of scrambled eggs. "Having my own transportation would be great. Then Stephen won't have to share." She looked across the table at Rick. "Is that plan okay with you?"

"No problem." Rick reached for another piece of toast. "Only time I drive a car is when me and Cassie take along someone else."

Stephen nodded. "I'm in favor, too, Nina."

Katie clapped her hands. "Now we can go to the library, huh, Nina?"

"You bet." Nina shifted in her chair to face Katie. "We'll find the perfect book for your Story Mates' program."

"I appreciate your giving Katie special time," Judy told Nina later as they cleared the table. "With all of us so busy, she's often on her own."

Judy's solemn eyes reflected her concern.

"I don't mind at all." Nina set a stack of plates on the counter. "I love sharing books and stories, especially with children."

Half an hour later, Nina and Katie arrived at the library. After parking the car and while crossing the lawn, Nina allowed her gaze to stray past the fountain and the carved wooden statues of animals to the bench where Angie and David sat. Was their meeting only three days ago? So much happened since then.

Nina and Katie climbed the steps to the library's front door, and Nina turned her attention to today's outing. She and Katie were about to have a fun adventure. Once inside the building, Nina gazed around and breathed a sigh. She was at home now. Here, order ruled, and order made her feel safe and secure.

Katie appeared comfortable here, too. She led them past the checkout counter and the row of computers to the children's room, where low shelving provided easy access for small users. A story pit occupied one corner, and beanbag chairs provided comfortable seating for adults and children alike.

"How about a fairy tale?" Nina picked up a copy of *Snow White and the Seven Dwarfs* displayed atop a shelf. The colorful pictures were the work of a well-known children's book illustrator.

Katie's brow wrinkled, and she propped her chin in her hand. "Hmmm. A fairy tale might be okay."

Nina replaced the book and gestured to the shelves. "Let's see what other fairy tales we can find to get ideas." She and Katie located the section and examined the books.

Katie put aside the stories she liked.

After choosing a dozen or so, Nina helped her carry the books to a secluded corner for further examination. "Look for a tale with good characters for puppets." She held up an edition of *The Three Bears* with appealing illustrations. "But most of all, choose a story you like."

A woman approached and stopped beside Katie's chair.

Nina studied the newcomer. In her early thirties, she had short, curly black hair and wore beige slacks and a matching tunic top that complemented her brown skin tones.

"Hello, Katie. Nice to see you today."

Katie looked up, and a grin spread across her face. "Hi, Miz Springer. My friend is helping me find a book for our Story Mates' program." She gestured toward Nina. "She's a librarian, too."

The woman's gaze moved to Nina. "Hello, I'm Cora Springer." She fingered her nametag.

"I'm Nina Foster. My friend, Stephen Kraslow, is Katie's uncle. We're here from Richmond, Washington, to attend the All Class Reunion."

"So sad about that poor man who died at the picnic." Cora sank into a nearby chair. "I didn't know him. My husband and I moved here only a few years ago, and so, we weren't part of the reunion. But, of course, I heard about his death."

Nina nodded. "Mark McTeague and Stephen were classmates and good friends. We're staying to attend his memorial."

Leaning forward, Cora gestured toward the array of books. "Have you chosen a story yet? Anything I can help with?"

"I like this one." Katie held up *The Three Little Pigs*. "What do you think, Nina?" She handed her the book. "Nina said she'd help me make the puppets," she added to Cora.

"Wonderful." Cora clapped her hands.

Nina paged through the book. "Hmmm, this appears to be the traditional version, which I think would work just fine. Let's check it out." She returned the book to Katie and then addressed Cora. "Storytelling is one of my favorite activities."

"Mine, too." Cora's eyes lighted.

"Who says I can't use the computer?"

The loud, whiny voice carried across the room. When Nina looked to see who made the complaint, she spotted Oswald Farrington sitting at one of the patrons' computers.

Oswald glared at the young man standing over him. "I have the right to be here." He poked a long forefinger in the man's face.

"Oh, oh, him again." Cora's brow furrowed. "I need to help Alan. Please excuse me." She stood and hurried to the computers.

Craning her neck, Nina waited to see what would happen.

Katie put down her book and turned toward the computers, too.

Some of the patrons followed the altercation while others ducked their heads or turned away and went about their business.

Cora and Alan, whose badge indicated he was a library employee, spoke to Oswald in low tones.

Oswald bellowed his responses, fragments of which floated back to Nina. Judging from what she'd seen of Oswald at the Museum Mommas meeting, today's display of temper was no surprise.

"Outrageous…You can't tell me… My rights violated…"

A uniformed security officer, stationed near the checkout desk, rose from his chair and joined the group. Grasping Oswald's arm, he lifted him to his feet and led him toward the front door.

Oswald held his head high and marched along beside the officer. As soon as the two disappeared out the door, calm settled over the library.

"Wow." Katie's eyes were wide. "He was mad."

Nina pressed her lips together and nodded. "Rude, too."

Taking along *The Three Little Pigs*, Nina and Katie moved to another section of the library where they chose several books on making puppets. Then they took their choices to the checkout counter where Cora was on duty.

Katie pulled her library card from her backpack and laid it on the counter.

Cora ran a wand scanner over Katie's library card and then over the bar codes on the books. "Looks like you're all set to prepare for the program, Katie. Making the puppets will be fun, especially when you have Nina to help you." Cora winked at Nina.

"Help is the key word." Nina patted Katie's shoulder. "I'm looking forward to our project and to the program." She turned to Cora. "Oh, by the way, I've met the man who gave you trouble. He came to a meeting of the Museum Mommas I attended yesterday."

Cora frowned. "Today isn't the first time he's caused a disturbance. Of course, everyone is welcome to browse, but using the computers requires a card."

"At the meeting, he said he's moving here, so I wonder why he hasn't applied for a card."

"We offered him one, but he declined. We also offered a guest pass, but he didn't want to show ID." Cora finished checking out Katie's books and slid the stack with her card on top across the counter. "He wants to use our system because his computer is being repaired, which is fine, but rules are rules."

Nina gave Katie her card and a few of the books to put into her backpack. She tucked the remainder of the stack into her tote. "Let's hope he gets his computer fixed soon."

Cora nodded. "He is a challenge. Good thing Mike was on duty to escort him out." She leaned her elbows on the counter. "Say, while you're in town, I'd love to get together and compare notes on our libraries."

"A get-together would be fun." Shoptalk with a colleague always interested Nina.

"Give me a call when you're free for coffee or lunch. Thursday is my day off, but my staff is flexible." Cora took a business card from a holder, handed the card to Nina, and then turned toward Katie. "Nice to see you today, Katie. I'm excited about our Story Mates' program, aren't you?"

"I am, 'specially now I have a partner." Katie smiled at Nina.

"Yes, partners." Nina returned the child's smile, pleased their outing was a success. Outside the library, Nina looked around to see if Oswald Farrington lurked nearby. Sure enough, he stood under a maple tree a few yards from the steps. He wasn't alone.

Lexie Duggan, one of the Museum Mommas, accompanied him.

Oswald gestured with his long arms.

Lexie propped her hands on her hips.

Were they arguing? Neither looked around, and Nina and Katie passed by without their notice.

"I saw that man before," Katie said as she and Nina headed for the parking lot.

Recalling Oswald's statement he'd recently come to town, Nina studied Katie. "You have? Where?"

"At Daddy's bank. Mom and I went last week, and he was there. I remember 'cause he sat by us while we waited for Daddy."

"Did he speak to you?" Nina guided them onto the shady path leading to the lot.

"No, he didn't. I noticed him because he jumped up whenever an office door opened. When no one came to him, he'd mumble and plop down in his chair."

Had Oswald's search for his roots led him to the bank? "Did anyone finally talk to him?"

Katie adjusted the strap to her backpack. "I don't know because then we saw Daddy and went to his office."

Oswald Farrington certainly made himself known

around town, Nina mused as she and Katie returned to the Barlows'. What was he up to? Had he really come to Parkers Landing to search for his roots? Or did he have some other, less honest, reason? What was Lexie's interest? Perhaps she offered her genealogy services. Yet, the two appeared to be arguing. Why? Were they involved in another, more secret, way?

Chapter Eight

As planned, on Nina and Stephen's way out of town that afternoon, they stopped at the police station.

Since Chief Cal was out, Officer Tony Garcia took Nina's report. He led them to an interview room where the three sat at a long table, Nina and Stephen on one side and Garcia on the other.

In his late twenties, his hair in a crew cut and his jaw clean-shaven, Tony Garcia radiated the intensity of a rookie eager to do a good job, which was fine with Nina. Maybe he'd take her more seriously than had Cal.

"Could you tell whether the person was a man or a woman?" Fingers poised over his computer keyboard, Garcia studied Nina.

Recalling the incident sent a shiver down her spine. "I was shoved from behind. The voice was low and guttural and could have been disguised. By the time I recovered my balance and turned around, the person disappeared into the darkness."

The officer nodded and punched the keyboard. "What was the person wearing?"

Closing her eyes, she pictured her assailant. "Pants, a long coat that came below the knees, and a baseball cap."

"Could you see hair under the cap?"

Nina opened her eyes. "No. But anyone with long hair could've tucked it up."

"Of course. Just askin'." Garcia's fingers moved over the keyboard.

Stephen leaned forward. "Were any other incidents like Nina's reported at the dance?"

Garcia sat back and folded both arms. "A couple guys' pockets were picked, but no assaults." He turned to Nina. "You said he didn't try to steal your purse, right?"

Nina fingered her purse strap. "He could've grabbed the strap, but, no, he didn't. He shoved me in the back and told me to 'get out of town.' "

Garcia finished typing and looked up. "Okay, I'll let Cal know about this incident. I'll print out your statement for you to sign, and then you're good to go."

The printer soon spit out the statement, which Garcia handed to Nina.

Nina read and signed the paper and then stood, eager to end the interview.

Stephen rose, too, turning to the officer. "Any news on Mark McTeague's death?"

Garcia closed his computer and shook his head. "We don't have the autopsy report yet. Only been a coupla days."

"I know, but I thought you might have heard something." Stephen folded his arms.

Garcia rubbed his chin. "Well…this isn't official, or for publication, but if you ask me, his death looks kinda suspicious."

Stephen's eyebrows rose. "As in…"

"Poison?" Aware Stephen overstepped his authority and yet wanting to hear what Garcia knew, Nina finished his thought. She studied the officer's expression, looking for clues he might give away.

"Maybe." Garcia stiffened and looked from Stephen to Nina. "Can't say any more. Nothing is official."

"Sure. We understand." Stephen waved a hand. "We'll wait for the autopsy report."

"Might take a while." Garcia walked Nina and Stephen to the door. "We had a poisoning in Prescott, where I worked before coming here. Took two months until the results were released."

Out on the sidewalk, Nina's heartbeat quickened as she turned to Stephen. "I was right. Mark was poisoned."

"Now, wait a minute." Stephen put out a hand. "Like Garcia said, they're still investigating. No official verdict yet."

"But if he was—"

"If he was poisoned, that still doesn't mean you need to get involved."

Nina placed a hand on his arm "I know you're concerned about my safety, but, Stephen, I already am involved."

Stephen slowly shook his head. "I suppose there's no use arguing. But for now, we'll get on with the rest of our afternoon." Grasping her elbow, he steered her along the sidewalk.

She fell into step beside him. "You still haven't told me where we're going."

"I'll explain along the way."

A few minutes later, Nina sat beside Stephen as he drove north on the four-lane highway and over the bridge spanning the Kokuskie River. Several kayaks, their occupants paddling in unison, sped along the water. She watched until they disappeared around a bend shaded by overhanging cottonwood trees.

"Another thirty miles, and we'd reach the Canadian border." Stephen pointed ahead. "Or we could turn off and go west to Montana. But we'll save both places for another trip."

The suggestion of more trips brought a smile, especially when this trip had not turned out as she'd expected. "I'll look forward to exploring under happier circumstances. I'm assuming today's outing isn't a pleasant memory?" Now over the bridge, Nina's side window revealed landscape that included farms growing hay and corn, separated by stands of cottonwood and evergreen trees.

"Yes and no. You'll understand when you hear the story. But I will give you some background."

"All right." Nina settled back in her seat, prepared to listen.

Stephen took a breath. "In high school, Mark and I belonged to the hiking club. Mr. Lozier, a math teacher and also a professional climber, sponsored the group. A dozen kids were members, and we took weekend hikes. One trip was to Rocky Ridge, where we're going today. Here's the first turnoff." Stephen slowed the car and swung onto a side road.

Nina turned her attention to the landscape, spotting a country store with an outdoor display of fresh fruit and bouquets of flowers, and then a gas station, with several vehicles lined up for service. Farmlands followed, where houses and barns and other outbuildings marked the territory. Eventually, the farms disappeared, and the road climbed, with woods enclosing them on either side.

After several miles of twists and turns, Stephen

finally reached a clearing. Pulling off the road, he cut the engine. "We hike from here."

Nina stepped from the car and gazed around. A forest of evergreens, similar to those at home, surrounded them. The tangy scent of pinecones filled the air. All was silent, except for the rustle of the wind in the trees and the twittering of birds.

"Been awhile since I was here, but the path looks the same." Stephen pointed toward a trail leading into the woods.

Nina tilted her head. "I hear water flowing."

"Cricket Creek. We'll follow it for a while. The path's overgrown in places but not steep."

"I'm sure I'll be fine." She'd hiked enough at home to feel comfortable with these surroundings.

The path was narrow, though, and in places Nina and Stephen climbed over fallen logs and pushed away overgrown foliage. The woods thickened, blocking out the sun and cooling the air. The creek, piercing the silence with a cheerful burble, kept the atmosphere heavy with moisture. Ferns, ivy, and other low-growing plants lined the path.

Stephen waved a hand. "Of course, Mr. Lozier taught us all along the way, naming the trees and the plants."

"Of course, you and Mark paid attention." Nina's light tone teased.

"More or less." Stephen chuckled. "As much as the other kids." He stopped and looked around. "We should be nearing a cabin. Yes, I see the roof through the trees." He pointed ahead.

Nina followed Stephen into a clearing. The cabin was a crude structure of weathered wood with ivy twining up the walls. A stone chimney atop the shingled roof appeared ready to crumble. Stepping through a patch of weeds, she approached a window. Cupping her hands around her eyes and peering through dust-coated glass, she made out a table and chairs, a stone fireplace, and a door leading to another, smaller room. "This cabin reminds me of the cabins I stayed in at Girl Scout camp. I can't imagine anyone living here permanently."

Stephen came to stand beside her. "Right. A place for campers and hikers to rest or to stay overnight, or a few days, at the most."

Nina and Stephen looked around for a few more minutes.

Then Stephen pointed toward a trail. "The end of our journey is only a short distance away."

As she followed Stephen along the path through the woods, Nina's curiosity grew. What could he possibly want to show her? Finally, she stepped from the shadows and the shelter of the trees into the bright sunlight. Shading her eyes with a hand, Nina took in the view. Directly ahead, a cliff dropped off into a canyon. Across the canyon, far in the distance, the snow-covered Rocky Mountains lined the sky. Her breath caught. "Wow. I feel like I'm on top of the world."

Stephen grinned. "Spectacular, isn't it? We all were awestruck. Along with most of the other kids, I whipped out my camera and took pictures. Mine were for a school newspaper article. We stayed another half hour or so, while Mr. Lozier gave us a geography lesson, and then we left."

"Sounds like a fun trip, but I'm guessing your story's not finished." Slanting him a glance, she saw his smile fade.

"You're right. Now comes the hard part. When I got home, I discovered the photos I took didn't turn out. I really needed them for my article, so I decided to make another trip for retakes. Mark said he'd come, too, and the following Saturday I drove us here."

Nina gazed again at the mountains across the canyon and thought how far away they were. "Did anyone else know about your trip?"

"We told our parents where we were going. We invited a few of our friends, but no one wanted to go, so we came by ourselves."

"You hiked to this same spot?" She pointed toward the cliff's edge.

"Yes, although we followed another, shorter cutoff that bypassed the creek. I took my pictures. Mark brought his camera, too, and he snapped some shots. Everything was fine until—until…" He took a deep breath and closed his eyes.

She laid a hand on his arm. "Are you okay, Stephen?"

He opened his eyes and blinked. "Yeah, I'm okay. Been a long time since I've talked about this place. Talking's difficult."

"You're sure you want to continue?" Of course, she wanted to hear the rest of the story, but the distress she heard in his voice concerned her.

He waved a hand. "Yes, I've come this far, and I want you to know…everything." He sucked in a deep breath. "I stood just about there"—he pointed toward a spot on the ridge—"taking my pictures. I took several shots of the canyon and the mountains, and then I turned around to snap a few of the path and the woods." He swallowed hard. "I stepped backward to frame a shot when all of a sudden, the earth slid out from under my feet."

Sensing what came next, Nina pressed fingers to her lips. "Oh, no…"

He nodded, his mouth tight. "Yep…I fell into the canyon."

"Stephen, how awful." Nina gave silent thanks that the results of his fall weren't disastrous.

"As I slid down with my face toward the wall, I wrapped my hand around a sapling. I yelled, of course, and Mark came running. When he saw what happened, he went flat on his stomach and reached down with one hand while anchoring himself to a rock with the other. I couldn't see him, of course, but he told me later. Anyway, I grabbed onto his hand with my free hand. He pulled, and I climbed, digging my toes into footholds. Miraculously, I reached the top and fell onto solid ground." His shoulders sagged. "I suffered some scrapes and my clothes were ripped, but otherwise I was okay."

Nina clutched her churning stomach. "What a frightening experience."

Stephen swiped a hand over his forehead. "Mark and I didn't tell anyone what happened. We knew if we did, we wouldn't be allowed to hike alone anymore. We did hike again with the club but never here. Since that day, I haven't been back. For a long time afterward, I had nightmares about my narrow escape."

"Maybe we shouldn't have come." Nina stepped close and put an arm around his waist.

"I wanted to share the experience, so that you'll understand my loyalty to Mark, even with all his flaws." He gazed down at her. "He saved my life."

Tears burned Nina's eyes. "I'm glad you told me, and yes, knowing helps me to understand. You and Mark went your separate ways after high school, though."

Stephen nodded. "He joined the Air Force, as he planned, and I went to college. We got together when we both were in town at the same time, like the high school reunions. But for the most part, our lives were too different to often cross paths. I've missed him, though. On this trip, I planned to ask him and Gloria to come to Richmond and stay so the four of us could hang out. Now, that won't happen." He shoved both hands in his slacks pockets and looked away.

Nina gazed at the mountains across the canyon. Their snowy peaks, silver in the sunlight, stood outlined against a vivid blue sky. Then, as a thought occurred, she turned back to Stephen. "You never got the photos you wanted."

Stephen gave a harsh laugh. "No, but I found some pictures on the Internet for my article. My camera is probably still at the bottom of the canyon."

"You could take some pictures today…" She gestured toward the canyon.

Several moments passed while Stephen faced the canyon. Then he pulled his phone from his jacket pocket. "Yeah, I think I will. I've never wanted photos of this scene, because they would only remind me of a terrible experience. But now, I think pictures will be a way to keep Mark's memory alive."

"I'll give you a few moments alone while I look around."

His lips curved into a smile. "Thanks, Nina."

"Stay away from the edge, though." Hoping to

lighten the moment, she grinned and patted his arm.

"You bet." He chuckled. "Hanging in that canyon is an experience I don't want to repeat."

Thinking to take photos, too, especially of the wildflowers she noticed along the way, Nina pulled out her phone. She found the flowers, their pink petals a vivid contrast to the surrounding greenery. As she straightened from snapping a shot, she spotted something shiny lodged under a pink blossom. Curious, she plucked a rectangular piece of burnished brass from its hiding place. The fragment probably belonged to an artist's sculpture. The find was of little value and of doubtful consequence, yet, always looking out for the environment, she slipped it into her jacket pocket. She could discard the piece later.

During the return drive to town, Nina broke several minutes of silence. "Do you still doubt Mark was murdered?"

He shot her a glance. "I'm not sure what I think. The warning you received at the dance—if the threat was a warning and not just a crazy person's rambling—plus what Garcia hinted about poison, tell me murder is a possibility. If so, of course, I'd want the murderer found and brought to justice. But I still don't want you in danger."

"I'll be careful. I promise. No more wandering around by myself at night, especially."

"All right, and I'll help you as much as I can. But, if nothing conclusive turns up by the time we need to leave, then…"

"I'll let the matter go." *Maybe.*

She needed to get busy. Having a time constraint made her more determined to solve the puzzle.

****

After returning from Rocky Ridge, Nina helped Judy prepare the evening meal.

George arrived home from work, and he and Stephen joined them.

Rick and Blaine appeared, and Katie, too. Now, everyone contributed to the meal preparation.

Nina marveled at how the Barlows functioned as a family. They seemed truly to enjoy one another. Oh, they weren't perfect. The kids sometimes argued, and on occasion, Judy and George disagreed, too, but none of the dissention lasted long, with harmony soon restored.

At first, Nina felt very much the outsider, but with each passing day and each occasion they were together, she became more a part of the group, part of a *family*. Of course, Nina had her grandmother, Jessica, whom she loved dearly, but one person wasn't the same as a group. This experience with the Barlows was unique.

When she finally went to her room that night, she again turned her attention to Mark's death. Encouraged by Officer Garcia's hints Mark had been poisoned, she renewed her intent to conduct her own investigation. In the event she was wrong and he'd died of natural causes after all, what would be lost, other than her own investment of time and effort?

While preparing for bed, Nina recalled the scrap of metal she found in the grass while photographing the wildflowers. She retrieved the piece from her jacket pocket and studied it under the light, thinking again it came from a piece of artwork, such as a sculpture. Perhaps someone staying at the cabin lost it. The bit of metal had no value, but for some reason, she was reluctant to discard it and instead placed the fragment on her dresser.

Next, she took out her tablet and reviewed her list of suspects. With nothing new to add, tonight might be a good time to research poisons. Since he hadn't appeared ill at the Meet-and-Greet, she surmised Mark was given the poison the following morning before the picnic lunch. The substance must be fast acting to kill him by lunchtime. Nina loved to do research, and tonight she dug eagerly into the topic of lethal substances. An hour later, her head spinning with the names of the various poisons, she sat back and blew out a frustrated breath.

Without knowing what the autopsy revealed, her chances of hitting on the correct poison were slim. She felt confident ruling out arsenic and cyanide, though. Arsenic left a yellowish skin tone and traces in the digestive tract. Cyanide released a bitter almond odor. The attending physicians would certainly have noticed those clues. Perhaps her best procedure would be to look for other clues and motivations.

She reviewed the conversation fragments overhead at the casino. Oren passed off the exchange as the Dead Man's Tag game he and Mark and their friends played as kids. Maybe. But for now, Nina would take seriously the threat that Mark had to "turn over the rest of the stuff" or he was a "dead man." Was Mark blackmailing someone? Was someone blackmailing him?

Nina studied her still-sparse list. Not much to go on. Perhaps she was wrong, after all. But whenever tempted to give up her investigation, she recalled Mark's distress and desperation when they passed in the hallway. No, she was certain he was murdered. Trouble was, the time for proving her theory grew short. Only a few more days until Mark's memorial and a couple days after that, she and Stephen would leave Parkers Landing. She must make more discoveries—and soon.

Chapter Nine

"How was your trip to Rocky Ridge yesterday?" Judy asked Nina as she drove them to town for the Museum Mommas' meeting at Curly Locks Beauty Salon. "Did Stephen tell you what happened there?"

Nina pulled her gaze from the colorful flower garden of a house they passed to focus on Judy's question. As she recalled Stephen's story, her chest tightened. "He did, after we arrived. What an ordeal."

"I didn't learn about his accident until years later, after our parents passed away. When he finally told me, I was horrified." Judy shivered.

"I was upset, too, even though I'm thankful he shared the experience."

"I'm glad you know, but I sense you two are in conflict over Mark's death." Judy's brow wrinkled. "I'm sorry. None of my business." She slapped the steering wheel. "But, okay, yes, it is. He's my brother, and I care about him. I care about you, too, Nina. You're already like one of the family."

Judy's words warmed Nina's heart. "Thank you, Judy. You've all made me feel welcome. But, although he says he'd accept proof, Stephen doesn't want to believe Mark was murdered. I don't blame him, but my gut feeling tells me I'm right. What do you think?"

Judy frowned. "Not sure I want to take sides. I considered Mark a good guy, but probably not as perfect as Stephen saw him, especially after the Rocky Ridge incident. Mark always needed to prove himself to be not just good, but the best. He didn't want just to fly, but to be an ace pilot in the Air Force, which he was. Then he successfully flew for another outfit until the accident that killed Mary Ellen's fiancé, Harmon. Mark made a comeback with FlyGuys. His and Oren's company is a highly rated charter service."

Nina glanced out the window again to see they'd reached downtown. Elevated signs identified the establishments—Delphon's Drugs, Sparkles Jewelry, Weyland's Western Wear—so many places to explore. "What do you know about Mark's upbringing? Was he born and raised in Parkers?"

"Yes. His father worked at the mill and his mother was a housekeeper at Greystone. They're both dead now. Mark's two brothers and sister moved away, like so many kids do, as soon as they graduated high school. None of them has ever been back for a reunion. But Mark always comes, and he always has something to brag about."

"Gloria's not from Parkers, is she?" Nina pictured the woman in her designer clothes and expensive hairstyle.

"No. He met her in California. She came from a wealthy family and bankrolled Mark and Oren in their fledgling charter plane business."

Judy's information matched what she'd heard elsewhere. "Gloria helped Mark to realize his dream."

Judy stopped for a red light. "Uh huh. I always got the feeling he resented using her money, but he wanted the business badly enough to swallow his pride and take what she offered."

"What did she see in him? Their backgrounds were so different." Nina idly watched a woman lead her German Shepherd across the street.

"He was good-looking and had a reputation as an ace pilot. She could show him off on the social scene."

"I don't see Oren fitting into their lifestyle. He's so—so—*rustic*." A vision of Oren in his Hawaiian shirt and tugging on his scraggly beard came to mind.

Judy tossed back her head and laughed. "You're too polite, Nina. I've heard other, less flattering terms. He and Mark knew each other in the service and discovered they shared a dream. Of course, in the Air Force, Oren had to shape up, as far as dress code, anyway. But now he's out and can be a bum again. I've heard he's a good pilot, though."

"He seemed competent when he took me and Stephen for a plane ride on Sunday. Does he have a girlfriend?"

The light changed to green, and Judy stepped on the gas. "From time to time. One was a casino hostess, and another a waitress at The Rusty Spur. Nothing serious." She ducked her head. "I'm being gossipy. But maybe knowing this background will help you—in whatever."

"What you've told me does help. I'm really learning about Mark, especially."

Judy waved a hand. "Basically, he was a good guy—I think. Who knows, really? Don't we all have a shadow side? Maybe Mark's got him murdered—if he was murdered."

"What do you think, Judy?" Nina studied Judy's profile, eager for her answer.

"I don't know." Judy shrugged. "But if I hear

anything I think will help one way or the other, I'll let you know."

"When we talked to Officer Garcia yesterday, he hinted the autopsy is taking so long because poison is suspected." Nina settled back in her seat.

"Then Mark was murdered—unless he poisoned himself, which I would doubt."

"I'll never forget how he appeared when I saw him in the hallway at the Meet-and-Greet." Nina tensed and hugged her arms. "He was definitely threatened."

"I understand your concern—and your involvement. If he was murdered, then the killer should be caught and punished."

"Thank you, Judy, for your support." Having at least one person on her side encouraged Nina.

Judy slowed to turn a corner. "Stephen's caught in the middle. If Mark was murdered, of course he wants to see the killer arrested and justice done. But if you're sleuthing, he worries you'll put yourself in danger."

"I know." Nina heaved a sigh. "My need to help seek justice often causes conflict between us."

"He loves you."

The simple statement brought tears to Nina's eyes. "I love him, too." Turning again to the window, she saw they'd reached Main Street.

"We're almost there." Judy nodded toward her side window. "Curly Locks will be on the left."

Skimming her gaze over signs for Val's Variety, The Rusty Spur, and Artorama, Nina spotted a yellow sign with Curly Locks spelled out in cursive writing. She looked forward to being with the Museum Mommas again and helping with their project. Hopefully, she'd also gain information to aid her investigation. A bell on the door tinkled cheerfully as Nina followed Judy into the salon.

In the waiting area, several customers sat in green vinyl chairs chatting and perusing magazines.

Behind the counter, an employee in her twenties rang up charges for a woman ready to show her new hairdo to the world.

Blown-up photos of models sporting trendy hairstyles decorated the walls, and the scents of permanent wave solution and shampoo wafted along the airwaves.

Not surprisingly, Judy knew everyone, exchanging greetings and introducing Nina. Two of the waiting women were Quilting Queens, the third worked at the drugstore, and the newly coifed patron lived next door to the Barlows. The young woman behind the counter was Bettina, Tilda's daughter from her first marriage.

Three stylists, including Tilda, worked with clients at their stations.

Tilda looked up and waved. "The Mommas are in the storeroom." She pointed her comb toward a hallway. "I'll join you soon."

Although Tilda's client's face was turned away, the woman's bright red hair looked familiar. "Isn't that Gloria with Tilda?" Nina whispered to Judy.

Judy craned her neck and then nodded. "Sure is. She's getting her hair styled for the memorial."

Nina and Judy continued on to the storeroom, an area at the back of the building large enough to house chair hair dryers and glass display cases. As Tilda indicated, Mary Ellen, Lexie, Mona, and Della were already at work.

Mona stepped forward. "Glad you could come

today, ladies. I'm in charge until Tilda joins us, so I'll put you to work. Tilda made individual inventories of items we're collecting." She handed Nina and Judy each a clipboard. "When you find something on your list, check it off and pack it in those boxes." She pointed toward a stack of cardboard boxes. "When we're finished, we'll load our cars and caravan to the museum."

The first item on Nina's inventory was a vintage, handheld hair dryer with an attached funnel. A few minutes search revealed the dryer hidden under a pile of plastic capes. She wiped off the dust, wrapped the dryer in newspaper, and added it to one of the boxes. A pair of curling tongs from the 1930s turned up, and then a package of hairbrushes. Next was a permanent wave kit called Curl Me. She searched the shelves and located four of the kits, each in a box showing a model with short, curly hair.

Della passed by, stopping to look over Nina's shoulder. "Oh, yes, Curl Me, one of those home perm kits. Remember those, ladies?" She turned to the others.

"My mom gave me that perm." Mona waved turquoise bejeweled fingers. "Dad always complained how it stank up the house, but it sure curled my hair."

"Home perms never worked well for me." Della's nose wrinkled. "My hair always frizzed." She smoothed her upswept hairdo.

Lexie looked up from sorting combs. "Probably because you left the solution on too long. You need to follow directions, people."

"The perms will be a fun part of the exhibit, anyway." Mona folded a plastic apron. "How many boxes are there, Nina?"

Nina consulted her inventory and then looked up. "Hmmm, my list says there should be six, but I've found only four."

"The remaining sets are around somewhere." Della's wave took in the entire room.

"We'll all keep an eye out. Right, ladies?" Mona's gaze swept the group.

Everyone nodded and made affirmative replies.

Nina spent the next ten minutes searching for the missing permanent sets but with no luck.

Tilda entered the storeroom through the open doorway. "How're you all doing?" Both hands on her hips, she gazed around. "Are you finding everything on the inventory?"

"I'm missing two of these Curl Me home perms." Nina held up one of the boxes.

Tilda frowned. "That's odd. I'm sure all six were here last week. But don't worry, Nina, they'll turn up." She pointed toward her wristwatch. "Now, it's time to take what we have to the museum."

Nina helped Judy load her car. She had just tucked a box of cosmetics into the trunk when Lexie stepped to her side.

"Looks like you may be right in guessing Mark was poisoned." Lexie shifted her box of hairbrushes from one arm to the other.

"Really? Have the autopsy results been released?" If Lexie had definite news, Nina hoped she would share. She'd been forthcoming in their previous conversations.

"No, but rumors are flying. Have you done any research on poisons?"

"A little, but there are so many." Nina turned away

to push the cosmetics toward the back of the trunk.

"Gloria and Oren wanted a quick cremation, too. Gloria—"

"Gloria what?" said another voice.

Nina straightened to see the subject of her and Lexie's conversation standing behind them. Oh, dear, how long had she been listening?

"There you are, Gloria." Lexie's lips curved into a smile. "We hoped Tilda would finish your hair before we left so we could see the results. Looks good. Love the style."

"You don't think she cut my hair too short?" Gloria half-turned to reveal the back length.

"Absolutely not." Lexie shook her head.

"The length is very flattering." Nina spoke the truth. Tilda proved to be a talented stylist, at least with Gloria.

Gloria pulled car keys from her shoulder purse. "So much to do yet. Today was the only time I could work in an appointment, with only one salon in town and no time to drive to Sandpoint."

"Is everything coming together for the memorial?" Gripping her box, Lexie leaned against Nina's car.

"The event will be a wonderful tribute to Mark." Tears glistened in Gloria's eyes. "He was such a…a good man."

"He was." Lexie straightened and heaved a deep sigh. "We all will miss him."

Given Lexie's criticism of Mark on previous occasions, today's praise surprised Nina. But then, no one should tell a man's widow how much he was disliked.

Gloria jiggled her car keys. "Well, I can't stand

here talking when I still have so much to do." Without waiting for a reply, she turned and walked away.

Lexie pursed her lips and shook her head. "Like my grandmother used to say, crocodile tears."

Nina smiled at the term to express fake grief, which she'd also heard from her grandmother. But then, thinking again about Gloria's response, she let a frown replace her smile. "I don't know…she seemed sincere."

"That's because she's an actress."

Nina widened her eyes. "Seriously? In plays? Movies?"

"Movies, mostly. She was pursuing an acting career when she met Mark. But she never had more than bit parts. Finally, she gave up, married him, and put her efforts—and her money—into their flying business."

"She gave up acting for him?" This fact was news Nina hadn't yet heard.

Lexie shrugged. "I guess you could say she did."

Nina studied Lexie. "You don't like her very much, do you?"

"Do you?" Lexie stuck out her chin.

"I hardly know her." Nina folded her arms and leaned against the car's fender. "I'll admit she hasn't been overly friendly, but I've taken into consideration the circumstances."

"Huh. You're way more tolerant than I am, Nina." Clutching her box, Lexie turned away.

A thought occurred, and Nina straightened and hurried to catch up. "Lexie, wait. Didn't I see you and Oswald Farrington at the library the other day?"

Lexie's eyes narrowed. "You don't miss much."

"I was there with Stephen's niece, Katie. I'm

helping her with a storytelling project. As we left, I saw you and Oswald talking in the park." She could have said, "arguing," but instead chose to be diplomatic.

"He's blabbing all around town about searching for his roots, like he's expecting to be related to royalty. I offered to help, and he agreed. When I learned he wanted my services for free, our association ended." Her lips thinned.

"He's an odd one."

"Yes, he is, Nina. You should keep an eye on him."

Nina watched Lexie drive away, her thoughts lingering on their conversation. Oswald's refusal to pay Lexie for her services came as no surprise. The real news was that Gloria was an actress. Nina marveled at how she continually learned new information about the people of Parkers Landing. Like an onion, each person had layers. How much more would be discovered? Would peeling the layers reveal the murderer?

Chapter Ten

Nina and Judy joined the car caravan, leaving Curly Locks and traveling the two blocks to the museum. They unloaded Judy's car and carried the collected items into the museum and then down the hall to the beauty salon exhibit. Selene greeted the group, standing in the middle of the room like a policeman on the street corner, pointing this way and that, making certain all the treasures were put in the correct places.

Returning to the car for another load, Nina passed Director Hal's office. She had yet to meet the man. He was either out of the building or busy in his office, poring over books and photos. A glance in the window revealed he was there today. He wasn't alone, though. His visitor was none other than Oswald Farrington the Third. Oswald perched on the corner of Hal's desk, arms folded, glaring down in what Nina thought a bold and disrespectful pose.

Just then, Oswald glanced up and met Nina's gaze. He gave her a brief nod.

She returned the gesture and continued on her way. On her return trip from picking up another load, she again glanced in the window, but Oswald was gone, and Hal once again bent over his books. Was Oswald using Hal to help locate his roots? Or did he counsel with the museum's director for another reason?

"You're all invited to Lovin's for lunch," Mary

Ellen announced when the boxes were unloaded and placed in the exhibit room. "We have fresh huckleberry scones today."

Della placed both hands on her ample hips. "I'm on a diet."

"We have salads on the menu." Mary Ellen's dimple flashed. "And skinny rolls."

"Skinny rolls?" Mona hooted. "I've never seen anything in your bakery I'd call skinny."

"Well, you'll just have to come today and let me show you." Mary Ellen clapped her hands.

Judy stepped to Nina's side. "What do you think?"

"I'd love to visit her bakery." Mary Ellen was one of her suspects. Hopefully, a trip to her establishment would turn up clues either to further implicate her or to absolve her from involvement in Mark's death.

After discussion, the entire group accepted Mary Ellen's invitation. Since the bakery was only two blocks away, they left their cars in the museum's parking lot and walked to Lovin's.

Before entering the bakery, Nina stopped to look in the window at the attractively displayed assortment of pies, cakes, and sweet rolls. Her mouth watered. With all the morning's activity, breakfast had worn off and lunch beckoned.

Inside, enticing aromas floated along the warm atmosphere. The yellow walls with red trim provided a cheerful backdrop to the glass cases filled with the bakery's offerings. In anticipation of the Museum Mommas, tables in the center of the room were pushed together to make one large square.

Along with the others, Nina pulled out a chair and sat. Picking up the menu, she studied the selections. A variety of sandwiches were featured, including roasted chicken, turkey and cranberry, and grilled cheese. Salads and soups rounded out the menu.

A young woman server who wore her blonde hair in a single braid brought a tray of pastry. "Hi, ladies, here's our honey walnut scones fresh from the oven." She placed the tray in the middle of the table.

Leaning forward, Nina breathed in the sweet, nutty aroma.

"Thank you, Sara." Della, seated on Nina's right, waved to the woman.

The bracelet Della wore caught Nina's eye. Square red stones alternating with what appeared to be diamonds were set in a narrow band of gold. The red stones reminded Nina of the stone she found at the casino. "What an attractive bracelet."

Della beamed. "I love bracelets, and this is one of my favorites."

"Are the stones rubies?"

"Oh, yes, and the others are diamonds. The bracelet was a birthday gift from my husband. The ruby is my birthstone." Placing a forefinger on the bracelet, she rotated it around her wrist.

Nina spotted an empty setting where a ruby should have been. "Did you lose a ruby?"

Della's mouth turned down. "I did. But I wanted to wear the bracelet today, anyway. It matches my blouse and flower." She pointed toward her dark red blouse and then the rose in her upswept hair.

"Did you lose the ruby recently?" The stone Nina found was about the same size as the one missing from Della's bracelet.

Della's eyebrows peaked. "Why, yes. Why do you

ask?"

Nina shrugged, not wanting to share any more information. "No particular reason. I just—"

"Here you go, Nina."

Sitting on Nina's left, Mona passed her the tray of scones.

"Thanks, Mona." Nina selected a scone, placed it on her plate, and then slid the tray to Della.

"Yummy!" Della's eyes grew big. "Can I have two?" She looked up at Mary Ellen, who hovered over the group.

"Of course." Mary Ellen beamed and waved a hand. "We have more in the kitchen."

Della helped herself to the scones and then handed the tray to Selene.

Lest Della become suspicious, Nina dropped her questions about the lost ruby. Along with the others, she turned her attention to enjoying the treat. Picking up her scone, she inhaled the aroma and then took a bite. "Mmm, delicious." She caught Mary Ellen's gaze. "How do you get your pastry so puffy?" She poked a finger into the scone, making an indentation that quickly bounced back.

Mary Ellen smiled and fluttered her eyelashes. "Sorry, Nina, but my recipes are trade secrets... Oh, Sara." She beckoned her employee. "Will you bring us another carafe of coffee, please?"

"I bet I know what Mary Ellen puts in her pastry," Mona whispered behind her hand to Nina when their hostess moved on.

"You do? What?" Nina took another bite of the scone, eager to hear Mona's revelation.

"Potassium bromate."

Nina frowned. "What is that?"

Mona cast a sidelong glance around the table. "A chemical she adds to the flour, to make the pastry rise. The substance is still legal in this country."

Her curiosity aroused, Nina sat back and regarded Mona. "Legal here but not in other countries? Why?"

Mona's nose wrinkled. "A few have banned its use because it can be poisonous."

"Poisonous?" Nina stared at the scone, which suddenly lost its appeal.

"In quantities, of course. The baking process makes the chemical harmless. So, don't worry. We can safely eat Mary Ellen's scones. They *are* good." She took another bite of hers and chewed.

Nina studied Mona with new interest. "How do you know all these facts about baking?"

"I was a chemistry major in college." Mona smiled. "Of course, I can't prove potassium bromate is what she adds…"

"What would you like to order?"

Nina looked up to see Sara, pad and pencil in hand. Struggling to switch her focus from Mona's shocking news to what to eat for lunch, Nina studied the menu. "I'll have the…chicken salad croissant." She pointed toward the item.

Sara wrote on her pad. "The sandwich comes with a cup of soup. Today, we have potato or tomato basil."

"Tomato basil." Nina handed the menu to Sara and then turned back to Mona, intending to continue their conversation.

Just then, Selene clapped her hands. "We have a new bequest to the museum and need to decide how to spend it." Her gaze swept over the group. "Of course, the board will make the final decision, but Director Hal welcomes input."

Della raised her hand and fluttered her fingers. "I vote for the Comstock courtroom exhibit we've all been waiting for."

"*She's* been waiting for," Mona whispered to Nina. "Honestly, the woman has a one-track mind."

"New display cases in the main room would be a better use of the money." Tilda lifted her chin. "The cases we have are over-crowded."

"Just a minute, Tilda." Della frowned. "Judge Comstock was a brilliant man and worthy of honoring."

Tilda looked down her long nose at Della. "Oh, puh-lccze. What is interesting about a courtroom?"

Della stuck both hands on her hips. "Judge Comstock's courtroom would be a more popular exhibit than a beauty shop."

Tilda huffed. "Salon. Curly Locks is a *salon*."

"Now, ladies." Selene shook a forefinger. "I'll make a note of both your requests. As I said, the final decision is up to the board."

Nina listened with interest, but part of her mind still focused on what Mona told her about potassium bromate. She covertly studied Mary Ellen. Instead of joining the group at the table, she hovered, making sure everyone's water glass or coffee or teacup was refilled. Bright and bubbly, she appeared the perfect hostess. But could she have a dark side that prompted her to use the substance that enhanced her pastries to poison Mark? Nina had difficulty picturing her as a murderer. But then, she'd read enough murder mysteries to know appearances could be deceiving, and that killers were quite clever in hiding their evil under a pleasant demeanor.

Later, when Nina and Judy were on their way home, Judy heaved a sigh and cast Nina a quick glance. "What a busy morning. But we accomplished a lot, didn't we? Thank you so much for your help, Nina."

"You're welcome." Nina offered a thumbs-up. "I enjoyed the morning. But when we get home, I do plan to take a nap."

Judy stopped for a traffic light. "After I make some calls, I'll relax, too, but not for long. I'm on a committee to elect a city councilman, and we're meeting for coffee later to plan our strategy."

Nina slowly shook her head. "How you juggle all your outside activities with family life amazes me."

Judy laughed and pressed the accelerator. "I do keep busy. George warns me, sometimes, to slowdown."

"But he's very proud of you. I can tell." Nina shifted her tote in her lap to a more comfortable position.

"You think?"

"I do. You two have a wonderful relationship."

A soft smile tilted Judy's lips.

"I'm so lucky we met."

"How did you two meet?" How couples got together always interested Nina.

Judy turned onto the road leading up the hill toward the residential neighborhoods. "George was passing through town on his way to a new job at a bank in Coeur d'Alene, but car trouble stranded him overnight. He ate dinner at The Rusty Spur where I was a waitress. He said he took one look at me and knew he'd never leave Parkers Landing." She laughed. "After turning down the job in Coeur d'Alene, he hired on at Parkers First National. I took a few courses at junior college, but when Rick and Blaine came along, I chose to be a stay-at-home mom. Katie's birth brought us the daughter we wanted, and our family is now complete."

Nina clapped her hands. "What a lovely story, Judy. Thanks for sharing."

"Of course. Now, what about you and Stephen? How fortunate for both of you that he moved to Richmond."

The memory of her and Stephen's first meeting brought warmth to her cheeks. "We met at a writer friend's book launching party, but our relationship hasn't progressed as smoothly as yours and George's. My fault, I'll admit, but I do love him. I'm afraid of commitment, though."

"You'll work out things. Every relationship has problems, even George's and mine. Adjusting to small town life wasn't easy when he had his sights set on a city larger than Parkers Landing."

"Stephen and I don't have that problem. We both love our small town. But when he arrived and we first met, I'd just ended a relationship and wasn't interested in a new one. He persevered, though, and now I'm so glad he did. I don't know what I'd do without him."

Judy nodded. "You're a good match."

Hearing Judy's remark encouraged Nina. "Thanks, Judy. But even so, now that David's in the picture... Well, I can't help worrying about how Stephen's new responsibility will affect our relationship."

"Judging by the way you and Katie took to each other, I'm betting you'll fit right in with whatever develops between Stephen and David."

Judy's encouragement buoyed Nina's spirits, and she smiled and straightened her shoulders. "Thanks, Judy. I hope you're right."

However, when Nina and Judy reached the Barlows' and Nina found Stephen and David on the front porch, their heads bent over a map spread out on the table, her doubts returned. Stephen had gained not only a son but also the son's mother. What would be Angie's role in this new situation? Would Stephen feel obligated to include her in his life? Where would that leave Nina? Stephen professed his love, but still…

Stephen looked up, and his eyes lighted. "Nina. We've been waiting for you."

His warm welcome relaxed her tension. "Hello, Stephen." She turned to David. "How're you, David?"

"I'm good."

David offered a shy smile and then looked away. Perhaps he, too, felt insecure in this new situation. Despite having had several fathers, adjusting to yet another one, along with the man's significant other and ready-made family, had to be a challenge. She turned back toward Stephen. "Looks like you're planning another outing."

"Yes, this time, on bicycles. This path along the river looks promising." He pointed toward the map. "Very scenic and with interesting stops along the way. We're waiting for you, so that you can come along, too."

"I, ah—" She was tempted to beg off, saying she was too tired, which was true—sort of. She also wanted to spend time researching poisons, especially potassium bromate. Her conversation with Mona at the bakery stirred her curiosity. Still, she'd already turned down several of their outings. She didn't want David to think she didn't like him and wanted to avoid his company. "Yes, I'll go. Sounds like fun."

"Good, I'm glad we waited. We've got our bikes." Stephen gestured toward the bicycles, with helmets hanging on the handlebars, parked near the bottom of the porch steps. "We'll find a bike for you in the garage."

"Okay, just give me a couple minutes to change my clothes. Why don't I meet you in the kitchen? Judy and I brought home doughnuts from Lovin's."

Stephen rubbed his hands together. "Hey, good idea. I could go for a snack. How about you, David?"

David grinned. "Mom and I went to Lovin's the other day. Good stuff."

Half an hour later, Nina, Stephen, and David cycled down the road toward town. Allowing the other two to lead the way, Nina brought up the rear. They rode through town to the river, catching the bike and pedestrian path Stephen indicated on the map. The beautiful setting captured Nina's attention. Overhanging trees shaded the path on one side, and on the other, a grassy bank led to the river. Cars swept over the bridge in both directions, with those traveling north soon disappearing around a curve in the highway. Despite all the action, the scene evoked peace and relaxation. At a lookout, Nina joined Stephen and David when they stopped at an historic marker.

Stephen read aloud the inscription. "*The original site of Parkers Landing where Phineas Parker began his ferry service, transporting settlers across the river on a raft. He charged twenty-five cents per person and fifty cents for luggage. Horses swam alongside.*"

Nina shaded her eyes with a hand and gazed at the river, imagining crossing the waters on a raft. "I read about Mr. Parker in my pre-trip research, and yesterday at the museum I saw photos of him and his ferry service. What an interesting beginning to the town."

"I've read about him, too." David wheeled his bike alongside Nina. "His story was in a library book I checked out."

Stephen leaned forward, resting his forearms on the bicycle's handlebars. "Parkers had its heyday when the mill was active and the main place of employment. When the mill work slacked off, the town felt the effects. Growth came to a standstill. Lots of old-timers were here but not many new people."

Stephen's mentioning the mill brought a memory to Nina's mind. "Judy told me Mark's father worked there."

"He did." Stephen nodded. "He got into some trouble, though, and ended up in prison."

"Really?" Judy hadn't included that fact. Nina turned to look at him. "What kind of trouble?"

Stephen's forehead wrinkled. "The incident happened after I left town for college, and I'm not sure of the details."

Always interested in anything concerning Mark, Nina filed away the information, intending to research the subject later. Back on the path, she turned her attention to enjoying the ride. Being with Stephen and David turned out to be easier and more relaxing than she anticipated.

A few minutes later, David pulled off the path, stopped, and took out his cell phone.

Nina and Stephen joined him.

"What's up?" Stephen gestured toward the phone.

"A text from Mom. She says, 'Tell your dad dinner here tonight.' " He looked up at Stephen and smiled.

Stephen's gaze moved to Nina and then back to David. "She means Nina, too, of course."

David shrugged. "Dunno. She doesn't say." He tapped the phone's screen.

"I'll assume she did include her. Okay, we can have dinner at your house. Right, Nina?" He faced her, eyebrows raised.

Join them for a meal at Angie's house? Nina's stomach clenched just at the thought. She still didn't know how she fit into Stephen and David's life, but where Angie was involved, she definitely wanted to keep a distance. "Oh, no…I, ah, promised to help Katie with her puppets for the library's storytelling program." True enough. Maybe not the tonight part, but the promise part applied.

Stephen spread a hand. "Can't you two get together tomorrow? I'd really like you to come with us."

Determined to avoid joining them, Nina shook her head. "Tomorrow she'll be at day camp."

"What should I tell Mom?" David pointed toward his phone.

Nina held her breath. She hoped Stephen would accept her decision without more argument, especially in front of David.

Finally, Stephen turned back to David. "Tell her you and I are coming."

"Okay." David turned away to text his reply.

"I really wish you were joining us tonight," Stephen told Nina. "I'll tell Angie to make clear you are included in whatever she plans for me and David."

Nina shook her head. "Stephen, I appreciate your wanting to include me on those occasions, but, please, don't make that demand."

"Why not? If you're with us, we can—"

"—Be one happy family? Do you really think that's possible?" Nina's stomach tensed, and she couldn't help the sarcasm that crept into her voice.

Stephen frowned. "Now isn't the time for a discussion about what I hope will happen in the future. We'll talk more later." He rode ahead to catch up with David.

With Angie's request, today's outing took a sour turn, and Nina wished she could leave Stephen and David to continue on their own while she returned to the Barlows'. But abandoning them now would only create more stress between her and Stephen. With a resigned sigh, she followed them down the path.

Chapter Eleven

Nina sat at the dining room table with Stephen's family, eating fried chicken, mashed potatoes, and sautéed green beans. As usual, the food was tasty and the conversation lively.

George related an embarrassing situation at the bank that involved hiring two people for the same position.

Judy told about her and Nina's morning at Curly Locks and lunch at Lovin's Bakery.

Blaine and Rick discussed a friend's experience buying a new car.

Even Katie, who usually was quiet, had a story from day camp.

If Stephen were present, he and Nina would talk about their bicycle tour along the river. But Stephen was having dinner with David and Angie. *You could have gone, too.* No, Angie's invitation had not included her. Nina heaved a sigh and took another bite of chicken.

Kitchen cleanup, as usual, was a family affair. Nina joined in, helping to store the leftovers.

Then Rick rode off on his motorcycle to visit his girlfriend, Cassie.

Blaine disappeared into his room.

George and Judy settled in the living room, she with her quilting and he with the newspaper.

Nina approached Katie about working on the puppets, but she was on her way to visit her friend, Risa, who lived next door. Left on her own, Nina took her tablet to the porch and sat in a wicker chair. The evening air was cool and refreshing. She turned on the device, intending to do research but then, experiencing a sudden longing for home, instead phoned her grandmother, Jessica. When the call connected, the sight of her relative's image on the screen brought a rush of warmth and affection.

"Hi, honey." Jessica smiled into the camera. "Been thinking about you."

"My mind's been on you, too, Gran. I miss you."

"Hello, Nina!" Several familiar faces popped up around Jessica.

Nina recognized Lily Ciliano, Mabel Whiteside, and Selma Bellari, her grandmother's friends. She became acquainted with the three last winter when they helped her establish a library at Marley Manor. Seeing them tonight made her feel lonely. "Hello, ladies."

"Tonight's our game night. We're setting up the board." Jessica held up one of the well-known game's lettered squares.

"Oh. Sorry to interrupt. I'll call another time—"

"No, no." Jessica shook her head. "Everyone wants to talk to you. How are you doing with your investigation?"

"Jessica told us you're solving another murder." Lily peered at Nina through her thick-lensed eyeglasses.

"You'll find out whodunit." Mabel pulled her paisley shawl tighter around her shoulders. "That TV sleuth—what's her name?—has nothing on you."

"You mean Wilma Wimple on *Murder She*

Solved." Selma laughed and patted her gray topknot. "I watched last night's episode. The killer was—"

Lily put her hands over her ears. "Don't tell us. I recorded the program and haven't seen it yet."

"How *are* you doing, Nina?" Jessica's brows knit. "Anything to report?"

With nothing certain, she'd best not share rumors. "No. I just wanted to say 'hi.' I miss you—all of you." She meant the sentiment. Jessica's friends were her friends, too.

They chatted awhile longer, mostly about happenings at Marley, including the upcoming picnic at a nearby park and a bus trip to a neighboring town's summer festival. The call ended with promises to talk again soon.

Nina took a few moments to savor the conversation and take comfort in making contact with home. Then, she opened her favorite search engine and researched potassium bromate. Was Mona correct in calling the substance poison? Nina soon discovered potassium bromate was an odorless, tasteless white powder and, yes, added to dough it created fluffy, soft, white pastry and bread. The chemical was classified as a poison, but during the baking process, it became potassium bromide, which was deemed harmless. Still, again as Mona had said, while some countries banned the substance, the U.S. allowed its use.

Several instances of accidental poisoning were documented. The symptoms included those exhibited by Mark, especially kidney failure.

Nina made a few notes on her tablet. Then, as a scenario spun through her mind, she sat back and gazed into the distance. Mary Ellen's anger over Mark's involvement in her fiancé's death, whether justified or not, reached the breaking point. She couldn't stand to see him successful and happy when her own happiness was destroyed. As a baker, she knew all about potassium bromate and its lethal effects when misused. What better way to revenge her fiancé's death than to make Mark suffer and die, too?

Mary Ellen plotted how to administer the poison. Perhaps Mark and Gloria visited Lovin's the morning of the picnic. They ordered coffee with their pastry. Seizing the opportunity, Mary Ellen added a hefty dose of potassium bromate to Mark's brew. Because the powder was odorless and tasteless, Mark had no clue his drink was tainted.

Returning to her research, Nina learned that once administered, the poison was fast acting, which would account for Mark's collapse only a few hours later at the picnic. Mary Ellen counted on kidney failure being declared the cause of death and, even if poison were suspected, the authorities would need to test specifically for potassium bromate to discover traces in his body.

Still, Mary Ellen took a big risk. Nina closed her eyes and pictured the woman, with her wide, dimpled smile and her cheerful, chirpy voice. Mary Ellen the ruthless murderer was difficult to believe. Still, what Nina imagined could be the truth. Obtaining proof that the baker did indeed use potassium bromate would help. But, how to obtain that proof?

****

The following morning on her way to breakfast, Nina met Stephen in the hallway. Although she was happy to see him, she hoped he wouldn't feel obligated to share details of his dinner with Angie and David.

He took her hand and fell into step beside her. "We're spending the day together."

She warmed to the idea of just the two of them on their own. "What do you have in mind?

"I don't care, as long as we're together. But I suppose what we do will involve your investigation." He tilted his head and studied her. "You are still looking into Mark's death, aren't you?"

"I might be." Fearing his disapproval, she kept her tone light. "If I am, I'll need an assistant."

"I'm your man—in more ways than one."

She laughed and squeezed his hand. "Good to know."

A few minutes later, Nina and Stephen joined the Barlows at the breakfast table, all except Katie, who ate earlier and left for camp. Bright sunshine beamed in the nearby window, glinting off the silverware and the pewter milk pitcher. The atmosphere held the enticing aromas of freshly brewed coffee, buttermilk pancakes, and scrambled eggs. Nina eagerly accepted the offerings passed around, loading her plate and digging in. She especially enjoyed the huckleberry syrup on her pancakes.

For a few minutes, everyone was silent while sampling the food.

Nina picked up her coffee cup and took a sip.

Sitting across the table, Judy caught her eye. "I wanted to take you downtown today to the stores you haven't visited, but I have to attend a city council meeting."

"No problem, Judy." Stephen pressed a thumb to his chest. "Nina has me as a guide. I need to catch up on what's happened around town since I last visited."

"Not a whole lot." George touched a napkin to his lips. "We're still a quiet small town."

"Until someone is murdered." Rick's brows drew together as his gaze swept the table.

Nina stared at Rick, wondering where he obtained his information.

Judy raised a hand. "Now, Rick, we don't know for sure…"

Rick shrugged. "The word's not official yet, but if murder isn't suspected, why isn't Mark's autopsy finished? Because they're lookin' for a cause of death, that's why."

"Al, my boss at Greystone, is really upset." Blaine poured syrup on a second helping of pancakes. "He says that if Mark was poisoned, he'll be under suspicion. Our restaurant provided the hot dogs, the baked beans, and the potato salad."

Blaine made a good point, Nina thought.

Judy pressed her lips together and shook her head. "I don't see how Mark could be poisoned from any of those dishes without others being affected, too."

Rick's eyebrows peaked. "Unless a server slipped the poison into only Mark's food."

"Server." Blaine frowned and tapped a forefinger on the table. "That would be me. I didn't do it, honest." He shook his head.

Nina followed the conversation closely, hoping to learn new theories.

"Of course, you didn't." Judy picked up the platter of scrambled eggs and added a spoonful to her plate. "Besides being a ridiculous idea, you don't have a motive."

"Some might think you do." Rick put down his

fork and folded his arms. "Remember last year when a bunch of us went to the airfield to help out on Free Fly Day? Mark got on your case because you kept him waiting."

Blaine shrugged. "I couldn't help being late. I ran out of gas."

"Still, he embarrassed you in front of everyone. I remember you said you'd get back at him sometime."

Behind his eyeglasses, Blaine's eyes blazed.

As she looked from one brother to the other, Nina widened her eyes. She'd never seen them argue before, but, obviously, this subject was touchy.

"By poisoning him? Are you crazy, bro? Yeah, he was a jerk, sometimes, but so are a lot of other guys, and I haven't poisoned any of them."

Rick spread his hands. "Of course, I'm not accusing you, but someone else who witnessed your argument might. I'm just making a point."

Blaine stabbed a piece of bacon with his fork, poked the food into his mouth, and chewed, all the while glaring at Rick.

"Cool the argument, you two." George frowned at Rick and then at Blaine. "We'll just have to wait until we hear the autopsy results."

Nina listened to the conversation with interest but, of course, she agreed Blaine was the most unlikely person to poison anyone. Still, similar situations involving Mark might exist. How many other people experienced his anger, and of those, who was angry enough in return to murder him?

After breakfast was over and cleanup accomplished, the Barlows went their separate ways, leaving Nina and Stephen alone in the kitchen.

Stephen folded his arms and leaned against the counter. "Now that we have the day to ourselves, what would you like to do?"

Nina hung up a dishtowel and then faced him. "I'd like to explore the downtown shops, but first, I want to stop at Greystone."

"Don't tell me you've caught the gambling bug."

The teasing glint in his eyes brought a laugh. "No, but I've been thinking about the Meet-and-Greet and the conversation I overheard in the hallway. I just can't accept Oren's explanation about the Dead Man game."

Stephen tilted his head. "You think he was the other person and he threatened Mark for some other reason?"

"Or he's covering for someone else." Nina folded her arms against her chest. "If I revisit the area, maybe something new will come to mind. I'd like to show you where the encounter happened. You might have suggestions."

Stephen nodded. "Your idea's worth a try. Let's go."

On the drive downtown, Nina gazed out her window at the sky filled with bright sunshine. Beyond the town and the river, the faraway hills beckoned. One of her and Stephen's goals this trip was to explore the countryside. Instead, they investigated a murder that at this point was only speculation. She glanced at Stephen. He accommodated her wishes today, but how long would his patience last if they turned up nothing to prove Mark was murdered?

At Greystone, full of the noise of people coming and going, Nina and Stephen headed for the hallway where she encountered Mark. On the way, she peered into a gambling room where the slot machines' glow gave the room a golden aura. Customers perched on stools, oblivious to their surroundings as they concentrated on the game. Nina shook her head. "Ten o'clock in the morning, and the casino is full. What about gambling attracts people?"

Stephen peered over her shoulder. "An escape, a challenge, and most of all, the opportunity to win money."

Nina pursed her lips. "Which doesn't happen very often."

Just then, bells rang, whistles blew, and shouts of "I won! I won!" floated into the hallway.

Stephen laughed. "Winning occurs often enough to keep people playing."

Nina was about to turn away when her gaze caught a familiar figure. She pointed a finger. "Check out the guy in the corner, the one with the scraggly beard and wearing a Hawaiian shirt. Isn't he Oren?"

Stepping closer to the doorway, Stephen peered into the room. "Sure is."

Oren pulled the machine's handle and leaned toward the spinning symbols. Then a grimace twisted his features, and he slammed a fist into the side of the machine.

Nina shook her head. "Oren's not having fun. He's angry."

"Yeah, he's losing instead of winning."

"Which is a good reason to leave. Why doesn't he just walk away and take care of his airplane or something else constructive?"

Stephen shrugged. "He's addicted and compelled to keep playing."

"Sad. Very sad." Nina truly felt sorry for Oren. But at the same time, she wondered if his habit were somehow connected to Mark's sudden and mysterious death.

Leaving the gambling area, Nina spotted the restrooms sign and led Stephen into the hallway. As before, the passageway was dark and the air cool. Locating the familiar area, she stopped and turned to Stephen. "This spot is where I overheard the two people talking. They were beyond the corner, and I couldn't see them." She pointed toward the curve in the hallway.

Stephen gazed around and then focused on Nina. "Tell me again what you heard."

"One person said, 'Just give me the rest of the stuff...' The end of his sentence was unintelligible. The second person answered, 'Not until you...' The first person replied, 'I'm warning you...you're a dead man, Mark McTeague...' Hearing the threat, plus a name I recognized, drew my attention. Then Mark came around the corner so fast we almost collided."

"Did he seem surprised to see you?" Stephen's brow wrinkled. "Embarrassed? Angry that you might have overheard a private argument?"

Nina propped her hands on her hips. "He was definitely upset. His face was red, and he barely mumbled a greeting. I told him I was looking for the restroom, and he pointed behind him toward the way he'd come. Then he rushed away. I continued on, expecting to see the other person, but the hallway was empty."

Stephen grasped her hand. "Show me."

Nina led him beyond the corner. The hallway widened, with one side leading to the men's room and the other to the women's. "No one was in the women's room when I went in, so I assumed Mark argued with a man who then went into the men's room."

"A woman could have exited around the corner." Stephen stepped to where the hallway continued on.

Nina knit her brow. "Oh, I didn't notice that way out." She waved a hand. "See? I knew having you along would be helpful. So, Mark's accuser could have been a woman. Hmmm." She pressed a finger to her lips. "Perhaps his wife? But why would she use his last name when addressing him?"

"You make a good point, but go on with your story." He waved a hand. "What happened then?"

"After I finished in the restroom, I retraced my steps toward the party." Nina led Stephen back along the hallway, stopping after they rounded another corner. "I was about here when the toe of my shoe hit something." She pointed toward the floor. "The object turned out to be the red stone. I wondered if Mark dropped it. I remember his hands were clenched, though, but in his distressed state, he could have lost his grip." A thought suddenly occurred, and Nina widened her eyes. "Or…maybe the stone came from Della Comstock's bracelet."

"Della Comstock?" Stephen's brow wrinkled. "I remember seeing her at the party, but what's the story about her bracelet?"

Nina repeated her conversation with Della at Lovin's Bakery. "She said she lost her stone recently, but I didn't have a chance to ask if she had any idea where."

"Does she have a motive for wanting to murder Mark?" Stephen rubbed his chin.

"I don't know. I haven't learned much about her, other than she's determined to have a special exhibit at the museum honoring her grandfather, who was a judge."

Stephen nodded. "I remember him—Harry Comstock. He had a reputation for being tough on criminals. But where is the stone you found?"

"I put it in my wallet." Nina dug into her purse and took out her wallet. Unzipping a side pocket, she pulled out the stone with thumb and forefinger and held it up. The gem—or piece of glass, she wasn't sure which—sparkled under the overhead light. "Perhaps I should have turned in my find to the casino, but my instinct said hold on to it for a while. I can always give up the stone later if it proves unrelated to Mark."

He frowned. "You didn't tell Cal about it, either."

"I know, and for the same reason. But what do you think? A gem? Or glass?" She held out the stone.

Stephen placed the stone in his palm and studied it. Then he shrugged and handed it back. "I'm no expert. We'll take it to Sparkles Jewelry. Drake Larson will know."

"Good idea." She nodded. "I need to follow up on this find. I have a dearth of clues in this case."

"I think you missed your calling, Nina." Stephen grinned. "Instead of a librarian, you should have been a detective."

Nina laughed and replaced the stone in her wallet. "No, the library is my first love."

"Huh! Where does that leave me?" Stephen's eyebrows peaked.

"Don't worry, you're at the top of my people list." She leaned forward to kiss his cheek.

On Nina's and Stephen's way to the casino's exit, they passed the office.

The door opened, and Oren, a scowl on his unshaven face, his hands balled into fists, stumbled out.

Another man appeared in the doorway. In his forties and solidly built, he wore black slacks, a white shirt, and a black vest. "Sorry, Oren, but that's the best I can do."

Oren whirled and stuck out his jaw. "Aw, stuff it, Al. I'll talk to the boss."

Al pointed a thumb toward his chest. "I *am* the boss." Turning his back, he marched into the office and slammed the door in Oren's face.

Oren jumped back and nearly bumped into Nina and Stephen. "Wha—Oh, it's you two." He peered at them. "Here to try your luck?"

Stephen slung an arm around Nina's shoulders. "I'm showing Nina the town today."

She nodded. "Shopping for souvenirs. We're checking out the casino's gift shop."

"Yeah?" Oren's eyes narrowed. "Well, you're way off. The gift shop's on the other side of the main lobby." He pointed ahead.

"Right." Nina turned toward the lobby. "We were just admiring the view from the deck."

"Speaking of luck, how's yours today?" Stephen tipped his head toward the hallway leading to the gambling rooms.

"My luck? I always have good luck." Oren turned and stalked off, disappearing down the hallway.

Nina stared after him, shaking her head. The man definitely had a problem with gambling. Did his addiction relate to Mark's death?

Chapter Twelve

From Greystone, Nina and Stephen drove downtown, parked in a public lot, and then headed down Main Street to visit Sparkles Jewelry. The blue neon gemstone on the store's sign made the establishment easy to spot. Nina stopped to admire the window display, featuring sets of matching earrings, necklaces, and bracelets artfully arranged on white satin cloth.

Inside, lighted display cases lined the walls, with several freestanding cases in the center. Hanging lamps with transparent shades brightened the room, and the aroma emanating from several bouquets of roses added to the store's ambiance.

A teenage girl with her black hair in a ponytail stood behind a display arranging rings in a velvet-lined tray. "Good morning. Can I help you find something?"

Returning her friendly smile, Nina stepped to the counter. "I'd like to have a stone appraised."

"Sure. I'll get Drake." She replaced the tray in the case, locked it with a key on a ribbon attached to her waist, and disappeared through a curtained doorway behind the counter. "Uncle Drake! Customers need you."

A dark-haired, middle-aged man pushed aside the curtain and came forward. Short of stature, he wore denim slacks and a blue cotton shirt with the sleeves rolled up. A jeweler's loupe hung from a cord around his neck.

"This lady needs an appraisal." The teen gestured toward Nina.

The man gave a slight nod. "I'd be happy to provide an assessment." His gaze moved from Nina to Stephen. "Ah...you look familiar."

Stephen offered a hand. "I'm Stephen Kraslow. I grew up in Parkers. My sister and brother-in-law are Judy and George Barlow."

The man's eyes lighted as he shook Stephen's hand. "Of course, I know Judy and George, and I remember you. You came for the reunion?"

"I did, and I brought my friend, Nina Foster." Stephen nodded toward Nina.

"Hello, Mr. Larken." Nina shook the man's outstretched hand.

"Welcome to Parkers Landing, and please call me Drake." Drake turned toward his employee. "This young lady is my niece, Jasmine."

Jasmine's brow wrinkled. "I heard about that poor man who got sick at the picnic and then died. Now, people are saying he was poisoned. I hope not. I don't like to think about a murderer being on the loose." She hugged her arms, displaying manicured nails painted a bright red.

"Now, Jas." Drake's lips thinned. "Don't spread rumors. We have to wait and learn what the authorities decide." He turned to Nina and Stephen. "You wanted my help with something?"

"I have a stone I'd like you to appraise." Nina opened her purse, pulled the stone from her wallet, and held it in her palm.

Drake grasped the stone with thumb and forefinger and examined it with his loupe.

Anxious to learn his decision, Nina shifted from one foot to the other. She glanced at Stephen and raised her eyebrows.

He smiled and shrugged, as if to say, "Gotta let the man do his job."

Drake finally let go the loupe and looked up at Nina. "Where did you get this stone?"

Nina stiffened. "Why, I found it."

"Here in Parkers?" His bushy eyebrows drew together.

"Yes." Reluctant to reveal exactly where, she kept her answer brief. "Is it a ruby?"

Drake shook his head. "Glass. A good imitation but only glass."

Nina let her shoulders sag. She hadn't realized how much she hoped the stone was a genuine ruby, not just because of the value, but because, well, she wanted it to be real. "The stone has such a brilliant color, I thought it was genuine."

Drake took a white cloth from underneath the counter, spread it, and placed the stone in the center. "Good imitators are skilled in their craft. The stone will make a nice ring. I'll put it in a setting for you. Take a look at some examples." He turned to his niece. "Jas, bring the gold, please."

Jasmine unlocked a nearby case, removed a black-velvet-lined tray, and set it next to the cloth displaying Nina's stone.

Drake bent over the tray. "Let me see… Here, look at this." He picked up a ring and held it out. "Very pretty setting, don't you think?"

Focusing on the etched gold setting, Nina regarded the ring. "The ring is attractive, but—"

"If you like fancy, how about these?" He replaced the ring and picked out several more. "Which one do you like the best?"

Nina shook her head. "The rings are all beautiful, but I haven't decided what to do with the stone."

"I could set it in a pendant."

Nina put out a hand. "No—not today." She kept her tone firm.

He leaned over the counter. "I'll buy the stone from you. How about fifty dollars?"

He wanted to purchase the stone? Nina dropped her jaw. "An imitation is worth that much?"

"This one is. Like I said, it's a good fake." He picked up the stone and, using the loupe, studied it again.

Nina glanced at Stephen. "What do you think?"

Stephen shrugged. "Your choice, but if it were up to me, I'd probably keep it."

"I agree." She turned back to Drake. "I'll keep the stone as is—for now. Maybe I'll have it set later—after I've had time to give the matter more thought."

Drake let the loupe drop and gave a slight nod. "As you wish."

Nina held out a hand with palm up, ready to accept the stone.

Instead of returning the stone, Drake took a step back. "Why don't I wrap it for you? I have a nice box in the back." He turned toward the curtained doorway. "Wait here, please."

Suddenly suspicious of Drake's offer, which would remove the stone from her sight, Nina leaned over the counter. "I don't need a box. Please, just give me the stone."

His jaw set, Drake met her gaze.

He hesitated so long Nina was about to repeat her request.

Finally, he placed the stone in her hand. "May I show you something else today?"

Nina secured the stone in her wallet. "I have nothing special in mind, but I do want to look around."

"Of course. Jasmine will be glad to help you." He turned to Stephen. "Nice to see you again."

Stephen gave a salute. "You, too, Drake."

With a slight bow, the jeweler disappeared into the back room.

Nina turned her attention to browsing. She really was interested in finding gifts for the people at home, especially Jessica. At one display, a pair of earrings caught her eye. She looked up at Jasmine, who had remained nearby. "May I see the pearl earrings, please?"

"Of course." Jasmine unlocked the case and removed the tray. Picking up one of the earrings, she held it out.

Nina pressed the earring to her ear, looked in a nearby mirror, and then turned to Stephen. "Do you think Gran would like these earrings?"

He tilted his head. "Nice. And, yes, I'm sure Jessica would be pleased to have them."

By the time she finished browsing all the displays, Nina had selected gifts for her library co-workers, as well.

Drake did not reappear.

Jasmine completed the transaction, placing each

gift in a separate box, wrapping it, and then putting all the boxes in a plastic bag decorated with the store's blue stone logo.

When Nina and Stephen were outside, Stephen grasped her elbow and led her along the sidewalk. "Too bad your casino find turned out to be only glass."

"*If* it's glass."

Stephen frowned. "You don't believe Drake?"

"I don't know." Nina pressed a forefinger to her cheek. "He was awfully eager to buy the stone from me. On the whole, I thought his behavior odd."

Stephen rubbed his chin. "Hmmm, he was pushy, now you mention it. Maybe we need another opinion. We'd have to go to Sandpoint, though. Sparkles is the only jewelry store in our town."

Nina waved a hand. "Never mind for now. Let's use our time today to visit other stores here. How about Race LaMott's Treasure Trove?"

"Sure. Race's store is on the next block." Stephen pointed ahead.

On the way, Stephen encountered several people he knew, and he and Nina stopped to exchange greetings and introductions.

Finally, Nina stood in front of the Treasure Trove's display window. In contrast to the neatly arranged jewelry at Sparkles, a jumble of objects decorated this window. A set of flower-patterned dishes, chairs draped with towels, a scattering of silverware, and several vases filled with artificial flowers were among the items.

The merchandise in the store's interior showed similar disarray, with shelves crowded with knick-knacks, furniture haphazardly thrown together, and clothing racks jammed with vintage apparel. "I can see why Tilda calls this a junk store." Nina stepped around a fireplace grate filled with tools.

"The place could use organization." Stephen picked up a bookend in the shape of a rearing horse. "Hmmm, nice bookend." He turned the piece upside down, and his eyes widened. "Wow, nice price, too."

"That's because it's cast iron bronze."

Hearing the comment from behind her, Nina looked around to see Race approach. He wore black slacks, a cream-colored shirt, and a bolo tie displaying a large, black-and-white onyx stone. The tie reminded her of those she saw at Sparkles, and she wondered if he bought the jewelry from Drake.

Stopping beside Nina and Stephen, Race picked up the matching bookend. "This set was made by Charles Teaksberry and is highly collectible—if you're a collector."

"Good to know." Stephen put down the bookend and shook Race's outstretched hand. "How are ya, Race?"

"Doing well." He turned to Nina. "Out on the town today?"

"Yes, Stephen's showing me around. What an interesting store." She made a wave at the surroundings.

Race nodded and propped both hands on his hips. "Keeps me busy while Tilda's doin' hair."

Picking up a teddy bear from a display of stuffed animals, she straightened its bow tie. "I'm curious to know how a person gets into this business. Do you mind sharing your experience?" She looked up at Race.

He shrugged. "I was out of the Army and roamin' around the country when I met Lexie Duggan in

Arizona. You know her, Stephen."

"Sure. I know Lexie." Stephen nodded. "She works in the mayor's office at City Hall and researches genealogies on the side."

"I've met her, too." Nina replaced the teddy bear. "She's in the museum group helping to establish the Curly Locks exhibit."

"Right. They call themselves the Mommas." Race chuckled. "Anyway, she invited me to visit her home town. I figured what the hell, and so I came. Lexie introduced me to a bunch of her friends, including Tildy." He grinned. "I've been here ever since."

So far, his story matched what Judy told her, yet hearing him relate more of his history might reveal something new. "Then you established Treasure Trove?"

Race nodded. "I took over the business from Jess Geller."

"I remember him." Stephen stuck both hands in his slacks' pockets. "He told stories about traveling the world and collecting all the stuff he used to start this store."

"When Jess said he wanted to retire, I made him an offer." Race planted his feet apart and folded his arms.

"I bet Tilda had something to do with your decision." Nina wondered how much he would reveal about abandoning Lexie and marrying Tilda.

"She sure did. Married five years now. Tildy's first husband died ten years ago. Her daughter works at Curly Locks, and her son lives in Spokane."

"Do you have children?" Nina kept her tone casual, hoping Race would think she was still making polite conversation, rather than, well, interrogating him.

He pointed a thumb toward his chest. "Me? Hell, no. Never been married before. Managed to escape the ball and chain until I met Tildy."

She wanted to ask if he chose Tilda over Lexie because she had more money, as Judy suggested, but feared that question exceeded the bounds of polite inquiry. "Do you like living in one place, after all your roaming?"

"I needed to settle down. Tildy's tied here, too, with Curly Locks."

"I understand she does a good business." Nina shifted her feet. "The salon was busy the day Judy and I helped clean out the storeroom."

"Tildy's the best. She learned from her mother, who learned from her mother. Doin' hair must be in the genes." He laughed.

The front door opened, and a middle-aged man and a woman entered.

Race waved. "Hey, Fred and Janice. Your table's refinished and ready to go." He turned to Stephen and Nina. "Excuse me, gotta take care of these folks."

"Of course." Stephen stepped aside, allowing Race to pass. "We'll be okay looking around on our own."

Race glanced over his shoulder. "If you need help, Dirk's around."

After Race and his customers left, Nina turned her attention to browsing. A box of books revealed an early edition of *Black Beauty* for her collection, as well as another story she thought Katie would like. Shelves of knickknacks beckoned. Maybe she could find items for her special friends at Marley Manor. Her gaze roved over eggcups, glassware, miscellaneous silverware, and figurines, including a selection of birds made of burnished brass. Each about four inches in height, they included an owl, a sparrow, and a cardinal. The burnished brass reminded her of something, but she couldn't bring the reference to mind. Then she spotted figurines made of porcelain and decided on those for Jessica's friends. She joined Stephen, who explored the other side of the store. "Find something interesting?"

He held up a model car made of plastic. "Here's a Chevy like the one we used to have. I remember when Dad bought it. I'd just learned to drive and worried he wouldn't let me get behind the wheel. But he did, and I drove the car around town until I got my own."

Nina admired the classy red sedan. "Maybe you should buy the model and start a collection."

As he rotated one of the car's wheels, he smiled. "I think I will. Now that I have a house, I have room for collections."

When she and Stephen were ready to go, Nina looked around for Race. He was nowhere in sight, apparently still busy in the back room with the customers.

Race's employee, Dirk, appeared. He wrapped Nina's and Stephen's purchases and rang up the sales.

Out on the sidewalk, Nina turned to Stephen. "Was I too obvious in questioning Race?"

Stephen chuckled. "Well, maybe a little, but he didn't appear offended or suspicious. Like a lot of people, he loves to talk about himself. Is he on your suspect list?"

"At this point, nearly everyone is—except you." She laughed and touched his arm. "I want to find out as much as I can about people who knew Mark. I never know when something important will turn up. But now, what's our next stop?"

Stephen glanced at his wristwatch. "We have time for one more before lunch. How about visiting the *Parkers Landing Post*? I'd like you to meet Len Dubrowski. He was my mentor when I edited the high school newspaper. I worked part time for him, too."

"Good idea. I'd like to know him." So far, their tour of the town was interesting and informative. Would the newspaper office have additional information she could use in her investigation into Mark McTeague's mysterious death?

Chapter Thirteen

On the way to the newspaper office, Nina and Stephen stopped at Stephen's car to drop off their purchases. The *Parkers Landing Post* sat on the corner of Main and Maple Street. Inside, in addition to chairs and tables, the waiting area included framed photographs lining the walls.

Behind a counter, a woman sat at a computer.

A man stood over her, pointing toward the screen.

"Hey, Len, Hazel." Stephen waved to the couple.

The couple both looked up, grinning and waving in return.

Len came around the counter with an arm outstretched. He was in his fifties, slightly built, and a bit stoop-shouldered. A ring of white hair encircled his otherwise bald head, and rimless eyeglasses perched on a snub nose.

Smiling, Stephen shook Len's hand and then introduced Nina.

"Pleased to meet you, Len." Nina accepted the man's firm handshake.

"Heard a lot about you, Nina. All good, all good." Len grinned. "This is my wife, Hazel." He gestured toward the woman.

Hazel nodded and smiled. "Welcome to Parkers Landing, Nina."

Bright red lipstick added color to Hazel's pale

complexion. Her neatly coifed gray hair made Nina think she'd recently been to Tilda LaMott's Curly Locks Beauty Salon. The couple's warm greeting put Nina at ease. They obviously held Stephen in high regard and were genuinely glad to see him.

Stephen folded his arms and leaned against the counter. "I'm showing Nina around town today, and of course, the *Post* was high on our list."

"Stephen tells me he worked here while in high school." Nina wanted to hear more about Stephen's early newspaper training.

Len nodded. "The job earned him credit toward graduation. He was the best student assistant ever. I tried to talk him into coming back after college, but he chose the big city instead."

"True." Stephen straightened and stuck both hands in his slacks' pockets. "But I always remembered working here and, eventually, I felt the call to return to small town reporting."

"Now you own your own newspaper. Proud of you, Stephen." Len laid a hand on Stephen's shoulder. "But, hey, got time for a cup of coffee and some gab?" He stepped to a table holding a silver coffee urn and a stack of paper cups.

Stephen raised his eyebrows at Nina. "Okay with you, hon?"

"Of course. I'd like to take a closer look at the photos on display."

Len filled cups of coffee for Nina and Stephen and one for himself. Then he guided them to the photos. "These pictures give you a good history of the town, like this one of our founder, Phineas Parker." He nodded toward the first photo in the display.

Similar to the one Nina saw at the museum, the picture showed Phineas Parker standing on his raft and using a long pole to transport several passengers across the Kokuskie River.

"Parker was a controversial character." Len sipped his coffee. "Some liked him, while others didn't. But you gotta admit he was an enterprising guy, and he performed a valuable service for the early settlers."

The next picture was of the town's lumber mill. Painted brown with black trim, the buildings included one with a chute extending from a high window to the ground. Stacks of lumber surrounded the buildings, along with a tractor and several trucks and wagons.

Len gazed at the photo. "Parker might have put the town on the map, but we're known mainly for the mill." He turned to Nina and Stephen. "Did you know that at one time our mill was one of the largest in the world?"

"Quite a claim to fame." Nina stepped to another picture of the mill that included a group of employees, along with a list of their names. "Here's Ian McTeague." She pointed toward a man in the front row. Like all the others, he wore blue overalls, a long-sleeved shirt, and sturdy work boots.

"Mark's father." Len joined Nina. "This picture is the last we have of him before he went to prison."

Nina looked toward Stephen and nodded. "I remember you telling me Mark's father spent time in prison."

Stephen studied the photo and then turned to Len. "He died there, too. Right, Len?"

"Correct. Ian was accused of giving thieves information that allowed them access to the mill's office after hours. They cracked the safe and stole a sizable amount of money. He went to prison along with the bad guys. Judge Comstock threw the book at the whole gang."

"I heard Comstock was a tough judge." Stephen frowned.

Len adjusted his eyeglasses with thumb and forefinger. "Some respected him, and others thought him too harsh."

"I met his granddaughter, Della, at Museum Mommas." Nina directed her comment to Len. "She wants an exhibit room dedicated to the judge."

Len rolled his eyes. "The Comstocks think they own the town, and maybe they kinda do. Burton was mayor awhile back, Norman runs the mill, and Phoebe's a lawyer. She's following in her grandfather's footsteps, aiming to be a judge, too."

"Did Mark talk much about his father?" Nina sipped her coffee, enjoying the rich brew.

Stephen shrugged. "Just claimed his innocence in the mill robbery."

Len set his empty cup on the counter. "When I covered the reunion's Meet-and-Greet at the casino, Mark and I spent a few minutes gabbing. He told me he would very soon clear his father's name and finally reveal the truth about Judge Comstock."

"No kidding?" Stephen's eyes widened. "Do you have any idea what he meant?"

Len shook his head. "We were interrupted before I found out more. I planned to follow up with him, but then he—well, you know." His voice dropped, and he lowered his gaze.

Nina listened carefully to Len's voice. Was he the person who argued with Mark? Although she was pretty sure he wasn't the one, she'd add him to her list of suspects. "I wish I knew what Mark had on Judge Comstock."

"Sorry I can't help you." Len's brow wrinkled. "I'd like to know, too."

Nina and Stephen spent a few more minutes talking to both Len and Hazel and then, after promising to visit again before leaving town, said their good-byes.

Once out on the sidewalk, Stephen turned to Nina. "How about lunch?"

She matched his grin. "Lunch sounds like a good idea."

"The Rusty Spur's around the corner." He pointed ahead. "Or do you want to try a new place?"

"The Rusty Spur will be fine. I enjoyed the dinner we had there the other night."

The restaurant proved to be a popular lunch spot, but the hostess found them a booth. After studying the menu, Nina chose a turkey club sandwich with a side of potato salad, and Stephen opted for a hamburger and fries.

Nina sipped the coffee the waitress poured, savoring the hazelnut flavor, and then put down her cup. "I sure am curious to know what damaging information Mark had on Judge Comstock."

Stephen's brow knit. "He never mentioned he'd discovered something about the judge. But, like I told you, except for meeting at reunions, we haven't communicated much during the past few years."

Nina held up a forefinger. "Here's a theory. Suppose Mark told Della he knew something bad about her grandfather, and he wanted money to keep quiet…"

Stephen sat back and raised both hands, palms out.

"Another instance of Mark as a blackmailer? Oh, Nina, I don't think so…"

Stephen's loyalty brought a soft smile. "Maybe he would sink that low if he was about to lose FlyGuys. Della wouldn't want anything to reflect badly on the Comstocks, especially the judge. To prevent Mark from ever revealing what he knew, she poisoned him."

"No, no. Mark wasn't…he wouldn't…" Stephen shook his head.

"I know you think highly of him." Nina leaned forward. "He saved your life. You were good friends. But he was determined to rescue his company from disaster."

"I still can't believe Mark would do something so…"

"Don't forget he has another motive, too—revenge for Judge Comstock's stringent sentence served on his father."

"Okay, for the sake of argument, I'll put aside my personal feelings." Stephen folded his arms against his chest. "If Mark blackmailed Della, then maybe she was the person you overheard threatening him at the casino, and the stone you found is hers."

"Hmm." Nina tilted her head. "She could be the person who argued with Mark, but her lost stone is a ruby. Drake said the one I found is glass."

Stephen rubbed his chin. "What if her husband lied and gave her fake, instead of genuine, rubies?"

"Or, Drake lied, and the stone is real after all." Nina lowered her voice.

Stephen's eyes widened. "Why wouldn't he be truthful?"

Nina drummed her fingers on the table. "I don't

know, but I have trouble believing he would pay fifty dollars for an imitation."

"Like he said, because the stone's a good fake." Stephen turned up a hand.

"Maybe so. I don't really know the man." Nina shrugged and took another sip of coffee. "Still, his behavior seemed odd, especially when he wanted to take the stone into the back room to get a box."

"Your list of suspects is growing. Oren and Gloria, Della…"

Excitement surged through Nina's veins. "Don't forget Mary Ellen, because she blamed Mark for the accident that killed her fiancé. Oh, and I now know how she could have poisoned him." She told Stephen what she learned from Mona and from researching the potassium bromate Mary Ellen might use in her bakery products.

"That theory sounds more likely than the one involving the Comstocks." Stephen leaned back against the booth.

"Maybe. But unless the authorities test for potassium bromate, they won't find it in Mark's system." Nina shook her head and heaved a sigh. "I wish we'd hear the results of the autopsy."

Nina's and Stephen's meals arrived, and for the next few minutes, Nina turned her attention to enjoying her sandwich, made of freshly roasted turkey grilled on sourdough bread. The tangy potato salad made a perfect side dish. The Rusty Spur was fast becoming a favorite eating spot.

Stephen's phone rang. He pulled it from his pocket and looked at the screen. "Angie. I'd better take her call."

"Of course." Nina's shoulders tensed.

Stephen put the phone to his ear. "Hey, Ang, what's up?" He listened, his gaze on Nina.

She looked away, watching the hostess lead diners to a table. Voices drifted from the booth behind them but not loud enough to drown out Stephen's conversation.

"Batteries? Sure, I can pick them up. Nina and I are downtown now... Of course, it's no trouble...Talk soon. Say hi to David for me." He punched off the call and returned the phone to his pocket.

Nina pasted on a smile. "Sounds like she has a job for you."

"Uh huh. She wants me to buy extra batteries for the drone David and I are building. The hobby shop's just around the corner, only a slight detour to the parking lot." He gestured toward their plates. "Are we ready to go home?"

"Almost." Nina picked up her purse. "I'd like to stop in Weyland's Western Wear and say hello to Mona. Why don't I go there while you purchase the batteries? We'll meet at the car."

"Okay. See you at the car." Stephen picked up the bill and pulled out his wallet.

Nina and Stephen left the Rusty Spur and went their separate ways. At Weyland's, she found Mona behind the counter finishing a sale.

Mona handed the customer her package and then turned to Nina. "Hello. Nice to see you." Her turquoise rings caught the light as she waved a hand.

"Hi, Mona. Glad I had the opportunity to visit you today."

Mona came from behind the counter and stood

beside Nina. "We feature locally made clothing and accessories, creations you won't find anywhere else. Let me give you a quick tour."

Nina followed Mona down aisles filled with racks of blouses, skirts, and slacks, then to a section featuring jackets and other outer wear, and then to one with footwear featuring boots of shiny, embossed leather. A display of scarves with silver clips especially caught Nina's eye. "These scarves are beautiful."

"They're made by a husband and wife team." Mona held up one featuring red roses. "She hand prints the fabric, and he designs and casts the silver clips." She fingered the ornament holding together the scarf ends.

"I must have this one." Nina picked up a scarf printed with bright yellow sunflowers against a dark green background. "Sunflowers are my favorite flower."

"Good choice." Mona smiled and nodded.

When the tour was over, Nina and Mona returned to the cash register. The scarf sale completed, Nina tucked the package into her purse. "I'll return another day when I can spend more time."

"I'll look forward to another visit. In the meantime, I'll see you at the Museum Mommas." Mona leaned against the counter and folded her arms. "Before you leave, though, I want to make clear what I said at Lovin's about Mary Ellen using potassium bromate. I never meant to imply she used it to poison Mark." Her brow wrinkled. "I don't want to start any rumors and get her into trouble."

"I understand." Nina slung the purse strap over her shoulder. "I mentioned what you said to Stephen, but

I'm sure he'll keep the information to himself."

"If Mark was poisoned, a more likely person would be his wife."

Although Nina heard the derision in Mona's voice, she kept her expression neutral. "Gloria? Why?" Although Gloria was already on Nina's suspect list, she wanted to hear Mona's reason for believing the woman might be the murderer.

Mona waved a hand. "She was fed up with taking second place to his business."

"I've heard how involved Mark was in FlyGuys."

"Uh huh." Mona nodded. "Gloria bankrolled him to begin with but recently told him no more money."

"What did she think of Oren's gambling debts?" Since Mona introduced the subject of FlyGuys, Nina figured she might as well pursue it.

Mona tilted her head. "You know about his problem?"

Nina shrugged. "Oren's habit seems to be common knowledge."

"Keeping his behavior a secret is difficult since when he's in town, he practically lives at Greystone. Still, Gloria might be on Oren's side because his debts would help to sink the business." Mona sighed. "Just listen to me. I didn't want to gossip about Mary Ellen, and now I'm gossiping about Gloria and Oren."

Nina put out a hand. "Don't be hard on yourself, Mona. The possibility that Mark was poisoned has everyone upset. The idea of a murderer being someone you all know is scary."

Mona straightened and smiled. "You're right, Nina. I wonder if we'll ever discover the truth about Mark's death."

With Mona's words ringing in her ears, Nina left the store. *The truth about Mark's death.* She wanted to know, too. Although she hadn't told Mona, Nina would keep Mary Ellen on her list of suspects. Gloria, too. In fact, if what Mona said were true, Gloria had more motive than Nina first realized. Excitement rippled through her. Was she at last on the right track to solving the mystery?

Chapter Fourteen

Still thinking about her conversation with Mona, Nina headed down the street, intending to meet Stephen at the car and return to the Barlows'. Reaching the end of the block, she waited for traffic to clear and then stepped into the crosswalk. Halfway down the next block, she realized she'd passed the street leading to the parking lot. She noticed an alley between Quiller's Barbershop and Delphon's Drugstore. The alley would provide a shortcut to the lot. Why not?

Adjusting the purse strap on her shoulder, she ducked into the alley. The buildings on either side blotted out the sunlight, and shadows stretched from doorways and dumpsters. The temperature dropped, too, sending a sudden chill rolling down her spine. She paused and glanced over her shoulder to see if anyone followed her. No one was in sight. Shrugging off her apprehension, she continued on.

Still, she stepped up her pace and hurried toward the end of the alley. One more dumpster to pass and she'd be on the street again. From there, the parking lot was only half a block away. Maybe Stephen was already at the car.

Just then, someone darted from behind the last dumpster and ran toward her. A baseball cap pulled low and a checkered bandana around his neck all but hid his face. He reached her and grabbed her purse strap.

"Gimme that!" Grunting and cursing, the person yanked the strap with both hands.

"No! Get away!" Her heart pounding, Nina kept a tight grip on her purse.

"Shut up and gimme the bag!" A deep growl accompanied the command.

"Help!" Nina's hold on the purse loosened, and the strap slid over her fingers. Still, she managed to hang on.

A dark-haired man burst from the back door to the barbershop and ran toward them. "What's going on?"

"Thief!" Nina yelled.

"Get outa here, you bum!" The man doubled his fists and swung at Nina's attacker.

Letting go Nina's purse, the would-be robber turned and ran toward the opposite end of the alley.

Exhausted and breathless, Nina sagged to the ground.

Passersby entered the alley from the street where she came in and crowded around Nina and her rescuer.

"What happened, Mitch?" someone asked.

"Mugger. Call the cops, while I help the lady." Mitch held out a hand to Nina. "You okay? Come sit over here." He helped her to stand and then led her to a chair near the barbershop's door.

Nina slumped onto the seat, took a deep breath, and looked up at her rescuer. In his forties, he had curly salt-and-pepper hair and wore a white cotton jacket over black slacks. "Thanks, Mitch. You arrived just in time."

Mitch grimaced and stuck both hands on his hips. "Yeah, good thing I was takin' my break between customers."

Two policemen ran into the alley. One was Stephen's friend, Chief Cal Donovan. The other was Officer Tony Garcia. After clearing the area of onlookers and making sure Nina did not need medical attention, Cal remained with her and Mitch while Officer Garcia searched the alley.

"Do you think the guy was the same person who attacked you at the street dance?" Cal stood over Nina, notebook and pen in hand.

Nina shook her head. "The person at the street dance was older and had a deeper voice. The guy today was a teenager."

Cal turned toward Mitch. "Any idea who the kid is? Ever seen him before?"

Mitch rubbed his jaw and shook his head. "His face was covered, and I didn't recognize his voice."

Tony Garcia approached. "No sign of him, but I found these in the dumpster at the end of the alley." He held out a plastic bag.

Glimpsing the blue baseball cap and a checkered bandana, Nina nodded. "He wore those items."

"Nina!"

Seeing Stephen break through the group of onlookers at the alley's entrance brought a flood of relief. She turned to Cal. "Okay if Stephen joins us?"

"Sure." The officer waved at Stephen.

Brow furrowed, he ran to her side and leaned to put an arm around her shoulders. "Are you all right?"

Stephen's embrace brought Nina comfort. "I am, thanks to Mitch." She gestured toward the barber. "He scared away the thief."

Stephen straightened and held out his hand. "Hey, Mitch."

Mitch accepted Stephen's handshake. "Heard you were in town. Good to see you." His mouth turned down. "Well, not under these circumstances."

Cal gave Stephen the details of the assault. Then, after asking Nina and Mitch a few more questions, he tucked away his notebook and stepped back. "Okay, we're done here. You think of anything more, give me a call. If we catch a suspect, we'll get in touch with you to identify him."

Stephen helped Nina to her feet. "Thanks, Cal, Tony, and you, too, Mitch." Keeping an arm around her waist, he led her down the alley.

Nina leaned against him, so thankful for his comforting presence and grateful, too, that she wasn't injured in the assault. When she and Stephen reached his car, she let him tuck her in. Exhausted from the ordeal, she took a deep breath and leaned back against the seat.

After traveling in silence for a few minutes, Stephen took his gaze off the road long enough to nod at her purse. "What would the guy have got away with, if he had stolen your purse?"

Nina straightened and unzipped her purse. "My ID, credit cards, and phone would've been the main losses." She pulled out the package from Weyland's. "A scarf I bought at Weyland's. A few cosmetics. A notebook and pen." She dug deeper. "Oh, and the stone we took to Sparkles that's in my wallet. But if the stone is glass, as Drake said, its loss wouldn't be significant."

"I shouldn't have left you on your own." Stephen frowned.

"Don't blame yourself." She laid a hand on his arm. "If I'd paid attention to where I was going, I wouldn't have cut through the alley."

Stephen turned onto the road leading to the Barlows'. "Maybe you were specifically targeted."

"You think someone wants to scare me?"

"I don't know. I'm just sayin' that I worry about you."

At the Barlows', Judy met Nina and Stephen at the door. "Are you all right?" Wrinkling her brow, she reached out and drew Nina inside.

Warmed by Judy's concern, Nina mustered a smile. "I'm okay."

"I heard what happened—"

Stephen shook his head as he pocketed his car keys. "Town grapevine scoops the story."

Judy gave a short laugh. "Mindy called me. She was downtown and saw the police in the alley with you two. She hung around long enough to learn what happened and then called me on her way home. I've been so worried. Come, sit, Nina, and I'll get you something. Coffee? Tea?"

"A cup of tea would be nice." Nina offered a weak smile.

The tea Judy brought restored Nina's calm. However, dinner later with the family rekindled her stress. George, Rick, and Blaine all had heard the news, and Nina's encounter with the thief dominated the conversation. Everyone had a theory.

Rick knew of a gang that went from town to town, committing a few robberies and then moving on.

George named two families whose kids were in trouble for shoplifting.

Blaine thought Nina's assailant might be a teen released from juvie in Boise who visited his Parkers

Landing relatives.

Finally, Katie put down her fork and, mouth turned down, stared at her plate. "I don't want to go downtown anymore."

Judy patted her shoulder. "Don't worry, honey, the police will catch the thief. Besides, you won't be alone. One of us will always be with you."

After dinner, Nina and Stephen sat on the porch. The peaceful evening, with the sunset turning the sky shades of orange and yellow, and the soft breeze threading through the pine trees, calmed Nina. She thought more rationally about the mugging and what it might mean. Was the attack random because she was in the wrong place at the wrong time? Or was she a specific target? If she was targeted, did the assault have to do with Mark's death and her investigation? The connection seemed unlikely, but experience taught her not to discount anything until proven, one way or the other.

****

Although memories of the attempted mugging lingered, on the following day Nina recovered enough to help Katie with her hand puppets. She sat with the child at the dining room table. The patio door stood open, allowing a fresh breeze to cool the room.

Katie wore shorts and a sleeveless T-top. Her thick hair hung down her back in her usual single braid. "What color do you choose for the pig's jacket?" Katie held up several squares of felt.

Nina finished cutting a piece of pink felt to serve as a pig's face and regarded the swatches. "Hmmm, since the other two pigs are wearing blue and green, how about red? Bright colors show up well."

Katie nodded. "I think so, too. Red's my favorite color. What's yours, Nina?"

"Blue." Nina spoke without hesitation.

"Why do you think people have favorite colors?" Katie placed the paper jacket pattern on the swatch of red felt and, with a pencil, traced the outline.

"I'm not sure why." Nina tilted her head. "Your question is interesting and deserves research, which is a specialty of mine."

"Do you like being a librarian?"

"Yes, I love my job." Nina smiled. "Do you know what you want to be when you grow up?"

Katie put down her pencil and looked up. "Not yet. I like to sing. But Mom says singing's no way to make a living."

Stephen strode into the room. "How're you ladies doing on your project?"

"We're having fun." Katie held up the patch of red cloth.

"We are. Take a look at the finished pig." Nina pointed toward the puppet sitting on the table.

Stephen picked up the puppet and smoothed the felt jacket. "Nice work, you two. But don't forget about the big bad wolf."

"He's almost finished, too." Katie nodded toward the wolf's felt head lying nearby.

Stephen ran his fingers over the wolf's pointed ears. "Hey, good job. He looks really fierce. But, since you two are making such good progress, how about joining me and David this afternoon?"

Nina put down her scissors and gave him her attention. "What do you have planned?"

"A trip to the fairgrounds to test our drone. After

that, we're going to Yoggie's."

"I love Yoggie's." Katie licked her lips. "They have the best ice cream."

Stephen nodded. "I agree. So, what do you say?"

"Yes!" Katie bounced up and down in her chair.

"Nina?" Stephen tilted his head in her direction.

Nina smiled. "Your plan sounds like fun, and you can teach us all about drones."

"Great." Stephen grinned and rubbed both hands together. "We'll pick up David at one o'clock. That schedule should give you more time to work on your project and for us all to have lunch."

Nina looked forward to the outing, which would finally give the four of them a chance to be together. Plus, they would be at the fairgrounds where Mark met his tragic death. Perhaps she would find an undiscovered clue to help determine exactly what happened.

****

At the county fairgrounds, sitting on a bench beside Katie, Nina shaded her eyes against the bright sun and watched the drone soar into the sky. With its four wings and square shape, the device resembled a large bug.

Stephen held the control box, carefully keeping the drone under the four hundred foot limit and not allowing it to stray. On this initial flight, he and David were extra careful but, judging by their beaming smiles, having fun, too. She turned to Katie. "What do you think, Katie?"

The child nodded, keeping her gaze overhead. "The drone is awesome."

Stephen passed the controls to David.

After David flew the vehicle for a while, he and

Stephen approached Katie. "Want to take over?" David pointed toward the control box.

Katie beamed. "Yes!" Then her smile faded. "But I don't know how."

"Don't worry." Stephen put out a hand. "We'll help you."

Accepting his hand, Katie stood and followed him and David to the center of the field. Soon, she had the drone flying. Judging by the big grin on her face, she enjoyed herself, too.

After Katie, Nina took a turn. "This is fun," she told the others and meant the sentiment.

Each of them flew the craft one more time, and then Stephen landed the droid. "I'd say our initial flight was very successful, don't you think, David?"

"Yeah, our drone had a good run today." David tucked the device into his backpack.

Stephen placed a hand on David's shoulder. "How about a walk around the grounds before we leave? I'd like to show you where I did my rodeo riding."

"Our 4H has an exhibit in the fair." Katie caught up with David and fell into step beside him. "Last year, I entered a patchwork pillow cover Mom helped me make, and I won first prize."

"Cool." A grin lit David's face.

Seeing the two children bond despite their age difference gave Nina a warm feeling. Jessica's friend, Joe, had the right idea when he suggested making their outings a foursome. Nina and the others reached the arena and stopped at the fence.

Stephen talked about the rodeos he'd been in, and David chimed in with his horseback riding in Denver.

Nina listened but then couldn't keep her gaze from

straying across the field to the picnic pavilion. The awful memory of seeing Mark collapsed over his lunch filled her thoughts. Where had he been just prior to the picnic? If he had been poisoned—and more and more she was sure he was—then where did he ingest the substance and how long before he collapsed? Whom had he been with? The murderer? The poison had to be something Mark ate or drank. When he went through the buffet line, had someone slipped a poison into his food or drink? If so, the lethal substance needed to be fast acting, for only a few minutes elapsed between ingestion and collapse.

Examination of the area might turn up a clue. Stephen, David, and Katie were still at the arena, deep in conversation.

Just then, Stephen looked around and caught Nina's eye.

She pointed first toward her chest and then toward the pavilion.

He nodded and gave an okay sign with thumb and forefinger.

Appreciating his agreement, Nina started on her mission. She passed fire pits and picnic tables, several people pushing strollers, and a group of children playing catch with a baseball. Reaching the pavilion at last, she studied the area, recalling the placement of the buffet line and the route to the tables. She searched the ground to see if perhaps something relevant escaped the cleanup.

Finding nothing of interest, she heaved a disappointed sigh and set her steps to return to the others. A different route led her past the exhibition buildings. The double doors to one of the long structures stood open. She stopped to peek inside, and when her vision adjusted to the dim light, she spotted a middle-aged man loading boxes into a wheelbarrow. His blue overalls identified him as a fairgrounds employee.

Finished with the chore, he pushed the wheelbarrow through the door, stopped, and eyed her from under the bill of his baseball cap. "Hey, there. Need help?"

"No, thanks. I'm in town for the reunion and out exploring today."

The man nodded. "Big event."

Hoping he might have information that would help her investigation, she stepped to his side. "Were you here the day of the picnic?"

"Yeah, we all got extra time. What a day, with that guy dyin' and all."

"Did you witness his collapse?"

The man let go the wheelbarrow and propped both hands on his hips. "No, but I heard the commotion and come running. I recognized him as a guy I seen earlier."

Nina's pulse quickened. "Here at the fair grounds?" She made a sweeping gesture to include the field and arena. "Or somewhere else?"

"Here. But, look, I gotta get this load to the office. They're waitin' for these boxes." He pointed to the wheelbarrow and then bent to grasp the handles.

"I'll walk along with you." Not about to let him go until she learned more, Nina fell into step beside him. "I'm Nina, by the way."

"Name's Chester. Anyway, I seen the guy—"

"Mark McTeague."

"Okay, Mark. I was gettin' extra folding chairs

from storage"—he nodded toward a nearby building—"and he come by just as I'm backin' out my cart. I almost run into him."

"Did you exchange words?"

"I asked was he okay, and he said he was. He held up a paper cup and asked where could he dump it. I pointed toward a garbage can in plain sight. He tossed the cup and mumbled something then headed for the picnic. Next thing, I hear screamin' and yellin' at the pavilion. When I get there, I see the same guy with his face in his plate."

Nina filed away the possible clue she'd just heard. "Did you tell someone about talking to him beforehand? The police? Anyone?"

Chester shook his head. "Just my wife. Nobody else asked. Then I hear the rumor he's maybe poisoned. Some woman from out of town—" He stopped and frowned. "You're from out of town, you said. I bet you're the one, and here I am, goin' off at the mouth. What are you, a detective?"

Nina saw no reason to lie. "No, just someone who wants to know the truth. The person I came to the reunion with was a special friend of Mark's."

He tilted his head. "So whaddya think?"

"I don't know." Nina shrugged. "But I appreciate hearing your story."

"I ain't telling the cops. Haven't always had the best relationship with them, if ya know what I mean." His mouth turned down.

"Don't worry about me passing on your information." She tilted her head. "But, did the cup Mark had indicate where it was from?"

"Hmmm." Chester pursed his lips. "Yeah, the Big

Bear Coffee Company."

Nina's heart beat faster. "You're sure?"

"Can't miss that big ol' bear plastered on the side. They know how to advertise."

Nina looked around. "I suppose the garbage can where he tossed his cup has long been emptied?"

"Oh, yeah." He nodded. "You oughta seen the garbage haul after the picnic."

"Where does the refuse go?" Nina figured she knew but had to make sure.

"To a big dump outa town. Finding his cup would be one of them needle-in-a-haystack searches. You're not thinking of..." His eyes narrowed.

Nina spread her hands. "No, not at all. I was, ah, just wondering."

At the office building, Chester pulled the wheelbarrow up to the door. "Here's where I'm leaving these boxes."

"Nice meeting you, Chester. Thanks for the info." Encountering him had been a lucky break.

"No problem." Chester touched the bill of his cap and then turned back to his wheelbarrow.

Looking around, Nina spotted Stephen, David, and Katie heading in her direction. She hurried to join them. "How's the tour?"

"We're ready for Yoggie's. Right, you two?" Stephen gestured toward David and Katie.

"You bet." David slung his backpack strap over his shoulder.

Katie clapped her hands. "I'm hungry for ice cream."

On the way to the car, Nina thought about her encounter with Chester. Although she still had no proof

Mark was poisoned, she now knew he drank coffee before the picnic. Coffee tainted with poison? She wished she had the answer to that question. Time was running out. Only a few more days remained until Mark's memorial, and then she and Stephen would leave Parkers Landing. If she were to prove Mark was murdered, she'd better come up with the evidence—and fast.

Chapter Fifteen

That evening after dinner, Nina and Stephen took their coffee to the front porch and sat in the swing. Nina brought her tablet, intending to review her notes with Stephen and add what she learned from Chester. For a while, though, she just relaxed, sipping her coffee while contemplating the twilight view of the peacefully flowing river.

"Good day, wasn't it?" Stephen broke the silence. "I'm glad the four of us finally had an opportunity to be together."

Nina touched a toe to the floor, setting the swing in motion. "Me, too. Despite the age difference, David and Katie relate well. He's a very nice young man."

"He is well adjusted, considering all the changes and insecurities in his life. I hope I can provide some stability." Stephen tightened an arm around her shoulder.

"I'm sure you can." She meant the words, too. She'd no doubt Stephen would do his best to raise his son. The part she would play, which was still to be decided, brought tightness to her chest. She lapsed again into silence.

The low rumble of the TV drifted out the open door behind them, and from the street below came the sounds of cars passing by. In the distance, Greystone's neon sign brightened the darkening landscape.

Finally, Nina opened her tablet. "Want to see my notes?"

Stephen straightened. "Of course. Did you learn anything about the picnic, or about Mark, from the worker you talked to at the fairgrounds?"

Nina suppressed a smile. "What makes you think we discussed Mark?"

He laughed and patted her shoulder. "I know you too well, Nina, dear. But, seriously, I'm glad you took the opportunity to investigate."

"Chester did have an encounter with Mark." She related the man's story. "He said Mark carried a paper cup of coffee from the Big Bear Coffee Company. Was that drink where he got the poison?" Frustration tightened her stomach. "I wish I could examine the cup, but it's long gone now, buried in the city's dump."

"Maybe the poison wasn't in the coffee but in a drink he got at the picnic. The punch, for example. If someone tainted just his drink, of course."

Nina nodded. "The substance needs to be fast-acting, though. I have a list." She scrolled to another page and pointed toward the screen. "In addition to potassium bromate, I found arsenic, ricin, and potassium chloride. Oh, and anti-freeze, which has a sweet taste and can be mistaken for a sweetener."

Stephen rubbed his chin. "Hmmm, Mark always added sugar to his coffee. Maybe he put the poison in his coffee himself. Wouldn't that be ironic?"

"So many possibilities." She gave the list a final review and heaved a sigh. "How will we ever discover the truth?"

"I don't know...but I do know you won't rest until you've explored every angle, which brings me to tomorrow. What's on your agenda?" He turned to face her, eyebrows raised.

Nina rested the tablet on her lap. "Lunch with Cora Springer."

"Ah, the town librarian."

"After lunch, we're visiting The Book Nook."

"Two librarians in a bookstore—that sounds dangerous." He chuckled.

"How about you? Does Angie have plans for you and David?" She stiffened as she waited for his answer.

He sobered and slanted her a glance. "You still don't like her much, do you?"

"I don't know her well enough to like or dislike." Avoiding his look, Nina scrolled to a new page in her notes.

"You could get to know her…"

Nina shrugged. "Why? We'll both be leaving town soon and heading in opposite directions."

"True. But she's our link to David."

Nevertheless, she still distrusted Angie's motives. Pressing her lips together, she held up her tablet. "I thought you wanted to review my notes on my investigation."

"Okay, I get the message." Stephen ran a hand through his hair. "I had no idea attending this reunion would present so many problems. I wish we hadn't come."

With a rush of sympathy, she placed a hand on his arm. "Stephen, don't. You've found someone who will be—who already *is*—a wonderful addition to your life. And if we weren't here, who would find out the truth about Mark's death?"

He straightened and offered a smile. "You're right.

If anyone can discover the truth, you can. I have great confidence in you."

His compliment warmed her. "Thanks, but I need help. Your help."

"Right. Read again about arsenic…"

Nina and Stephen finished reviewing her notes without reaching any conclusions, and she finally put away her tablet. Then she settled back to watch the setting sun spread bands of gold, orange, and red across the sky. Still, tension kept her nerves humming. Time was running out. She needed to find the answer to Mark's death soon. If she returned to Richmond without knowing the truth, the mystery would continue to haunt her.

****

"I'm so glad we could get together today." Nina smiled at Cora Springer, who looked neat and trim in navy slacks, a print top, and a white jacket that set off her dark, curly hair. Nina and Cora sat at a window table in Greystone's dining room, enjoying selections from the lavish buffet.

Outside, guests strolled the lawn under a bright sun shining on the Kokuskie River and the hills beyond.

Cora nodded. "I'm pleased, too. I've looked forward to visiting and comparing notes." Picking up a roll, she broke it open and spread butter on one half. "Where did you take your library training?"

Nina finished a bite of baked chicken, savoring the creamy sauce. "The University of Washington's Information School. How about you?"

"The University of Illinois. I landed my first job at the Chicago Public Library." Her eyes lighted. "I was so excited."

"What brought you and your husband to Parkers Landing?" Nina sipped her iced tea.

"Zel's a park ranger. We've always wanted to see this part of the country, and when he heard about an opening with the park department, we jumped at the opportunity. We're glad we did. We love living here."

"The area is beautiful." Nina gestured out the window. "Stephen took me to Rocky Ridge. The view of the mountains was spectacular." She didn't know Cora well enough to share Stephen's story and so pushed away the other, sad memories of the trip.

Cora nodded. "I know the area you mean. An old cabin is in the vicinity, right?"

"Stephen said hikers stay there." Nina sliced another piece of chicken.

"As well as illegals sneaking over the Canadian border. Zel and his men caught a couple of trespassers just last week." Cora added the contents of a sugar packet to her iced tea.

"What happened to the illegals?" Her interest piqued, Nina leaned forward.

"I don't know their fate." Cora shrugged. "Zel notified the Border Patrol, which completed his responsibility."

The talk turned to their jobs, with mutual agreement that working with the public had both rewards and challenges. "Especially patrons like Oswald Farrington." Nina recalled the man's tantrum she and Katie witnessed.

"He was in again the other day."

"Still searching for his roots? He told the Museum Mommas about his quest."

"Apparently. He swept through the section on the

town's history like a hurricane." She pursed her lips and shook her head. "I asked if I could help, but he said no, he knew where to find what he wanted."

"He's an odd one, all right." Oswald was on Nina's list of possible suspects, although she hadn't discovered any link he had to Mark.

Later, as Nina and Cora left the casino, they encountered Oren.

In a hurry, he barely stopped to say "hello" before disappearing into the nearest card room.

Nina turned toward Cora. "So, you know him? He was Mark's partner in FlyGuys."

Cora nodded. "Zel introduced me." She opened the casino's front door and waved Nina through. "Zel met Mark, too."

Nina waited outside to let Cora catch up. "What did your husband think of him?"

"He considered Mark's dedication to flying impressive."

"Yes, I keep hearing about his passion... Shall we leave our cars here and take the underpass into town?" Nina gestured toward the nearby tunnel under the highway.

"Good idea. The Book Nook's only a couple blocks down Main Street."

Inside the tunnel, Nina breathed in the cool atmosphere, a welcome break from the hot sun.

"Have you discovered anything to indicate Mark was murdered?" Cora asked.

"I have a theory, but no proof." Nina told Cora about her research into poisons.

Cora scrunched up her shoulders. "Poison. Ugh. Such a horrible way to die."

Leaving the tunnel behind and stepping once again into bright sunlight, Nina and Cora traveled the two remaining blocks to Main Street and The Book Nook. After browsing the books displayed on a table outside the door, as well as those in the window, Nina and Cora went inside.

A man in his fifties stood behind the checkout counter sorting a stack of paperback books. He peered from under bushy eyebrows, and a grin lit his face. "Well, here's my favorite librarian."

Cora approached the counter. "Hello, Ed. You get double trouble today. This is my friend, Nina Foster." She gestured toward Nina. "She's also a librarian, from Richmond, Washington, and here for the reunion. Nina, meet Ed Smythe, Book Nook's owner and book expert."

Ed held out a hand toward Nina. "Welcome to The Nook."

Nina shook Ed's hand, at once liking the friendly proprietor. "Bookstores are always special. I visit them wherever I go, along with the local library." She waved in Cora's direction.

Ed nodded. "Thanks to Cora, we have a top-notch library. I'm a big fan myself... By the way, Cora, the book you ordered arrived. I was just about to call you." He reached under the counter, pulled out a hardcover book, and held it out.

"*The Mystery of the Crooked Mile*." Nina read aloud the title, set in bold, white typeface against a dark background. "Sounds like my kind of story."

As she accepted the book, Cora's eyes lighted. "I ordered it for the library and then decided I wanted my own copy. I collect mysteries."

"How about you, Nina?" Ed turned toward her. "I bet you're a collector, too."

The thought of the book-filled shelves in her home office brought a smile. "Yes, but my collection centers on children's books. The only mysteries I acquire seem to be real life ones."

Ed rested his arms on the counter and leaned forward. "We have a real life mystery right here in Parkers—the man who collapsed at the reunion picnic. Talk around town says he might have been poisoned."

Cora nodded toward Nina. "She's already on the case."

"Really?" Ed's bushy eyebrows peaked.

"Mark was a special friend of my friend, Stephen Kraslow." Not wanting to reveal too much about her theories, Nina waited for Ed to volunteer more information.

"Mark was a customer. He collected books, too, on flying and airplanes." Ed tilted his head. "No surprise there, huh? Whenever he was in town, he'd stop in to see if I had anything new. I always kept my eye out at garage and estate sales. I'll miss him." His voice dropped, and he looked away.

Ed's heartfelt show of emotion impressed Nina. "I'm sure he will be missed by many."

A moment passed, and then Ed turned back toward them and pressed his palms on the counter. "Now, how can I help you ladies today?"

"Hmmm." Nina looked around, her gaze landing on an area decorated with posters of children's books. "I'll check out your children's section."

"I'll look at biographies." Cora pointed toward the back of the store. "My aunt's birthday is coming up, and she loves to read about famous people."

Nodding, Ed stepped back and folded his arms. "Okay, I'll leave you two to browse. Holler if you have questions."

In the children's area, Nina joined several women and children, some sitting at a table and others on the carpeted floor. She perused the shelves and found several titles by authors popular with her library's patrons. After pulling the books, she spotted a section labeled "Collectibles." A study of the offerings resulted in three more books to purchase.

She explored the rest of the bookstore, encountering other browsing customers, and eventually reached the Crime and Mystery books. Locating the poison section, she found a volume to supplement her Internet search and added it to her stack. On her way to the front of the store, she met Cora.

Cora held up her choices, a biography of a past president for her aunt and a joke book for her husband. "He's always looking for new jokes to tell his buddies."

At the counter, Ed rang up their purchases and tucked them into tote bags sporting The Book Nook's logo. "Thanks for comin' in, ladies. Happy reading."

He'd no sooner handed them their bags than the front door flew open and a young man ran inside. "Ed! Drake Larken's dead!"

Chapter Sixteen

Nina stared at the newcomer who'd burst into The Book Nook. Drake Larken? The jeweler she met only yesterday?

"Drake's dead?" Leaning over the counter, Ed echoed Nina's stunned reaction.

"Yeah, just now. At Sparkles." The young man pointed toward the door.

The women and children from the children's area hurried to join them. Several other customers from the back of the store appeared, too. Wide-eyed, they gathered around the young man.

Ed put out a hand. "Take a deep breath, Reggie, and tell us what happened."

Reggie ran a hand through his rust-colored hair, making it stand on end. As he sucked in a breath, his broad chest expanded. "Somebody said heart attack. You can see his store from here."

Ed rounded the counter and approached the door.

Nina, Cora, and the others followed, crowding around to look over Ed's shoulder. What could possibly have happened to the jeweler?

Ed craned his neck. "Can't see much except a coupla cop cars and people standing on the sidewalk."

"All the action's in the alley." Reggie waved a hand. "I was takin' my shortcut to the grocery store when the cops stopped me. I saw the medics carry somebody on a stretcher out the store's back door and put him in the ambulance. The guy standin' next to me said it was Drake."

Was he still alive at that point? Nina wondered.

"I didn't hear a siren," a middle-aged woman said.

Reggie shrugged. "Maybe they didn't need one because he was already dead."

"He had a bad heart." A man at the edge of the group folded his arms and nodded solemnly.

"I remember when Drake was sick last winter," said a dark-haired woman in her twenties.

Speculation continued. Finally, though, The Nook's customers returned to their previous pursuits.

Carrying their totes, Nina and Cora said goodbye to Ed and left.

Once outside, Nina turned to Cora. "Can we walk by Sparkles? I'm curious about what happened to Drake." Was the stone she showed him somehow involved?

Slinging her book bag and purse over her shoulder, Cora nodded. "Me, too. We probably won't get close, but we might find someone who can give us more information."

"Did you know Drake?" Nina glanced at Cora as they crossed the street.

"I've bought jewelry from him. He's quite friendly and helpful. How about you?"

"He appraised a stone I thought might be a ruby—he said it wasn't—but that's been our only association."

At Sparkles Jewelry, a small crowd milled around the sidewalk, some peering in the store's window and others talking among themselves.

Cora approached one of the women. "What

happened, Hilda?"

Hilda adjusted the sun visor covering her gray curls. "Don't know for sure. Jasmine said when she came to work, Drake complained of not feeling well. Then he collapsed. She locked the store and went to hospital, too." Hilda gestured toward the Closed sign in the store's front window.

Nina and Cora lingered, speaking to a few others Cora knew but not learning anything to add to Hilda's account.

Later, after bidding Cora goodbye and returning to the Barlows', Nina went to her room where she thought about Drake Larken's sudden—or seemingly sudden—death. Could his demise be connected somehow to Mark's? Did they even know each other? Probably, since Parkers Landing was a small town. She recalled Drake's interest in the stone she showed him. Did her visit have anything to do with his death? Now, that idea was really far-fetched. Still, she took out the stone again and studied it. Glass, as he had said? Or ruby?

At dinner that evening, with the family all assembled around the table, not surprisingly, Drake's death was a topic of conversation.

While attending one of her meetings, Judy encountered a friend who was in Drake's store only minutes before he collapsed.

"Elsa was there to pick up a watch Drake repaired." Judy sipped her water. "He went to the back room to get it, she said, and when he returned, he didn't look well. She asked him if he felt okay, and he said his stomach was queasy, that he'd drunk some coffee that wasn't sitting right."

"Coffee?" Nina frowned and put down her fork.

"Did he say where the coffee was from? Or if he made it himself?"

Judy tapped her chin with a forefinger. "Hmmm. Elsa did say something about a paper cup he pointed toward when he complained. Anyway, she retrieved her watch and left. Later, when she was at Val's Variety, a woman came in and announced Drake was dead."

Blaine helped himself to the mashed potatoes. "I bet the coffee came from Big Bear. Whenever Drake has lunch at the casino, he complains that our coffee doesn't compare to theirs."

Big Bear Coffee Company. Chester from the fairgrounds said Mark drank from a cup with the Big Bear logo. However, not wanting to start more rumors, she kept the information to herself. Later, she and Stephen took a walk through the Barlows' flower garden.

"I noted your interest in Drake's coffee." Stephen led them around a bend in the gravel path. "Wasn't Mark's coffee from Big Bear, too?"

Stopping to admire a bed of pink roses, Nina breathed in their sweet scent. "Yes, according to Chester."

Stephen slowed his steps. "We don't know Drake's coffee came from there, too, though. We have only Blaine's guess."

"Right." Nina turned from the roses to focus on their conversation. "But if the coffee was from Big Bear…and it contained poison, then the same person might be the culprit. If, like Mark, Drake died of kidney failure, that's another similarity between their deaths."

Stephen shook his head. "Lots of suppositions, Nina."

She sighed and nodded. "I know. But I need to consider all the angles."

"Autopsies usually take a few days. Mark's memorial will be held soon, and then we're leaving town." He studied her. "You don't have much time to continue investigating."

"I'll do what I can." She straightened her spine. "I want to discover the truth."

He clasped her hand and drew her close. "I know. Your determination to see justice done is one reason why I love you. But I worry about you and your safety."

Grateful for his support, she snuggled against his shoulder. "Thank you for understanding. I'll be careful. I promise." Although she meant the vow, guilt niggled. She would be careful, but, if faced with a situation offering a solution to the crime, she would investigate, dangerous or not.

****

The following day, Sunday, was uneventful, as far as Nina's investigation was concerned, but not without activity. She attended church with the family and afterward enjoyed a brunch at Diamond's, a nearby restaurant. Other church members joined them, which made a festive occasion.

Stephen spent the afternoon on Internet conference calls with friends and associates in Richmond.

Nina, too, had an online visit with her grandmother, catching her and Joe between games of pool in their retirement home's recreation room. When evening rolled around, Nina and Stephen joined the Barlows to watch favorite TV programs.

On Monday morning after breakfast, while the

Barlows went their separate ways, Nina and Stephen cleaned up the kitchen.

"What's on your program today?" Stephen rinsed a pan and placed it in the dishwasher.

Nina transferred a carton of milk to the refrigerator. "I have more shopping to do, but if you and David have an activity planned, I can go alone." Actually, she hoped they scheduled something because she wanted to be on her own. "Shopping" was really "investigating," and, although she always welcomed Stephen's help, she feared today's agenda would not meet his approval.

"We're driving to Sandpoint to the game arcade." Stephen added a plate to the dishwasher. "You're welcome to come along and shop while we're at the arcade. Sandpoint has interesting stores."

"Thanks, but I'd rather stay in town. I know my way around now."

He grinned and waggled a forefinger. "Okay, but keep away from the alleys."

Although said in jest, Stephen's warning held a serious note. Recalling her recent ordeal, Nina gave a solemn nod. "Right. No alleys."

Stephen's cell phone rang. He pulled it from his pocket and looked at the screen. "Angie."

Nina wrinkled her nose. "She probably has an errand for you and David."

"We'll see." Stephen held the device to his ear. "Hey, Angie." He listened, his gaze on Nina. "Uh huh. She's right here." He placed a hand over the speaker. "She wants to talk to you."

"Me? Why?" Nina frowned as she accepted the phone. "Hi, Angie."

"Hello."

Angie's soft voice came over the line.

"Since Stephen and David are going to Sandpoint today, I thought you and I could get together."

Taken by surprise, Nina fumbled for a polite refusal. "Ah, I've already planned to do some shopping…"

"Okay, but you can meet for lunch, can't you?"

"Lunch?" She didn't want to meet Angie, period. She glanced at Stephen.

He smiled and nodded.

Nina gave an inward sigh. "All right. Do you have a place in mind?"

"Kelly's Kitchen, on Sixth and Woodlawn, just around the corner from Main. See you there at noon."

Nina disconnected the call and handed the phone to Stephen. "I can't imagine why she wants to get together."

"To become more acquainted." Stephen pocketed the cell. "You two have something in common."

Nina tensed and placed both hands on her hips. "Really? What?"

"Me."

His eyes twinkled with teasing, but then his brows drew together in a frown.

"Seriously, I know she can be difficult and, okay, demanding. But for David's sake…and mine, I hope you two will get along." Stepping close, he put an arm around her shoulders.

She leaned against him, comforted, as always, by his nearness and his touch. "I'll give our meeting my best effort."

"Thanks, Nina." He planted a kiss on her cheek.

As she returned to cleaning the kitchen, Nina

focused on her upcoming lunch with Angie. Stephen assured her the woman just wanted to know her better, but, judging from what she already knew about Angie, Nina suspected she had something else in mind. She'd better be on her guard.

****

Later, while driving downtown, Nina put aside her worries about meeting Angie and turned her attention to today's first mission—visiting Sparkles Jewelry.

She half-expected to find the store closed, but the neon-lighted Open sign in the window indicated otherwise. As she entered, the bell over the door tinkled, and the air, the other day so redolent of flowers, smelled stale and flat. No one was in sight, though, which again raised her doubts, but then Drake's niece, Jasmine, appeared from the back room. Her eyes were red-rimmed, and she held a tissue to her nose.

"May I help you? Oh, it's you, the lady from the other day, with the ruby…"

"Ruby?" Nina frowned and shook her head. "Your uncle told me the stone was colored glass."

Jasmine bit her lip, but then she smiled and waved a hand. "Right. Of course, I remember now. Your stone looked like a ruby but wasn't genuine. What can I help you with today?"

Nina approached the counter. "I'm looking for a couple more gifts, but I also wanted to tell you how sorry I am to hear about your uncle."

"Thank you. His death is very sad." Jasmine dabbed her eyes with the tissue.

"Had he been ill?"

Jasmine shrugged. "He always said he had a bad heart."

"Then he died of a heart attack?" The young woman's willingness to talk encouraged Nina to pursue her questioning.

"I don't know. I wasn't here. I opened the store, like I usually do." She gestured toward the front door. "He came in the back door, with his morning coffee, just like he usually does." She turned and nodded toward the back room. "He sent me on an errand to the office supply store. On the way back, I saw a couple friends at a table outside Lovin's Bakery. They asked me to join them. I knew I shouldn't, but I did." Shaking her head, she blew her nose into her tissue. "When I finally returned, I found Uncle Drake lying on the floor." Stepping away from the counter, she pointed toward a spot near the curtained entrance to the back room. "When I saw he wasn't breathing, I called 911. Then I gave him the CPR I learned in school, but it was too late."

Nina tapped her chin with a forefinger. "Hmmm. You said he came in with a cup of coffee."

"He always stopped for coffee on his way to work." Jasmine twisted her tissue between her fingers.

"Where did he buy his coffee?" Nina held her breath.

"At Big Bear." She frowned. "Why are you asking so many questions about Uncle Drake?"

Nina was tempted to blurt the truth—that she wanted to know if Drake's death was related to Mark McTeague's. But, of course, she couldn't admit the real reason. "After our conversation the other day, I felt I knew him."

Jasmine put out a hand. "I'm sorry. I didn't mean to be rude. I'm just so upset."

"Of course, especially since his death was so sudden. Unless he hadn't been feeling well." She slanted Jasmine a glance, and then, fearing she'd pushed too far, she stepped back.

Jasmine hugged her waist and looked away. "He was upset about something. I don't know what." She shrugged. "Business has been good, but, still, something bothered him. The day before he died, I overheard him arguing with someone on the phone." She gestured toward the back room. "When he hung up, he was red in the face and mumbling about birds. He didn't say who he talked to, and I didn't ask."

Nina tucked away that bit of information and then waved a hand at the surroundings. "What will happen to the store now?"

Jasmine plucked a tissue from a nearby box and dabbed her wet cheeks. "I don't know. Mom and Dad will decide. They're arriving later today from Boise. Dad is Uncle Drake's brother."

"Your uncle had no family of his own?"

"He was married a long time ago, but they didn't have children. Uncle Drake called me and my brother, Tommy, his kids. Tommy's in the Army in Afghanistan." Jasmine leaned her arms on the glass case. "Uncle Drake was always good to us, which is why I wanted to work for him this summer." She heaved a sigh. "But here I am, going on and on. What can I show you? Pins? Rings? Necklaces?"

Nina gazed around. "Hmmm, I have a friend who likes butterflies."

"We have some really cool butterfly pins." She led Nina to a display, opened the case with the key hanging from her waist, and removed a box of pins set on black velvet.

Nina spent a few minutes perusing the jewelry. "They're all beautiful, and choosing is difficult, but I'll take this one." She picked up a butterfly made of blue and green stones and held it out.

"Super." Jasmine wrapped the pin in tissue paper and placed it in a small white box. "I hope your friend likes her gift."

"I'm sure she will." Nina took out her wallet. She had just finished paying for her purchase when the door opened.

A middle-aged woman wearing a straw hat entered. "Oh, Jasmine, I'm so, so sorry…" Her gaze landed on Nina. She stopped and pressed a hand to her chest. "Excuse me. I just wanted to offer my condolences."

"Thank you, Hazel." Jasmine approached the woman and stepped into her outstretched arms for a hug.

Several more people arrived.

Nina tucked her package into her purse and moved away from the counter, allowing the newcomers to gather around Jasmine. She wanted to stay and hear what was said, but her watch showed eleven forty-five. On her way to meet Angie, she reviewed her conversation with Drake's niece, filing away bits and pieces that might be important. One, she had called Nina's stone a ruby then corrected her mistake. Or was her first call a mistake? Had Drake confided to Jasmine that the stone was in fact a ruby and cautioned her to keep the secret?

Two, before he died, Drake drank coffee from Big Bear Coffee Company, as had Mark. Were both coffees tainted with poison? If so, by whom?

Three, Drake argued over the phone with someone, afterward mumbling about birds. Were any of these facts significant? Right now, she could only add the information to what she'd collected so far, like pieces of a puzzle. Would she ever find all the parts and assemble the entire picture?

****

At Kelly's Kitchen, the photos of pop music and film stars decorating the walls indicated the restaurant catered to a young crowd. Nina spotted Angie waving from a table near the windows. With her long blonde hair and wearing sandals, black leggings, and a sleeveless blue T-top, she blended in with the other clientele. Taking a deep breath and steeling herself for what she feared would be an ordeal, Nina returned Angie's gesture and headed in her direction.

"You found the place." Angie beamed Nina a bright, red-lipped smile.

Nina pulled out a chair across from her and sat. "Your directions helped."

"I thought you'd like to see where Stephen and I hung out when we were in high school." Angie nodded at their surroundings.

Nina was tempted to say, "Not particularly," but determined to do her best for Stephen's sake, she bit back the words. "Kelly's looks like a popular place."

"Oh, yes. Being in town for the reunion brings back so many memories." She placed a hand on her chest and sighed.

"I'm sure it does." Nina picked up her menu. A quick look told her—not surprisingly—that burgers were featured.

Angie shifted in her chair. "Stephen and I met in

math class. I had trouble with algebra, and he was a student coach. He's very smart, don't you think?"

"Yes, he is." Nina kept her gaze on the menu.

"Anyway, that's how we met. Then when he was editor of the Parkers High newspaper, I was on the staff. We started dating."

"So he's told me." Actually, he'd barely mentioned his and Angie's high school association, and, not wanting to know the details, she hadn't asked. Still, perhaps indicating she knew would save hearing more.

The server, a young woman with a long, thick braid draped over her shoulder, appeared at the table. "Whatcha gonna have today?" She held a pencil poised over her order pad.

Glad for the interruption, Nina traced her finger under an item on her menu. "I'll have a build-a-burger with, let's see"—she reviewed the choices—"mustard and pickles."

"I want the happy burger and a chocolate shake." Angie tapped her menu with a red-nailed forefinger. "The happy burger was my favorite in high school." She smiled at the server.

The girl nodded and wrote on her pad. "Lots of reunion folk order that particular burger. Kelly's glad we kept it on the menu." Scooping up their menus, she tucked them under an arm and headed toward the kitchen.

Angie turned to Nina. "Where were we? Oh, yes, high school. Stephen and I were together all senior year, but after graduation, we went our separate ways. I'm so glad he and David are getting to know each other. After all these years…" She heaved a sigh.

"Yes, how…nice." Nina truly was at a loss for

words. She needn't have worried, though. With only a slight pause, Angie kept the conversational ball rolling.

"They are so much alike, and they are having such a good time. David will enjoy visiting Stephen in Richmond, too." Angie leaned forward. "You know about David's trip, don't you?"

Nina felt her stomach tense. "Stephen and I haven't discussed David's visit, but I assumed he would."

Angie tilted her head. "Have you and Stephen made plans?"

"Plans?" Was she talking about David's trip? Or something else? Nina gritted her teeth.

"You know, permanent plans—the two of you." Angie sipped her water but kept her gaze on Nina.

Nina pursed her lips. "Why don't you ask him?"

Angie put down her glass. "I have, but he's…evasive."

"So, you invited me to lunch to pump *me* for information." Nina pointed toward her chest. As she'd suspected, Angie had an ulterior motive.

"No, no, Nina." Angie's eyes widened, and she spread both hands. "I really want to get to know you… Well, okay, I'll admit the idea crossed my mind that if you and Stephen have no plans for a permanent relationship, then—"

Anger bubbled up inside. She folded her arms. "Then you'll pursue him yourself? Take up where you left off in high school?"

Angie shrugged. "For David's sake. To give him a family."

"Uh huh." Nina inwardly rolled her eyes.

"Stephen and I might, hopefully, renew our, ah, affection for each other." She looked down and smoothed her napkin on her lap. "David would have a father."

"Haven't you been married? I thought Stephen said—"

Angie raised her gaze and waved a hand. "I was married twice. Both mistakes were hard on David. He should know his true father. I'm sure you understand."

"I didn't know my father." Nina lifted her chin. "He left when I was five. My mother never married again."

"Well, then, you do know how important having a father is for David."

Nina searched her mind for her next response.

But, the server arrived with their meals.

Her appetite gone, Nina stared at her burger. Finally, she picked it up and took bite. The food stuck in her throat, but she managed to swallow and continue eating.

Angie dug into her meal. In between bites, she continued talking. How much Stephen and David looked alike. How much fun they had getting to know one another.

At last, Angie finished her burger and milkshake and sat back. "That was sooo good." She rolled her eyes. "They have great pie here, too, and ice cream sundaes. Shall we look at the menu?" She pointed toward the dessert menu wedged between the sugar bowl and the salt and peppershakers.

Nina patted her stomach. "I can't eat another bite." *If I do, I'll throw up. I might, anyway.*

"Where are you going now?" Angie touched her napkin to her lips.

Resenting Angie's probe into her personal plans,

Nina kept her reply vague. "More shopping—souvenirs for friends at home."

Angie smiled and tucked her napkin under her plate. "I could show you around."

Nina made a dismissive wave. "That's kind of you, but both Judy and Stephen gave me tours, and I'm familiar with the stores. I'm sure you have other things to do."

"True, I am busy. Time here is short, and David and I soon will return to Denver. But, anyway, lunch is on me." She reached for the check.

"Oh, no, thank you. Let's split the cost." She wanted no obligation to Angie, not even for a simple lunch.

"Uh uh. My treat." Angie held the check to her chest.

"I'll leave the tip, then." Nina took a few bills from her wallet and placed them on the table.

When Nina and Angie were outside, about to go their separate ways, Nina turned toward the other woman. "Thanks for the lunch."

"You're welcome." Angie slung her purse strap over her shoulder. "I'm so glad we could get to know each other."

Know each other? Hardly. But judging by Angie's satisfied smile, she was pleased with herself for letting Nina know her intentions regarding Stephen. Once free of Angie, Nina took a deep breath of fresh air. Still, her stomach churned. She needed a place to relax before continuing her agenda. Recalling City Park was a couple blocks away, she turned her steps toward her refuge.

At the park, she chose a bench under the shade of a

maple tree, facing the river. Sitting back, she contemplated the peacefully flowing water. Still, her thoughts wandered to her lunch with Angie. Maybe Angie, Stephen, and David should be a family. She knew Stephen wanted to be a good father. Was reuniting with his son's mother the best way to fulfill that goal?

Stephen made his intentions clear that he wanted to marry Nina, but she was afraid of commitment and put him off. Now, would he give up on her and instead choose Angie? Could she confront and deal with her own fears in order to preserve their relationship?

Thank goodness she still had the mystery of Mark's—and now Drake's—death to occupy her time and her thoughts. Otherwise, worry about Stephen and his situation would drive her crazy.

After a while, she left the park and returned to Main Street. She kept an eye out for Angie, planning a quick escape in case the woman changed her mind about returning home and remained in the vicinity. Thankfully, she saw no sign of the troublesome woman. Taking a deep breath, she set her steps in the direction of her next target establishment.

Chapter Seventeen

When Nina reached Lovin's Bakery, she stopped to look at the window display, not only because the pies, cakes, cookies, and doughnuts were appealing but also to allow a few minutes to review her plan. Then, taking a deep breath, she opened the door and went inside.

An assortment of sugary aromas filled the air. The bakery did a brisk business, with customers purchasing selections from the display cases while those at tables enjoyed a late lunch. Nina found an available table and took a seat.

Sara, who had served the Museum Mommas, approached with a glass of water and a menu tucked under an arm. A smile lit her face. "Hi. I remember you. You're Judy's friend. Here by yourself?"

"I am, and I've already had lunch elsewhere, but I saved room for dessert."

Sara's smile widened. "Can't beat Lovin's for pleasin' your sweet tooth. What can I bring you? Or do you need a menu?"

"No, I've already decided. I'll have a piece of apple pie and a cup of tea. Do you have mint decaf?"

"Sure do." Sara wrote on her order pad.

After Sara left, Nina gazed around planning her next move. She spotted the restrooms sign near the back of the bakery. Stretching her neck to see where the sign led, she located three doors. Two would be the men's and women's rooms. Hopefully, the third door led to storage.

Sara returned with a tray holding a piece of apple pie, a mug with a tea bag, and a pot of hot water.

"The pie looks wonderful." Nina inhaled the sweet scents of apple, cinnamon, and sugar.

"Baked fresh this morning." Sara poured water from the teapot into Nina's cup.

The aroma of mint soon mingled with the pie's sugar and cinnamon. Despite her recent lunch, Nina's mouth watered. "Thank you, Sara." She spread her napkin on her lap and picked up her fork. "Is Mary Ellen here today?" She hoped her question sounded casual.

Sara set the teapot on the table. "She's here every day."

"Oh…" That answer was not the one she wanted.

"But not at this moment. She had an errand at the post office." She frowned. "Did you need to see her today?"

Nina made a casual wave. "No, I just wanted to say 'hi.' " She was glad Mary Ellen was gone. Her absence made one less person to worry about when she carried out her plan.

"Well, enjoy." Sara tucked her tray under an arm and headed back to the kitchen.

Nina took a bite of her pastry and, as expected, the filling was both sweet and spicy, and the crust melted in her mouth. She sampled another taste while at the same time gazing around. The term "casing the joint" came to mind, which, despite her nervousness, brought a giggle. She watched a server ring up a sale at the cash register. Another employee waited on customers at the display cases, and Sara hadn't yet emerged from the kitchen. Now would be a good time to engage her plan.

Leaving her pie half eaten, Nina rose and wound her way through the tables to the restrooms sign. Bypassing the sign, she continued on to the third door, which turned out to be marked Storage. *Yes!* Just what she'd hoped. Glancing over her shoulder and not seeing anyone nearby, she opened the door and ducked inside. She paused to let her eyes adjust to the dim light. One side of the room had shelves of equipment—mixers, sheet pans, cookware—while the shelves on the other side held containers of various ingredients. Nina headed for those shelves.

Fortunately, the containers were clearly labeled. She quickly scanned tubs of flour, salt, cans of spices, and bags of nuts. She was almost at the end when she spied what she looked for—a glass jar of white powder labeled Potassium Bromate. Excitement quickened her pulse. Despite what Mona said about Mary Ellen's use of the chemical, Nina wanted to see for herself. Now she had that proof. She pulled out her cell phone and snapped a photo.

"What are *you* doing here?"

Stuffing away her phone, with her pulse racing, Nina whirled.

Mary Ellen stood with both hands propped on her hips, eyes narrowed to slits and mouth set in a tight line.

Nina swallowed and lifted her chin. "I was looking for the ladies room."

Mary Ellen's eyebrows peaked. "Oh, really? You didn't see the sign on this door that says 'Storage'?" She pointed toward the wording on the door.

Nina waved a hand. "When I realized my mistake, I thought I'd look around at all the interesting equipment. As a librarian, I'm always interested in other professions." Turning her back on the shelves of food, she stepped to a large metal box with a lid opening. "Like this machine. What does it do?"

"That machine makes bread."

Keeping her gaze on Nina, Mary Ellen bit out the words. "How interesting. How about that one?" Nina approached another device, where a glass window protected a metal saw.

"That's a dough divider."

Nina inquired about a couple more machines then stood at the door. "This tour has been very interesting, but I'd better make that visit to the restroom."

Still scowling, Mary Ellen opened the door wider and stood aside.

Nina swept into the hallway. She half-expected the woman to follow her into the restroom, but she didn't. When Nina returned to her table, she spotted Mary Ellen visiting with other diners. As she tossed back her head in laughter, her gaze caught Nina's, and her eyes narrowed and her mouth thinned. Then she was all smiles again, flashing her dimple as she welcomed new customers.

Nina pasted on a smile and then took a bite of her pie, but the pastry left a sour taste. Her tea was cold, and she had no desire to add hot water from the teapot. She pulled out money to pay her bill and stepped to the cash register. An employee accepted her money without comment. Once outside, she hurried from the vicinity, lest Mary Ellen pursued her. She traveled several blocks before slowing her steps.

Caught snooping, especially by the bakery owner herself, was unfortunate, but, otherwise, her mission was a success. Mary Ellen indeed possessed potassium bromate. Nina's entry into the storage room upset the woman. Why? Was she afraid Nina would discover the potentially poisonous substance? But, if that were the case, why was the potassium in a labeled container and in plain sight? Perhaps her anger was only because use of the potassium was a closely guarded secret she wanted to protect. Some customers might not approve of her use of the controversial substance. Or did she fear Nina would guess she also used the chemical to poison Mark?

****

After dinner that evening, Nina and Stephen sat in the swing on the front porch. The evening was peaceful, as usual, with twilight casting a soft yellow glow over the landscape. A light breeze swept through the trees, fluttering the leaves on a nearby aspen and cooling Nina's cheeks.

Stephen tucked an arm around her shoulders. "We've both had a busy day with much to discuss, but first, I'd like to hear about your lunch with Angie."

Nina gave an inward sigh. The topic was not one she would have picked. "Well, we met at Kelly's Kitchen…"

A smile crossed his lips. "Ah, our old high school hangout."

"So I learned. Angie told me you tutored her in math and later worked with her on the newspaper staff. In fact, you two were all she talked about, besides David, of course. Then, she asked if you and I have plans."

He drew back and frowned. "Plans?"

"For the future."

"What did you tell her?" One eyebrow peaked.

Nina folded her arms and looked away. "I told her she needed to ask you."

Stephen put out a hand. "Nina, you know we have plans—at least, I do."

"That's why I told her to talk to you." Despite her resolve to remain calm, she felt her throat tighten. She didn't want to lose him but how to handle Angie challenged them both.

"I'll set her straight. I just wish you were as certain about our future together as I am—as I want to be."

Nina's and Stephen's future was always a sore spot, with him wanting more commitment than she could give. Fearing further talk would lead to an argument, she remained quiet. She held herself rigid, though, expecting him to pursue the matter.

However, Stephen, too, fell silent, gazing into the distance.

The only sound was the creak of the swaying swing.

"Okay, we'll deal with our future another time." Stephen finally broke the silence. "Tell me what else you did while you were downtown."

Taking a deep breath and relaxing her tense muscles, Nina began with her visit to Sparkles Jewelry and her talk with Drake's niece, Jasmine.

Stephen rubbed his jaw. "You think his death is suspicious?"

She spread her hands. "Well, he collapsed shortly after drinking coffee, just like Mark, and both drinks came from Big Bear Coffee Company."

"Nina, people buy coffee from that outfit every day, and they don't collapse and die."

"Of course not." Nina pursed her lips. "But what if the same person bought the drinks and added the poison before giving the coffee to Mark and Drake?"

"Okay...." Stephen nodded. "But do you know what Mark and Drake have in common that would make someone want to poison them both?"

Nina shook her head. "All I have is a hunch the two men are somehow connected."

"Hmmm." Stephen's eyes narrowed. "I have to admit your hunches often turn out to be fact. You seem to have a sixth sense. But still—"

"Here's something that is fact." Nina raised a forefinger. "I now have proof Mary Ellen uses potassium bromate in her baked goods." She pulled out her cell phone and scrolled to the photo from Lovin's Bakery.

Stephen grasped the phone and studied the photo. "Hey, good shot. How were you able to take this picture?"

Nina explained the circumstances. "Mary Ellen was upset when she found me in the storeroom. Downright angry, in fact."

"Because she also used the chemical as a poison? Or because the area is off-limits for some other reason?" Stephen handed her the phone.

"I don't know." Nina studied the photo, looking for other clues. "But the coffee that poisoned Mark and Drake—okay, *might* have poisoned them—came from Big Bear. I need to pay them a visit..."

"If you have time. Only a couple more days until Mark's memorial, and then we'll leave."

The reminder brought tension to her shoulders. "We both have obligations waiting for us at…home." She slanted him a glance. Did he still consider Richmond his home? Or had being in Parkers Landing changed his mind about where he wanted to live? Now that he'd found a new family, maybe Denver would be his home. Her chest tightened.

Stephen shifted in his seat. "Nina, about Angie—"

Just then, the screen door burst open, and footsteps clattered across the porch. "Nina? Uncle Stephen? Are you here?"

Katie appeared, looking cool and summery in a white blouse, pink shorts, and with her hair in a ponytail. She carried a flat box.

"Hey, Katie." Stephen leaned forward. "Whatcha got there?"

"My puppets, for storytelling. I thought maybe we could work on them tonight?"

She cast Nina a hopeful look. A wave of guilt rolled through Nina. In her involvement with the mystery, she'd all but forgotten her promise to help Katie prepare for the library's storytelling program. "Of course, we can." She turned to Stephen. "You don't mind, do you?"

"Not at all. In fact, maybe I can help?"

"I know something you can do, Uncle Stephen." Katie grinned and shifted from one foot to the other. "You can listen to see if I'm changing my voice for each character."

Stephen nodded. "I can do that."

Nina and Stephen followed Katie into the house and unloaded the contents of her box onto the dining room table.

Settled into her chair, Katie recited the story.

Nina selected a pair of scissors and cut the felt for the wolf's clothing.

Stephen focused on his niece, but then he looked Nina's way and their gazes met. He smiled and winked.

Feeling warm inside, she returned his smile. Was this cozy evening what having a family with Stephen would be like? Maybe, just maybe, they could have such a life.

Then doubts chased away the warmth, leaving a cold chill. Stephen already had a family—if he wanted to claim them. He'd already acknowledged and accepted his son. Would he claim Angie, too, as the woman obviously hoped, and make his family complete?

Later, as Nina climbed into bed, her mind churned with the day's events. Reaching for her tablet, she powered it on and brought up the notes on her investigation. She added what she learned today about Drake and Mary Ellen. She'd yet to establish a link between Mark and Drake, but with the discovery of potassium bromate at Lovin's Bakery, the case against Mary Ellen gained strength. Right now, she was Nina's most likely suspect. Still, she'd learned from past experience that what at first appeared to be a solution didn't always prove true. She needed to dig deeper.

Next, she accessed her notes on poisons and after reviewing the information on the various substances decided potassium bromate was still the most likely one. Picking up the book on poisons she purchased at The Book Nook, she turned to the chapter on potassium bromate. Yes, the substance was a baking enhancer, but home permanents also contained the chemical. Nina tapped her chin with a forefinger. Home permanents…hmmm. The Curly Locks' museum exhibit included six old home permanents, and two were missing. Had Tilda mistakenly counted her inventory, or were the missing kits used for a more nefarious purpose?

If the latter was true, Tilda was the most likely culprit, but what motive would she have for murdering Mark? Or Drake?

Perhaps Della Comstock stole the kits and used the poison to prevent Mark from exposing the crimes of her grandfather. But why would she also poison Drake?

What about the other Museum Mommas, Mona and Lexie? Selene, too, could have learned about the toxic ingredient in home permanents. Nina could think of no motives for any of those three, but that didn't mean motives didn't exist. Tomorrow, she and Judy would attend a meeting of the Mommas at the museum. She would check on the missing home permanent kits. Were they found? Or still missing? If missing, were they used for murder? Although Nina disliked suspecting Judy's friends, if she wanted to solve the crime, she must adopt an objective approach.

****

"Can we stop at Big Bear Coffee Company?" Nina asked Judy the following morning while on the way to the Museum Mommas' meeting. Today was a typical summer morning in Parkers Landing, with the sun beaming down from a clear sky and the temperature already climbing.

"Of course." Judy steered the car around a corner.

Nina cast her a cautious glance. "Not that I don't like your coffee…"

Shaking her head, Judy laughed. "I take no offense. At our house, coffee is coffee. But at Big Bear—ah, so many flavors, so many variations."

"I thought sampling one of their special drinks would be fun." Nina hoped Judy would accept that reason for her request. Without more proof, she wasn't ready to share her suspicions that Big Bear's coffee played a role in Mark's and Drake's deaths.

Several blocks later, Judy pulled into the coffee shop's parking lot.

A carved wooden statue of a grinning bear holding a cup of coffee stood beside the front door. Inside, the walls of white stone with log beams gave the place a rustic look. Customers sat in overstuffed chairs grouped around a stone fireplace or at tables placed around the room. Nina and Judy joined the line at the order counter. While she waited, Nina studied the chalkboard wall menu with offerings such as Mucha Mocha, Lotta Latte, and Decaf Delight.

Judy's turn arrived, and she placed her order.

Then Nina approached the counter.

"What can I get you?" asked a young woman whose nametag said "Lois."

Nina pressed a finger to her cheek. "I can't decide. One of your drinks was recommended, but I don't recall the name."

"Hmm, who was the person?" Lois tilted her head. "If he's a frequent customer, I might know his order."

The unexpected opportunity to share Drake's name brought a silent cheer. Before responding, she looked around for Judy and spotted her at the end of the counter, waiting for her coffee. Satisfied she was out of earshot, Nina turned back to Lois. "Drake Larken, from

Sparkles Jewelry. The man who passed away two days ago."

Lois's forehead wrinkled. "I knew Drake. I was so sorry to hear about his death. He was a good customer—besides being a nice man. His favorite drink was Mucha Mocha."

Nina snapped her fingers. "That's the one. I'd like a Mucha Mocha, please."

"Short, Medium, or Tall?"

"Medium." Nina pointed toward the middle cup of the three sizes displayed. "Drake said he stopped here for his coffee each morning on his way to work. When I spoke to his niece, Jasmine, yesterday, she said he had his coffee even on his last day."

Lois shook her head and pulled a paper cup from a stack nearby. "He didn't. I watched for him because I have a broken necklace I wanted him to fix, but he never came. Then I heard he died. Heart attack, they said. So sad." Her mouth turned down.

Later, when she and Judy were on their way to the museum, Nina sipped her mocha, enjoying the rich, though strong, flavor. She reviewed Lois's news that on his last day, Drake hadn't stopped for his customary coffee. Yet, his niece, Jasmine, said he arrived with a drink in hand, as usual. If he didn't purchase the coffee, then who did? Someone who laced the brew with a potent poison?

Chapter Eighteen

"What do you think of the new shelving our Maintenance Department built?" Selene waved a hand toward the shelves lining one wall of the Curly Locks' Beauty Salon exhibit.

Along with the Museum Mommas, Nina inspected the new additions, running her hand over a shelf and breathing in the aroma of freshly varnished wood. "Very nice."

Della nodded. "The carpenter who remodeled our house couldn't have done better."

The others chimed in with similar comments.

Selene moved to a counter with glass display shelves. "We had this counter in storage, and I think it fits here."

"Good visibility." Mona tapped the glass with ring-laden fingers.

Judy nodded. "Perfect for the cosmetics display."

"Suits me." Lexie folded her arms.

Selene pointed toward Tilda. "You're the boss. What do you think?"

A smile lit Tilda's face. "I feel like I'm a little girl again and visiting Grammy's salon."

"Just what I wanted to hear." Selene lifted her chin and thrust out her chest. "Now, let's get to work."

"What's going on?"

Nina turned to see Oswald Farrington stride into

the room. Not having seen him around town for a few days, she'd all but forgotten about him.

A frown creasing his brow, Oswald planted both hands on his hips. "I didn't know you were meeting today. Woulda missed you if I hadn't stopped in to see Hal."

"You didn't get my email?" Selene gave him a wide-eyed look.

Oswald's lips thinned. "No, I didn't."

"Sorry about that."

Nina hid a smile. Selene's chirp sounded anything but sorry.

"Okay, put me to work." Oswald stepped farther into the room.

"We're just getting started. We need the boxes unloaded and the contents displayed." Selene ticked off the items on her fingers. "The mannequins must be dressed and placed, and the dryers set up."

"Della and I will arrange the dryers." Judy headed toward the row of cone-shaped dryers in one corner.

Lexie nudged Nina with her elbow. "Let's you and I dress the mannequins."

"All right." Working with Lexie would give Nina a chance to question her about Drake. Hopefully, she could do the same with the others later.

"Mona, you can unpack the boxes." Selene indicated the cartons set around the room. "I'll check the inventory, and Tilda will supervise."

"Wait a minute." Oswald raised his voice. "What am I supposed to do?"

Selene tapped a finger to her lips. "Hmmm, how about helping with the unpacking?"

Oswald issued a grumble. "Unpacking—anyone

can do that."

"Nooo, unpacking requires concentration. Certain items must be kept together. Mona has a list."

Selene's measured words indicated exaggerated patience.

Oswald frowned and folded his arms.

Silence hung in the air.

Nina held her breath. Would Oswald goad Selene into a fight?

Then Tilda waved both hands, flashing red, glitter-embellished nails. "Okay, everybody, let's get started. The boss is watching."

The tense moment passed, and the group, including Oswald, set to work. Soon, the room buzzed with activity.

Nina and Lexie chose a mannequin and then unpacked clothes from one of the boxes.

Lexie held up a navy-blue dress with a flared skirt and puffed sleeves. "Wow, look at this operator's outfit. Pret-ty fancy."

Nina helped Lexie slip the dress over the mannequin's head. "Sad about Drake Larken's sudden death, isn't it?"

Lexie straightened the skirt. "Uh huh."

"I was in his store only two days before he died." Nina picked up a blonde wig, smoothed the tousled strands, and held it out to Lexie.

"Really? Were you looking for something special?" Lexie took the wig and set it on the mannequin's head. "Does this hair piece look straight?"

Nina studied the model. "Maybe a little lower on her forehead. I asked Drake to appraise a stone."

"What kind of stone?" Lexie stopped adjusting the

wig and stared at Nina.

Ah, now she had the woman's attention. Did her interest signify something other than idle curiosity? "A red stone I thought might be a ruby."

Lexie's eyes narrowed, and she leaned closer. "Was it? What did he say?"

"He said the stone was only glass."

"Oh, that's too bad, huh?" Lexie's eyebrows furrowed as she drew back.

Nina shrugged. "I didn't have any money invested. I found the piece at the casino, the night of the Meet-and-Greet." Unwilling to divulge any more details about how she acquired the stone, she ran a comb through the mannequin's wig. "Do you know what caused Drake's death?"

"Heart attack. He had a history."

"No, he didn't."

Wondering who had spoken with such authority, Nina looked around to see Mona approach.

Mona set the box she carried on the counter and propped both hands on her hips. "Drake did not have a bad heart. My husband's his doctor, and he should know."

"What does your husband think caused Drake's death?" Nina put down the comb and focused on Mona.

"He's waiting for the autopsy results."

Nina gave an inward sigh. As she'd feared, another wait, just like with Mark's death. Well, in the meantime, she'd continue her own investigation.

Waving a clipboard, Selene joined them. "I'm checking inventory. Let me see what you have in your box, Mona."

Mona reached in the carton and pulled out a

handful of metal curlers. "Three boxes of these curlers."

Selene marked her list and looked up. "What else?"

Mona dug again into the box. "Three packages of combs, five of hairclips…"

"What about those old permanent wave kits?" Selene leaned forward and tapped her clipboard with a forefinger. "I have six on the list but only four checked off. I've already made sure they aren't in any of the other boxes brought today."

Feeling her stomach clench, Nina looked from Mona to Selene. "Four were all I found when I took inventory at the salon."

Selene searched the box and pulled out two permanent wave kits. "Now we have only two. Hmmm, I wonder what happened to the missing boxes." She raised her head. "Tilda!"

More kits unaccounted for? What could have happened to them in such a short time?

Tilda left supervising Della and Judy setting up the dryers and joined Selene. After listening to her complaint, Tilda checked the contents of the box without finding the missing sets. "Never mind." She made a dismissive wave. "We'll use the two we have."

Selene nodded and made another note on her clipboard. Then she looked up, her brow wrinkled. "But losing four out of six seems strange. Who would want old permanent wave sets? The new ones are much improved."

Who, indeed? Nina searched the faces of the other women, hoping to see a sign of guilt or perhaps fear of being exposed as the culprit.

While she straightened the mannequin's wig, Lexie's face was hidden.

Della and Judy returned to the dryers. Judy, of course, was not a concern, but Della was on Nina's suspect list.

Mona pulled other items from the box and placed them on the counter, ready to be displayed.

What about Oswald Farrington? Nina searched the room, but the man was gone.

"What happened to Oswald?" She waved toward the doorway.

Selene pursed her lips. "I expected him to duck out. He's not really interested in helping. He just wants to make points with Director Hal so he can have free run of the museum for his research. But never mind about him." She tapped her wristwatch with a forefinger. "It's noon, and we have a catered lunch waiting in the staff room."

Despite Selene's dismissal of Oswald, as Nina joined the group for lunch, she continued to think about him. Had he planned to stay only a short while and then leave? Or, when the missing permanent wave kits were discovered, was he afraid he'd be exposed as a thief? She hadn't considered Oswald as the poisoner, but why not? He certainly behaved suspiciously. Perhaps the search for his roots was a cover-up for something that involved Mark and Drake.

****

Later, when she and Judy returned to the Barlows', Nina took her tablet and a glass of iced tea and sat on the porch swing. She leaned back and relaxed a few minutes, and then she straightened and set to work. After the eventful morning, she had much to review and record. Stephen was spending the day with David, so she had time to work on her own.

She began with her visit to Big Bear Coffee Company and then moved to the meeting of the Museum Mommas, noting two additional permanent wave sets were missing. Were the solutions containing the potassium bromate used to poison Drake's coffee as well as Mark's? Her research revealed the substance was odorless and tasteless, but even if the permanent solution itself had a taste, the coffee flavor would mask it, especially in Drake's case. The Mucha Mocha Nina sampled was indeed strong.

If the permanent wave solution was used, then who stole the kits? The possible culprits were many. All the Mommas had opportunity. Della's fear Mark would expose her grandfather as a crook put her high on the list. But what would be her motive for poisoning Drake Larken?

Of the other committee members, Tilda appeared the most likely. Maybe Mark knew something about her worthy of blackmail or about her husband, Race. Lexie and Mona also might have hidden motives. Even Selene and Director Hal could be added to the list.

Nina heaved a deep sigh. The more she delved into the matter, the more complicated the puzzle became. Would she discover the truth before she ran out of time?

****

"This is Mark and Gloria's *vacation* home?" From the window of Stephen's car, Nina surveyed the two-story house set on a hillside overlooking the river. White siding gleamed in the sunshine beaming through the maple and pine trees. A stone walkway led to a porch supported by round, cement columns and furnished with wrought iron chairs and tables. The entire effect spoke of elegance and wealth.

"Some place, huh?" Stephen followed the line of cars traveling up the gravel driveway.

Nina and Stephen just attended Mark's memorial at a local church. Although brightened by flower arrangements and uplifting stories of his life, the service was a somber affair. Now they'd come to the McTeague home for the reception. "Hard to believe their flying service was in financial trouble." Still awed by the grandeur of the home set on this secluded bluff, Nina shook her head.

Stephen pulled into a parking spot at the end of the driveway. "Gloria and Mark built the house when the business was profitable. I'm betting she'll put the property on the market now."

Nina stepped from the car and joined Stephen and the others heading up the walk. At the top of the porch, the double doors stood open, and they went inside.

"The reception's on the patio." A man in the group gestured down a hallway.

Nina peeked into the rooms they passed, all tastefully furnished with expensive-looking, modern furniture. Another door soon led outside again, where people gathered on a stone patio set with padded lawn chairs and sofas, wicker tables, and in the center, a fire pit. Nina imagined cozy evenings spent around the fire, with the stars twinkling overhead and owls hooting from distant trees. Today, however, even though the sun shone brightly, the atmosphere held the chill of sadness.

Nina focused on the other guests. Unlike the Meet-and-Greet, where she knew no one, now she saw many familiar faces—Oren and Gloria, of course, and Tilda and Race LaMott, and the other Museum Mommas and, except for Lexie, their spouses. Director Hal was present, too. Greystone catered the occasion, and Blaine was on hand to help serve.

Wearing a stylish, powder blue slacks suit and with her Curly Locks hairdo still in perfect place, Gloria graciously greeted the guests. When Nina stepped up to offer her condolences, she noticed how tired Gloria appeared, with circles under her eyes and lines around her mouth. Her distress over her husband's death appeared genuine. But then Nina recalled Gloria was an actress before marrying Mark, which cast a new light on her behavior.

With Stephen engaged in conversation, Nina took the opportunity to investigate. Since this was Mark's home, perhaps the interior hid a clue or two to explain his mysterious death. Seeing an entrance to the kitchen, she approached the door and stepped inside. The room was a busy place, with restaurant employees preparing and dishing up food. She exchanged waves with Blaine, who rinsed dishes at the sink, and then headed down a hallway. If anyone asked, she'd say she looked for the bathroom—always a good excuse when one went snooping.

She passed a laundry room and then a storeroom stacked with boxes. Some were taped shut while others had the flaps open and ready to be filled, presumably with nearby piles of clothing. As Stephen suggested, was Gloria planning to move? Perhaps she didn't want to keep the house now that Mark was gone. Too many sad memories? Too expensive to maintain?

The roll top desk and file cabinet in the next room indicated a home office. Wooden shelves with glass doors displayed various collections. One had miniature airplanes, another pocketknives, and still another held books. Always interested in the reading preferences of others, Nina approached the books. Not wanting to disturb them, she tilted her head to peruse the titles. As might be expected, the subjects dealt with aviation and travel.

As she straightened, she spotted a figurine on top of the shelf. About four inches high, six inches in length, and made of metal, the sculpture resembled a robin with outstretched wings and an open mouth. The piece looked familiar. Had she seen it before? Or one similar?

"Looking for something?"

Her heart pounding, Nina whirled.

Gloria stood in the doorway with both hands planted on her hips and a frown wrinkling her brow.

Nina lifted her chin. "Yes, the bathroom."

"Really?" Gloria's eyes narrowed. "We have a guest bathroom just off the kitchen." She pointed over her shoulder. "You didn't see the open door when you came inside?"

"I must have missed it." Nina forced a smile. "Then when I passed this room, I noticed your book collection. Being a librarian, I'm always interested in books." She gestured toward the bookshelves.

"Those are all Mark's." Gloria's nose wrinkled. "Wherever we went, he looked for books on flying. He read every one, too."

Her comment encouraged Nina. "I know about collecting. My passion is children's books. I keep them in glass cases, too, similar to these."

"Uh huh." Gloria folded her arms and tapped a

foot.

So much for her attempt to relate. Maybe another tack would bring more results. "This bird is interesting." Nina pointed toward the metal robin on top of the shelf. "Very unusual. Was Mark starting a new collection?"

Gloria's lips twisted. "He brought back that ugly thing on his last trip. I didn't want it, but he said we had to keep it, and so I put it there on the shelf."

"I find metal sculpture intriguing. Mind if I examine this piece?" So, he insisted on keeping the bird. Why?

Gloria shrugged. "You can have it, for all I care."

"Oh, no. Mark gave the figurine to you." Nina shook her head.

"Not really. He just wanted me to keep it. I don't know why. He knew I'm not fond of crude sculpture." She made shooing motions with both hands. "Go on, take the bird. I'll be glad not to look at it anymore or have to dust it."

"Well…okay." Nina picked up the robin. "It's heavier than I would have thought, being made of metal."

"Probably has something inside to give it weight, so it doesn't topple."

Just then, Oren appeared in the doorway.

He'd dressed up for the occasion—sort of—wearing slacks instead of jeans with his Hawaiian print shirt.

"Oh, Gloria, here you are." Oren's gaze moved to Nina, and a frown knit his brow. "What's *she* doing in here?"

"Looking for the bathroom, or so she said." Gloria

tipped her head toward Nina.

"I'm also perusing Mark's interesting book collection. I'm a librarian, you know." Nina offered him a smile.

"Whatever." Oren turned to Gloria. "They need you in the kitchen. Something about extra dishes."

Gloria frowned. "I set out the dishes I thought might be useful. But all right, I'll see to the problem." She turned and headed down the hallway.

Not wanting to risk more of Oren's questions, Nina swept past him and followed in Gloria's wake.

His footsteps sounded from behind, though, and in the kitchen, he caught up and tapped her shoulder. "What have you got there?"

"Gloria gave me this sculpture." Nina held up the bird. "She said Mark brought it on their flight here, but she doesn't want it."

Oren's eyes narrowed. "She shouldn't be giving away his stuff."

Even though the bird was Gloria's to deal with, Nina wanted to avoid an argument. She took another step toward the door.

"Wait!"

Oren's sharp tone jolted. What now? Nina held her breath.

"Here's the room you were lookin' for." He pointed toward an open door nearby.

Nina glimpsed the outlines of a sink and a toilet. She blew out her breath. "Oh, right. Thank you, Oren." Stepping into the room, she shut the door and snapped the lock. By that time, her nerve-racking encounter with Gloria and Oren had brought on a true need for the facilities.

A few minutes later, with the bird figurine tucked safely in her purse, she was finally outside again. She looked around for Stephen, wanting to touch base. She spotted him and Angie, with David between them, sitting on a wicker sofa at the edge of the patio. Her breath caught. They looked so much like a family. David was obviously their child. He had Stephen's brown hair and straight nose and Angie's wide smile. How ingenious of nature to so skillfully combine the features of two people to create a third.

Seeing them together brought an ache to her chest. Although Stephen assured her the two of them had a future, would being with his son and his son's mother change his mind? Instead of joining them, Nina approached the buffet table, picked up a plate, and concentrated on the offerings.

"Nice service, wasn't it?"

Nina turned to see Lexie. "Oh, hello. Yes, even though I didn't know Mark well, I thought the service a wonderful tribute." Then she noticed Lexie's hair was cut shorter than usual with curls framing her face. "You have a new hairdo. You must have been to Curly Locks."

Lexie shook her head. "I go to Sandpoint for my hair care."

Lexie's choice reminded Nina of the contention she had observed between her and Tilda. "Well, the style is very becoming."

"Thanks." Lexie picked up a plate. "I suppose you and Stephen will leave soon, now Mark's memorial is over?"

Nina spooned strawberry salad onto her plate. "Yes, we're here for only three more days. We'll save exploring more of the countryside until another time. The area is beautiful, and I look forward to a return trip. Meeting Stephen's family has been great, too. What about you? Do you have any special plans?"

Lexie used tongs to select a roast beef sandwich. "Maybe. I hope so."

Watching Lexie's gaze stray to the others made Nina wonder if her "someone special" was here. She'd never learned the person's identity. Why did Lexie and her lover keep their relationship a secret?

"I suppose you've given up proving Mark was murdered." Lexie's eyebrows arched. "Especially now you're returning home."

Nina finished sampling a cracker topped with creamed cheese. "I might be leaving, but I'm not giving up."

Lexie snorted. "Huh, how can you solve a crime from a distance?"

"I don't know, but I won't rest until I'm satisfied." Nina stepped farther down the buffet line.

"You're wasting your time." Lexie added a spoonful of tossed salad to her plate.

Nina studied the woman. "I'm surprised at your change of attitude when all along you've encouraged me."

Lexie shrugged. "Mark's dead. End of story."

Not wanting to argue, especially at the deceased's memorial, Nina remained silent. After filling her plate, she sat at one of the picnic tables. Lexie and Mary Ellen joined her. They were engaged in idle small talk when Tilda and Race LaMott, glasses of wine in hand, strolled by.

Mary Ellen beamed a smile at Tilda. "All the

women here look gorgeous, thanks to you, Tilda."

Tilda fluttered her fingers, each nail painted blue with a gold star. "Making women look their best is my life's mission. Everyone needs a mission, right?" She gazed at her husband.

"You bet, honey." Race put an arm around Tilda's shoulders. "Mine is keeping you happy."

"Aw, you're so sweet." She patted his cheek.

Nina glanced at the others to see their reaction to the couple's public display of affection. Mary Ellen flashed her dimple and rolled her eyes. Lexie, however, frowned, her brows drawn into a tight V. Was the negative emotion aimed at Tilda or Race? Or both? She recalled Lexie's and Tilda's contention during the Museum Mommas' meetings. The two definitely didn't like each other. Why? Lingering childhood jealousy? Or something more?

Chapter Nineteen

Later that evening, after helping Katie with her puppets, Nina sought out Stephen. He wasn't with the rest of the family, who gathered in the living room to watch TV. She found him on the porch, sitting on the wicker sofa and staring into the growing darkness. A soft breeze cooled the air and rustled the leaves of a nearby aspen tree.

He looked up and patted the seat beside him. "Come join me."

Enough light remained for her to discern his bleak expression.

"You're sure? Would you rather be alone?"

"I do have a lot on my mind, but I'd like your company, anyway."

Nina crossed the porch and sat. Being close felt comforting, and she relaxed against his shoulder. Not sure what to say, though, she remained silent.

"This trip isn't the vacation I'd planned," Stephen said at last. "I thought you'd meet my family, we'd attend the reunion, and then explore the countryside. We'd return to Richmond happy and relaxed."

Nina sighed. In addition to Stephen's expectations, she hoped this special time together would deepen their relationship and help her to make a decision regarding their future. "Plans don't always turn out, but don't apologize. I've loved meeting your family. They're wonderful. I've enjoyed knowing your friends and classmates, too, despite the tragedy of Mark's death. David, though a surprise, is a fine young man."

He turned, his brows knit. "Then the whole trip hasn't been a bust?"

"Of course not." She wanted to say, "We will have other vacations," but bit back the words. Despite her encouragement, no doubt their lives were changed, and who knew what the future held.

He slanted her a glance. "Will you be okay leaving without having proved Mark was murdered?"

No, she wasn't ready to return without solving the mystery. She hadn't finished her investigation, either, and would pursue the matter until she discovered the truth. But why add to Stephen's worries? "When the time comes to leave, of course, I'll go."

The door to the house flew open, and Katie ran out. "Hey, Uncle Stephen and Nina, come inside. We're making popcorn." She grasped Stephen's hand and tugged.

Stephen scooted to the edge of the sofa. "We don't want to miss that treat, do we, Nina?"

"No, we don't. Popcorn sounds good." Although she enjoyed her alone time with Stephen, she liked being with the family, too.

Later, while preparing for bed and thinking of Mark and today's memorial, Nina recalled the tin robin Gloria gave her. She retrieved the figurine from her purse, took it to the round table, and studied it under the overhead lamplight. The sculpture was rather crude and amateur, but the piece had a certain charm. The bird's highly polished eyes twinkled, as if it withheld information. Nina leaned close. "What's your secret, little robin? Tell me."

The bird, of course, remained silent, but its eyes glittered even more than before.

As she set the sculpture on her dresser, she again noticed the robin seemed heavier than its tin construction warranted. The weight centered in the bird's bottom. As Gloria suggested, something was added to give the sculpture stability. Nina turned over the bird. The legs, thin sticks of metal ending in claws, supported a circular piece of tin plugged into the body. She shook the piece. Nothing rattled, so the weight must be secured to the insides. A sudden need to know what it was seized her. First, though, she must remove the legs. She rose and crossed to her closet.

When she first fancied herself an amateur sleuth, she enrolled in a course given by a private detective that included instructions for putting together a kit of tools and other investigation aids. Nina assembled a set and carried it nearly everywhere, including this trip to Parkers Landing.

Stepping into the closet, she retrieved the kit from her suitcase. Returning to the table, she sat and slid open the plastic case's zipper. Along with lock picks and a flashlight were miniature tools—hammer, pliers, and a screwdriver. Pulling out the screwdriver, she poked the tool at the tab securing the piece of tin forming the bird's bottom. After several tries, she loosened the piece and it popped free. Setting aside the fragment, she stuck her finger in the hole. Yes, something was hidden inside. Her heartbeat quickened.

Capturing the elusive object proved difficult, but she finally pulled out a small cloth bag with a drawstring. She opened the drawstring and poured the contents onto the table under the hanging light. A dozen small, red stones scattered across the table's surface. Nina stared in astonishment. They must be rubies and therefore valuable. Why else would they be hidden? Retrieving her wallet from her purse, she took the stone found in the casino hallway and laid it alongside the others. Not an expert, she couldn't tell for sure, of course, but her stone looked identical to those concealed in the bird.

Nina sat back, folded her arms, and let her mind work on her discovery. Mark must have smuggled the stones. Gloria said he brought the sculpture to Parkers Landing on his recent flight. Did Oren know? Nina would guess not; otherwise, he would have insisted she return the sculpture at the memorial. What had Mark intended to do with the stones? Pass them along to a contact? Who?

Picking up the small piece of metal from the bird's bottom, she gave it closer scrutiny. Something about the shape was familiar. She studied the fragment a moment and then snapped her fingers. The metal looked similar to the piece she found among the flowers the day she and Stephen visited Rocky Ridge. She retrieved that fragment from her dresser drawer and compared the two metals. When she saw they were alike, a smile tilted her lips. Did the piece from the ridge come from one of the birds, too? If so, was that fact significant? Or coincidence?

Nina turned her attention again to the jewels. Now what should she do? Turn over her find to the police was the obvious answer. That they were hidden indicated probable illegal activity. She couldn't in good conscience keep the gems to herself. On her own, she might never discover who else was involved in the scheme. As much as she hated to give up the search, the time to contact Chief Cal Donovan had arrived.

Still, even after making her decision, she spent a restless night tossing and turning. The tin robin, mixed with an owl, a cardinal, and a crow, haunted her dreams. She awoke with a start, sitting straight up in bed, the room dark except for the glow of the bedside clock. The other tin sculptures weren't just figments of her dream imagination. She'd seen them somewhere before—on this trip, here in Parkers Landing.

She wracked her brain. Sparkles Jewelry had figurines, as did Val's Variety and…Race's Treasure Trove. Yes! She'd seen the sculptures in his store and could go there tomorrow. No, she should deliver the stones to Cal at the police station and let him handle the matter. But why not first check Treasure Trove, to make sure her memory was correct? She didn't want to give Cal false information and waste his time checking invalid leads. Just one more investigation on her own, and then she'd share her discovery with the authorities. She only hoped they would give the matter their full attention.

****

The following morning, Nina joined the family for breakfast, as usual. Thoughts of the valuable stones now in her possession kept her nerves on edge. She wished she could share her news with the others, but knew she must keep the secret until she turned over the matter to Chief Cal.

For several minutes, the conversation revolved around the children's activities.

Then Judy turned to Nina. "What do you and

Stephen have planned for today?" She shifted her gaze to her brother.

Stephen shrugged. "I don't have any special plans."

Nina touched her napkin to her lips and carefully composed her reply. "I still have a couple more souvenirs to buy."

"Okay, we can go shopping again." Stephen flashed a smile.

She wrinkled her forehead. "You don't have to come along." If she revealed her reason for visiting Treasure Trove, she'd have to tell him about discovering the stones, and then he would want her to go directly to Cal. To carry out her plan, she'd best be alone.

"Sure, I do." Stephen sipped his coffee.

His emphatic tone indicated his reluctance to give up. "Wouldn't you rather do something else on your own? Is there someone—an old friend—you'd like to visit? I can drive the spare car. Right?" She shifted her gaze toward Judy and then George. *Please say "yes."*

"Of course." Judy spread huckleberry jam on her toast.

George nodded. "You bet. The extra driving has been good for the car."

"All right." Stephen helped himself to another piece of bacon. "I'll drop in on Len at the newspaper. We always have something to talk about. Then you and I can meet for lunch."

Despite a niggle of guilt, Nina breathed a sigh of relief. "I like that plan. I'll text you when I'm ready to get together." From her room, she called the police station, asking to speak to Chief Cal.

"He's not in yet," the receptionist said. "But I can

make an appointment for later this morning."

Nina agreed, and they settled on eleven thirty. She would turn over the stones with her explanation and then meet Stephen. Over lunch, she'd fill him in on her discovery.

Everyone went separate ways.

The bus for Katie's camp arrived.

George left for the bank.

Ryan roared off on his motorcycle to his job at the garage.

A friend arrived to take Blaine to Greystone.

Judy went to a meeting of the Quilting Queens.

When the time came for Nina and Stephen to leave, he led the way to the garage. Once there, he reached for his car's door handle then stopped and turned. "Maybe I should go with you, after all."

"Oh, no." Nina smiled and made a dismissive wave. "I know my way around town now, and you'll have a nice visit with Len. We'll meet for lunch, like we planned."

"Well...okay. But if you'll be *sleuthing*, I want to be with you."

"I'll be *shopping*, like I told you." The evasion brought more feelings of guilt.

Stephen frowned. "I never know what to expect where you're concerned, Nina."

She gave what she hoped was a casual laugh. "I like to keep you guessing. Then you don't take me for granted."

He pressed his lips together. "You know what I mean."

"I do know." She touched his arm. "I'm only teasing. I'll be fine. Really."

She thought to secure the bag of stones and the metal robin in the car's trunk. But fearing Stephen would inquire what she took into town, after making sure his back was turned, she put them instead in the glove box. Then she led the way down the hill. Stephen stayed close behind. When she saw him turn off at the newspaper office, she took a relieved breath. An hour remained before her appointment to meet Cal. She intended to make good her declaration to shop, but first, she wanted to visit Race's Treasure Trove to see if her memory about the metal bird sculptures was correct.

Not finding a parking place on the street, she drove around the corner and spotted an alley. Recollection of what happened the last time she entered an alley sent a shiver down her spine. She needed a parking place, though, and if the alley was the only place available, she'd have to make do. Still, she glanced around to make sure no one lurked. Reaching the back of Race's store, she found an available space next to a red pickup truck.

Race was just climbing from the vehicle. He stood by the truck's door.

She lowered the window and leaned out. "Okay if I park here? I couldn't find a place on the street."

"Sure. You can come in the back door with me." He pointed past a couple dumpsters to a door that said "Treasure Trove."

After parking the car, Nina followed him inside and down a narrow hallway with storage rooms on either side. She glimpsed shelves loaded with boxes and an office furnished with desks and computers.

In the showroom, Race's employee, Dirk, helped a woman customer examine a set of dishes, while several other people browsed.

Race stopped at the entrance to one of the aisles and eyed Nina. "You looking for anything in particular?"

"No, just doing some last-minute shopping." Nina shrugged, striving to appear casual rather than on a mission.

Race stuck his hands in his slacks' pockets and tilted his head. "I suppose now Mark's memorial is over, you and Stephen will be leaving."

Was it her imagination, or did he look eager? Or perhaps relieved? "Yes, in two more days."

"Okay, I'll let you look around on your own. Holler if you need help." He turned and headed toward the checkout counter.

Nina casually inspected a display of embroidered pillowcases and hand towels and then approached the shelf where she recalled seeing the metal sculptures. Other figurines were displayed but not the birds. She searched the shelves nearby but still didn't see them. Now what? She'd have to ask. She didn't want to draw attention, but if she wanted to inspect the figurines, she must find them. She joined Race at the counter.

He looked up from sorting a stack of papers. "Need help, after all?"

She nodded. "When Stephen and I were here the other day, I saw metal sculptures of birds, but today I can't find them."

"I'll show you where they are." He stepped around the counter and led her to a corner crowded with furniture. "These what you're looking for?" He pointed toward a knick-knack shelf attached to the wall.

When she saw the familiar sculptures, Nina smiled,

but then she realized only two sat on the shelf, an owl and a crow, not the grouping she'd seen before. She turned toward Race. "These are the ones, but you must have sold some."

He shrugged. "Yeah. Popular item."

Nina picked up the owl, which had big, black eyes and feathers of curled copper. "This is heavier than it looks, being made of tin."

Race took the crow from the shelf. "A weight inside keeps it steady." He turned over the bird and pointed toward the underside's metal circle.

Were rubies the weight in these sculptures, as they were in the robin? Surely not. Still, just in case they were loaded with gems, she would purchase them for delivery to Cal. "I'll take these."

His eyebrows peaked. "Both of them?"

She handed him the owl. "I know someone who collects metal sculptures." *Right. Me—as of today.*

Race clutched the two birds. "I'll ring them up."

Nina followed him to the checkout counter.

He'd no more laid the sculptures on the counter when his phone buzzed. Pulling the phone from his shirt pocket, he looked at the screen and frowned. "I need to take this call. Dirk can finish your sale." He beckoned across the aisle toward Dirk and then headed for the hallway leading to the back of the store.

Dirk rounded the counter. "Sure. You buyin' these?" He gestured toward the birds.

Nodding, she fingered the owl's stiff feathers. "Are the sculptures a new item, or have you had them awhile?"

"New." Dirk pulled a sheet of brown wrapping paper from a roll under the counter.

Nina reached into her purse for her wallet. "Where do they come from?"

He shrugged. "Dunno. We get stuff from all over. Race has a lot of contacts."

I'll bet he does.

The transaction completed, Nina grasped the handles of the paper bag containing the birds. "I parked in the alley, so I'll go out that way." She pointed toward the hallway. "Thanks for your help today."

"You're welcome. See ya." Dirk waved a hand.

Traveling down the hallway, she heard Race's deep voice coming from the office. She slowed her steps and tilted her head toward the open doorway.

"Yeah, I'll be there…ready to make a delivery. I'm leaving now."

Nina ducked into a nearby storeroom just in time to avoid Race as he emerged from the office.

"Dirk! I'm going out," he called down the hall. "Back in a couple hours."

Nina remained hidden, holding her breath, hoping that before he left, he wouldn't visit the room where she hid. When she heard the sounds of his footsteps echoing along the hallway, she peeked out just in time to see him leave through the back door. A black briefcase was slung over his shoulder. A minute or so later, a truck's engine roared to life.

Hurrying to the door, Nina stepped out as Race pulled from his parking place and headed down the alley toward Main Street. She ran to her car, jumped in, and started the engine. She reached the end of the alley just in time to witness him turning left onto Main.

Allowing a couple cars to pass by, she too made the same turn. He was sure in a hurry. Why? She glanced at the dashboard clock. Still half an hour before her appointment with Chief Cal. She would follow Race for a few minutes and see where he went. Judging by his urgency to leave, he was on an important mission. "Ready to make a delivery," he'd said during the phone call. Something to do with rubies? Her pulse quickened.

Race made a few turns that led them out of the business district and to the edge of town. She soon realized he headed toward the highway and the bridge spanning the Kokuskie River. Would he go north? Or south? South led toward the state's interior, while north led to Canada. The bigger question was should she follow him? The dashboard clock indicated she now had only twenty minutes until her meeting with Cal. She could hang on a few minutes longer. Although, if she couldn't follow Race to his destination, what good would a few more miles do?

Despite her arguments to the contrary, she remained on his tail even when he took the entrance to the four-lane highway that led north. Keeping his red truck in sight was easy enough, and the added traffic helped to shield her as his pursuer. He traveled the highway for several miles and then exited onto a two-lane road leading toward farmlands and an occasional store or gas station. After another turnoff, she realized they were on the road that, if followed to the end, led to Rocky Ridge, where Stephen had his accident. Why would Race go there to meet the person from the phone call? Why meet in such a remote spot instead of in town at a coffee shop or a restaurant? Why didn't the person come to Race's store?

A glance at the clock told her that even if she

turned around now, she would be late to her appointment with Cal. She should call and cancel, but manipulating the phone on the winding road was risky. If she pulled off the road, she might lose Race.

Returning to town would make her late for her meeting, anyway. Maybe she wouldn't even get to see Cal. Better keep on Race's trail and explain later. Hopefully, she'd then have something important to tell the police chief.

Not wanting Race to realize he was being followed, she slowed to allow more distance between them while still keeping the truck in sight. Now, she was fairly certain where he was headed. The deserted cabin at the top of the cliff was a perfect place to meet his contact. She also had a good idea what the meeting was about. Recalling the metal sculpture fragment she found near the cabin—if it had come from one of the birds—indicated this trip was not Race's first to Rocky Ridge.

When she'd gone far enough to be certain the ridge was Race's destination, she pulled into the brush where the car would be hidden from the road, which had now become little more than a track. After locking her purse, the robin Gloria gave her, and the birds from Treasure Trove in the car's trunk, she headed toward the cliff, keeping to the cover of the bushes and trees. Except for the occasional chirp of a bird, all was silent. The air was heavy and dry and hot. Sweat trickled down her forehead, and thirst dried her throat.

Nina finally reached the cliff. The cabin came into view, with Race's truck parked in plain sight. Beyond and across the canyon, the mountains stood outlined against a deep blue sky. Still seeking cover in the bushes, she crept to within fifty feet of the cabin.

Through the window, she glimpsed Race sitting at the small table. He had his back to her, studying his cell phone. The black briefcase lay at his elbow. Was he waiting for someone? The person he'd spoken to at his store?

Now what? She certainly wouldn't confront him. She wanted only to be a witness and report what she saw to the authorities. She wished now she'd alerted Cal's office to this meeting. But would prior notice have done any good? She couldn't expect the police to marshal their forces just on what she surmised about Race.

The minutes crept by. Her legs cramped, and she shifted her position, only to cramp again. A persistent fly tickled her nose, making her want to sneeze. Sweat trickled down her forehead, and her throat was as dry as the ground underneath her feet.

She glanced away for a moment, and when she looked back at the window, Race had disappeared. Uh oh. She'd better keep him in sight. She crept forward, focusing on the window where she last saw him.

"Stop right there!"

The command came from behind. Nina jolted to a halt, and when she turned and saw who spoke, her heart did a flip-flop. "Lexie! What—" She moved her gaze from the woman's angry face to the gun she held, and Nina froze.

"Shut up!" Lexie stepped closer. A breeze caught her flyaway hair, swirling curls around her face, and lifted the collar of her blouse. Rumpled slacks were tucked into her leather boots.

Nina's anger blazed, drowning out her fear. "Are you in on this scheme? Do you know what Race is up to?" She waved toward the cabin.

"Of course, I know." Lexie's eyes narrowed. "Too bad you do, too. Why didn't you keep your nose out of our business?"

"What the hell are you two doing here?"

Race's voice rang as he marched across the clearing. He stopped, planted both hands on his hips, and stared at Lexie then at Nina.

"She followed you." Lexie tilted her head toward Nina.

Race frowned. "Is that true?"

Nina shook her head. "I'm not following you. I'm out for a ride in the country, sightseeing on my own before Stephen and I leave town." She nodded toward the canyon where a flock of birds flew across the sky.

"You're lying." Lexie kept the gun aimed on Nina. "I pulled into the alley behind the store and saw you drive off after Race." Her brows drew together in a frown. "You think you know everything, don't you, Nina?"

Seeing no point in continued denial and instead wanting to learn as much as she could, Nina lifted her chin. "I believe I do. I know about the smuggling."

Race stared. "How the hell—"

Nina turned to Lexie while from the corner of her eye, she searched for an escape route. "But I didn't know you were involved."

"You shouldn't be here, Lexie." Race scowled.

Lexie's mouth turned down. "How can you say that? I had to protect you."

"I don't need your protection." He stuck out his chin.

"But you said that after this job you'd have enough

money that we could—you know—be together." She
focused on Race.

Her voice carried a plaintive note that under less
threatening circumstances might have elicited Nina's
sympathy.

"Shut up, Lexie! You talk too much." Race tipped
his head in Nina's direction.

The pieces to the puzzle continued to fall into
place. Race was the mysterious man Lexie often
alluded to—her "love interest" who couldn't be with
her now but would be soon. He originally came to town
years ago because of her, but then he met and married
Tilda. Instead of ending his relationship with Lexie, he
kept her dangling, promising to divorce Tilda and
marry her after all. "So you're the one who poisoned
Mark," Nina said to Lexie.

"Poisoned Mark?" Race's eyes widened. "What is
she talking about?"

Lexie waved her free hand. "She's just babbling.
She knows nothing."

"Oh, but I do." Nina straightened her shoulders.
"You poisoned Mark with potassium bromate-laced
coffee because he discovered Race's smuggling. You
stole the poison from Tilda's salon—or from Lovin's
Bakery. I think it came from the salon, though, because
if the poison was detected, the police would suspect
Tilda. Then you also poisoned Drake Larken. He was in
on the smuggling, too, although I'm not sure how. I'm
surprised you don't have a cup of coffee for me."

"Don't listen to her, Race." Lexie took a step
forward. "But she knows too much about you now.
Let's get rid of her before Mickey comes."

The two stared at each other.

Nina edged backward toward the path. If she had a head start, she might escape. Just then, a branch under her foot crackled.

Lexie whirled and fired her gun.

The bullet zinged over Nina's head. Her heart pounding, she scurried toward the bushes.

Race ran after her and grabbed her arm. "You're not goin' anywhere."

Nina struggled, but Race's grip held, his strong fingers digging into her flesh.

Lexie grasped Nina's other arm with her free hand, and she and Race dragged her to the clearing. "Toss her over the edge." Lexie pointed her gun toward the cliff. "Nobody'll find her, and if they do, they'll think she fell."

"Can't we just offer her a little somethin'?" He squinted at Nina. "How much ya want to keep yer mouth shut?"

"Don't be stupid, Race." Lexie's voice shrilled. "She fancies herself a detective and wants to solve the so-called crime. Dump her into the canyon."

His brow furrowed, Race looked from Nina to the canyon and back again.

Nina held her breath, her heart continuing to thump in her ears.

Finally, he turned to Lexie. "All right, but put away that damn gun. If she's got a bullet in her, folks'll know it wasn't no accident."

Lexie scowled but stuck the gun in her slacks' pocket.

Nina eyed the edge of the cliff, and a cold chill traveled through her. No, she would not let them carry out their evil plan. Twisting and turning, she struggled to break free.

Lexie and Race held her in an iron grip. Dragging her by the arms, they headed toward the cliff's edge.

Dust clogged Nina's nose and mouth and blurred her vision. Still, she made out the canyon just inches away. Her heart raced, and nausea churned her stomach.

"Over she goes." Lexie's grip tightened around Nina's arm

"Wait." Race dug his heels into the dirt. "We gotta make sure it looks like she fell on her own. Turn her over. She's walkin' along the edge, see, and slips—"

Lexie pursed her lips. "Oh, shut up, Race. Just get on with it."

As Lexie and Race argued, their grips on Nina loosened. With a lunge, she broke free and rolled over on her stomach. Digging her palms into the dirt, she drew up her legs to rise to her knees.

"No, you don't!"

The sharp toe of Lexie's boot hit Nina in the side. Pain arrowed through her. She swayed, arms flailing, feet shuffling—and then tumbled over the cliff. "Noooo!" Her voice echoed into the chasm.

She skidded down the wall, clawing the earth, grasping at plants and rocks, anything her fingers brushed. Then her feet hit something solid. Ah, relief at last. Glancing down, she saw she'd landed on a rocky ledge, no wider than the length of her feet, but enough to stop her fall. She reached up and grabbed a branch, first with one hand and then with the other. Taking a deep breath, she dared to look up.

Lexie and Race leaned over the cliff's edge.

"That takes care of you, Miss Nosy." Lexie's eyes

gleamed.

"I dunno." Race twisted his lips. "She could climb out."

"Not a chance. She'll finally have to let go, and that'll be her end. C'mon, let's go back to the cabin, meet Mickey, and then get outa here."

"Okay... You're right, Lexie."

"Of course, I am. Aren't I always?" Lexie straightened and grabbed Race's arm, pulling him from the cliff's edge. The two disappeared, their voices fading away.

The top of the cliff was no more than an arm's length away, and yet, the distance might as well be a mile. Would Lexie and Race really leave her here? What about Mickey, the man Race was to meet? What would happen when he arrived?

Summoning all her strength, Nina clung to her safe harbor. Safe now, but for how long? Already her fingers ached from clutching the branch, and bit-by-bit, her weight crumbled pieces of the ledge. Her heart pounded, and sweat broke out on her forehead. She thought of Stephen and now knew firsthand the fear he experienced in his fall. But he had Mark to rescue him, while she had...no one. Too late she realized the mistake of not letting either Stephen or Chief Cal know her plans.

Time passed, with each sixty seconds an eternity. Except for the wind whistling through the canyon and the occasional tweet of a bird flying by, all was silent.

Then, from up above came the sounds of vehicle engines and car doors slamming. Mickey arriving?

"Stop! Hands up!" Several voices shouted.

The police must have arrived. How had they

known where to come? Who tipped them off? "Help!" she yelled but feared all that happened topside drowned out her pleas.

"Nina! Nina!"

Stephen's voice. Hope surged through her veins. "Here I am! Down here!" The wind swept away her words. She yelled again but heard more shouting and yelling above, and again feared her plea was lost. Her fingers ached from gripping the tree branch. Pain spiraled down her legs and into her feet. Her entire body felt as though she were on fire.

"Nina, I see you!" Stephen's voice drifted down. "No, don't look up. Hang on."

Nina tightened her grip on the branch, pain shooting through her fingers and along her arms. Then hands closed over her wrists.

"We've got you!"

A different voice. Chief Cal's?

Nina felt herself being lifted. When her feet left the ledge and she dangled in air, fear arrowed through her.

But her rescuers held on.

Soon, she gained another foothold to help propel herself over the top. Strong arms pulled her to her feet. Breathless and with heart pounding, she staggered and fell into Stephen's arms.

Chief Cal and Officer Tony Garcia stood nearby.

She looked over Stephen's shoulder to see two other officers guarding Lexie, Race, and a grim-faced man Nina assumed was Mickey.

Sullen and stony-faced, Race stared at the ground.

Lexie set her jaw and met Nina's gaze with narrowed eyes.

"I-in the cabin," Nina choked out. "B-briefcase."

"We have the briefcase." Stephen held her close. "Don't worry."

"W-what? How did you find me?"

"Shh." Stephen brushed the dirt from her cheeks and put a finger to her lips. "Explanations later. Right now, we need to get you to hospital."

"No, no, I'm f-fine." Nina struggled to stand upright, but her legs shook, and she fell against Stephen. Her hands stung from scraping rocks on her way down the cliff and then from hanging onto the tree branch.

"We're going." His firm tone brooked no argument.

"All right." She was so thankful to see him and to be safe. Many questions still needed answers, but discussion could wait. Right now, having Stephen take care of her was all she wanted.

Chapter Twenty

"This is one place in town I haven't visited." Lying on the bed in an emergency room cubicle in Mountain View Hospital, Nina looked first at Stephen and then at Cal. A doctor had examined her and determined that except for cuts and bruises—mainly on her hands, which were treated and bandaged—she was unharmed. No broken bones or internal injuries. The faint smell of antiseptic hung in the air. From outside the cubicle came the sounds of voices and shuffling feet as patients arrived for treatment.

Sitting at Nina's bedside, Stephen shifted in his chair. "I gladly could have skipped this visit."

Cal, who stood on the other side of the bed, waved a hand. "Gotta say, I come here all too often. But just answer me a few questions, and I'll leave you two alone."

"May I ask one first? How did you and Stephen know where to find me?" She switched her gaze toward Stephen.

Stephen leaned forward to pat her arm. "When you didn't call to meet for lunch, I phoned you. The call went to voice mail, and I left a message."

"You must have phoned after I parked at the ridge and locked my purse in the trunk."

"Ah, so that's why you didn't answer. Anyway, then Cal called and said you were late for an

258

appointment and hadn't returned his call. I didn't know anything about your meeting, but I worried something had happened. After waiting a while longer, I knew I had to find you. I used a locator app to track the location of your cell phone."

Nina widened her eyes. "Pretty smart, Mr. Kraslow."

He grinned and squeezed her arm. "Good thing you left your cell phone on and that I had your account number and passwords to allow the connection. When I saw you were at Rocky Ridge, I figured something that had to do with Mark sent you to the area. So I phoned Cal and told him. We decided to follow you and bring reinforcements—just in case. Sure glad we did."

"I'm glad, too." She offered up a prayer of thanks for Stephen and his quick thinking.

"So let me get this straight." Cal folded his arms and planted his feet apart. "You suspected the stones we recovered from the trunk of your car today were smuggled rubies, and you planned to turn them over to me when we met."

Nina nodded. "But I went to Treasure Trove first, to see if other bird sculptures were still for sale. I bought the two remaining ones, thinking they might be added evidence. When I overheard Race's suspicious phone conversation, I followed him. Once we were on the mountain road, I thought about calling both of you, but the road was too winding to focus on the phone. If I stopped to make the call, I was afraid he'd turn off somewhere, and I'd lose him. So I kept going. He ended up at the cabin at Rocky Ridge. I watched him through the window, and then Lexie appeared."

"You didn't know she tailed you?" Cal frowned.

"I was too intent on keeping Race in sight. She undoubtedly knew where he was headed and kept her distance. The guy you found with Race must have been the one he was meeting."

"Yeah, he's in custody, too." Cal shifted his feet. "But that's all I can say about him right now."

"Cal, Lexie poisoned Mark." At last, she could finally give the information to the right person.

The chief's eyes widened. "What?"

"With potassium bromate in old permanent wave solutions she stole from Tilda's salon."

"Why would she poison Mark?" Cal's brow wrinkled.

"To protect Race. Mark brought the rubies in his plane when he came for the reunion. I don't think he knew he was smuggling. But then one of the birds broke and he discovered the jewels. He confronted Race, either with threats to turn him in or to pay him for his silence."

Cal rubbed his chin. "Doesn't that theory point to Race as the poisoner?"

"Logically, yes." Nina smoothed her covers. "But I believe Lexie was the killer. She found out about Mark's threats and got rid of him to protect Race. He's been stringing her along all these years, promising they'd go away together. But Race acted surprised today when I accused her, so I don't think he knew she'd poisoned Mark."

"Okay, we'll consider your theory when we question Race and Lexie." Cal folded his arms. "I can see you've done a lot of thinking about Mark and how and why he died."

"I have. I also think Drake Larken was involved."

"You think he was poisoned, too?" Stephen leaned forward.

"I do. He was also involved in the smuggling." Nina ran a bandaged hand over her forehead. "Maybe he checked the stones to make sure they were genuine—for a cut in the profits, of course. He acted strangely when he examined a stone I found at the casino. He told me it was glass, but then he wanted to buy it. Maybe he threatened to expose Race, and Lexie also poisoned him. She gave both him and Mark coffee from Big Bear laced with the potassium bromate."

Cal raised a forefinger. "That reminds me about you being mugged in the alley. Was that after you saw Drake about the stone?"

"The same day. Why?" Nina hoped he had news of her attacker.

"A couple days ago, we arrested a kid for purse snatching. He confessed to a number of such crimes, including the one involving you. I intended to tell you when we met today."

"Really? Was something more behind his attack?"

"Uh huh. He told us Drake hired him to steal your purse and deliver it with the contents intact."

Nina's thoughts spun as she put together more pieces to the puzzle. "Drake wanted the stone. He saw me put it in my wallet."

"Could be. He didn't tell the kid why he wanted your purse. But if he was involved in the smuggling and your theory about Lexie is correct..." Cal shook his head. "Okay, what you've told me will take some sorting. You've given me enough for now, Nina, but we'll talk more later."

"Of course. Just let me know when you're ready."

Nina took a deep breath and leaned back against the pillows.

After Cal left, Stephen moved closer and clasped both her bandaged hands. "You've done a fine bit of sleuthing, Nina. I'm proud of you. And I'm also thankful you're safe."

"Thanks, Stephen." His words of praise warmed her. "I'm happy to be on solid ground again, too. Now I know what you experienced when you fell off the cliff." She shivered at the memory of nearly plunging to her death.

"When I saw you in that canyon, my heart almost stopped." Stephen leaned to kiss her forehead then drew back and brushed a lock of hair from her cheek. "But now, let's get you discharged. You will rest better at home."

The word "home" brought to mind her condo in Richmond. When trapped on the side of the cliff, she thought she'd never see home or her grandmother again. But of course, Stephen's "home" meant the Barlows', and, surprisingly, the term fit their house, too. She visualized sitting on the front porch, a glass of iced tea at her side, contemplating the view of the town and Greystone, the lazy flow of the Kokuskie River, and the highway leading north to Canada. She gazed at him, a smile on her lips. "Yes, Stephen, please take me home."

****

Nina sat in the swing on the Barlows' porch, enjoying the afternoon breeze. Stiff and sore from yesterday's ordeal at Rocky Ridge, she was thankful to rest today. Yesterday had also been busy bringing the Barlows up to date with all that happened. As word spread around town, their phone rang with callers wanting to know more but also inquiring about Nina's welfare. She appreciated all the concern. Parkers Landing truly was a friendly town.

Stephen stepped onto the porch, tucking his phone into his shirt pocket. "I just talked to Cal." He sat beside Nina, pulling her into an embrace.

Glad for his affection, she snuggled close to his shoulder. "Are Race and Lexie still in jail?"

"They are, and a search of Lexie's home turned up boxes from the permanent wave kits that Tilda identified are from Curly Locks. The bottles containing the potassium bromate were empty."

"Wow. Stupid of Lexie to keep the evidence of her crimes."

Stephen patted her shoulder. "I agree. But when Cal confronted her with their discovery, she broke her silence and talked."

"What did she say?" Eager for more news, Nina straightened and faced him.

"She confirmed your theory. As a favor to Race, Mark brought the birds containing the rubies when he flew up for the reunion. He didn't know he was smuggling until he unloaded the boxes and one broke open. A bird was damaged, and he found the stones. He figured out Race was smuggling and threatened to expose him if he didn't get a cut of the profits."

Sadness filled Nina to hear Stephen's treasured friend was indeed a blackmailer. Still, having her theory confirmed brought satisfaction. "He wanted the money to save FlyGuys."

"Right, much as I hate to admit Mark would stoop to blackmail." Stephen drew in a breath. "Anyway, when Lexie found out, she plotted to get rid of Mark. The money Race made from smuggling was supposed to take her and Race away from Parkers Landing. Or so Race promised. Of course, he denies ever promising her anything."

Nina thinned her lips. How disgusting. Race and Lexie were a sorry pair. She could imagine what Tilda experienced, now she knew of her husband and her friend's betrayal.

"Lexie was the person who told you to "get out of town" at the street dance. She heard you informed Cal of your suspicions about Mark being poisoned."

Nina brought her attention back to Stephen's news. "Did Lexie tell Cal how Drake Larken was involved?"

Stephen pressed his foot to the floor and set the swing in motion. "She did. Before confronting Race, Mark took one of the stones to Drake to make sure it was a ruby. He didn't know Drake had been verifying the rubies for Race or that Race had ended the arrangement, telling Drake he was no longer smuggling."

"How did he know the ruby I found was one Race smuggled?" Nina knit her brow.

"With his expertise, he knew it came from Myanmar, the same area as the previous stones he'd examined. He called Race and demanded to be let in on the action again, or else he would go to the police. Race promised to include him, but Lexie didn't trust Drake to keep quiet, so she poisoned him, too."

Nina shook her head. Such greed in a small town. "How bold of her to use the potassium bromate from the permanent wave solutions again."

Stephen nodded. "Just like you figured, she thought

if the poison was identified, Tilda would be suspect."

"Did Cal find out who argued with Mark at the Meet-and-Greet?"

"Yep. Race. Mark followed Race to the men's room, with more threats to turn him in unless Race paid him off. Race told him he was a "dead man" if he exposed him." Stephen snapped his fingers. "Oh, I almost forgot the other big news. The coroner tested Mark for potassium bromate and, sure enough, traces were found. They plan to exhume Drake and test him, too."

"Sounds as though the case is about wrapped up." Nina sat back and relaxed into the swing's rhythm. "I'm sorry you had to find out Mark blackmailed Race."

Stephen tightened an arm around her shoulders. "Me, too. But I understand how his need to save FlyGuys could drive him to crime. The company was his heart and soul. His action doesn't change my gratitude for him saving me that day at Rocky Ridge."

"Of course not. I, too, will be forever grateful to him for rescuing you."

A few moments of silence slid by, then Stephen gave her shoulder a squeeze and drew her closer. "Well, Nina, you helped to solve another crime. You're becoming a real pro."

She nestled into the curve of his arm. "You're okay with my detecting?"

He ran a forefinger along her cheek and then lightly kissed her lips. "As long as you let me help. I'm here for you."

"Thank you, Stephen. I'm so thankful for your support." Nina gave thanks, too, that she had helped to discover the truth about Mark's and Drake's deaths.

Righting wrongs and restoring order—those ideals were what her sleuthing was all about.

****

The following morning, Nina sat beside Judy as she drove them to a Museum Mommas' meeting.

"I'm so glad you could be here for today's get together." Judy steered the car down the hill toward town.

Nina turned from gazing out the window at the homes they passed and furrowed her brow. "I'm pleased, too, although I'm also a little uncomfortable. How will the others feel about my exposing one of your group as a murderer?"

"I'm sure once they get over the shock, they'll be grateful. I know I am."

Still, when Nina and Judy arrived at the museum and reached the meeting room, Nina slowed her steps.

Judy grasped her arm and drew her forward. "Come on, Nina. The meeting will be just fine."

Inside the room, Mary Ellen, Mona, Della, and Selene stood in a tight group drinking coffee and eating doughnuts. When Nina approached, they drew apart and crowded around her.

"We're so relieved you're okay." Mona's forehead wrinkled, and she pressed her turquoise-ringed fingers against her lips.

"I've hiked at Rocky Ridge." Mary Ellen gestured with her free hand. "The cliff is a scary place."

"You were so brave." Della slowly shook her head. "I never could have done what you did."

Mona brought Nina a cup of coffee.

Mary Ellen held out a plate of miniature doughnuts, each one resting in a paper muffin cup. "Try my new creation—hazelnuts and honey."

"Thanks, Mary Ellen." Nina picked up a doughnut, inhaling the sweet scent. The memory of seeing the potassium bromate in the bakery storeroom flashed through her mind, but, remembering that the baking process rendered the bromate harmless, she relaxed and bit into the doughnut. The combination of nuts and honey tasted delicious. "Mmm, wonderful."

The women chatted a few more minutes, and then Selene motioned everyone to the table. "Time to start the meeting."

Once the group was seated, Selene tapped her gavel. "The meeting of the Museum Mommas will please come to order." She turned to Nina. "We're so glad to have Nina with us today and sorry about what happened to her at Rocky Ridge. We are shocked to learn about Race and Lexie."

Della folded her arms and sniffed. "I'm not surprised. I saw them together in Sandpoint too often to be a coincidence and suspected they were carrying on."

Mary Ellen nodded. "I spotted them, too, in Coeur d'Alene. Lexie told me they were just old friends, but I knew they were more. She never accepted his marriage to Tilda."

Realizing she hadn't yet seen the beauty salon owner, Nina looked around. "Where is Tilda?"

"She's with her daughter and family." Selene laid her gavel on the table. "She's quite shaken, as you can imagine."

The door flew open. Along with the others, Nina turned to see the new arrival.

Oswald Farrington the Third stood in the doorway, feet planted apart, both hands on his hips, and with his leather briefcase slung over a shoulder. A smile lighted his long, thin face.

Nina tensed. What now? The man was so unpredictable.

"I have reached the end of my search." His gaze swept the group. "I have found my roots."

"How nice for you." Selene's lips thinned. "But we are in the middle of our meeting—"

Oswald waved a hand. "I know. Your meeting is why I came to tell you all my wonderful news." He stepped farther into the room. "Thanks to the information provided by your museum archives, plus the folks at whosmydaddy.com, who analyzed my DNA, I am proud to announce that I am a direct descendant of Phineas Parker, for whom this town was named. I have the documentation to prove the lineage." He patted the briefcase.

Silence greeted his announcement.

Nina, too, felt a stunned surprise. Who would have guessed?

Oswald's eyebrows peaked. "Aren't you going to congratulate me?"

Everyone exchanged glances then looked toward Selene.

Along with the others, Nina waited for their leader's guidance.

"Of course, we're happy for you, Mr. Farrington…" Selene scooped up her stack of papers and tapped them into alignment. "Now you can return to Montana."

Oswald waggled a forefinger. "No, no, no. I'm staying right here. I have big plans for our town. I've already commissioned a life-size statue of Phineas to be placed at the river where he had his ferrying service."

Della coughed into her handkerchief.

Mona shaded her eyes with a ring-laden hand.

Mary Ellen made "tsk-tsk" noises and shook her head.

Selene glared.

Covering her mouth with her hand to suppress a laugh, Judy exchanged a look with Nina.

Nina shrugged. Oswald's memorial gift sounded like a generous gesture. Why did everyone appear so upset?

He took a few more steps into the room. "I have plans for the museum, too. I've already discussed with Director Hal about establishing a Phineas Parker room."

More choking sounds from the group.

Oswald pulled out a chair and sat. He looked around. "Now, what else is on today's agenda?"

Selene introduced other items of business, but the group gave little or no response, and none of her efforts were met with success. Finally, she declared the meeting adjourned.

Once Nina and Judy were in the car and on their way to the Barlows', Nina asked the question that puzzled her. "Why was everyone so upset about Oswald's plans for honoring Phineas Parker? I can understand not being particularly happy about Oswald staying in town, but his projects regarding Parker should appeal."

"Not really." Judy shook her head. "Phineas Parker was a notorious drunk and womanizer. I'm surprised Oswald could establish his lineage, even with the wonders of DNA testing. How Phineas got the town named after him is a mystery. We have a standing committee that every year petitions to change the town's name, but the citizens can't agree on a new name, so nothing's done."

"Looks like you're stuck with Oswald."

Judy's smile was grim. "I'm guessing he won't stay long. He's the kind who flits from one thing to another. Once winter sets in, he'll be gone."

Nina wasn't so sure. Judging from what she'd seen, when Oswald set his mind to something, he persevered. But then, she could be wrong. Time would tell.

****

That afternoon, Nina, Stephen, and David joined the Barlows at the library for the Story Mates' program. The puppet theater, complete with curtained stage, stood ready for the animated stories. Lively background music added to the festive atmosphere.

Presently, the music faded, and Cora Wilson appeared. She wore a long, navy-blue dress decorated with silver stars and moons. A sorcerer's conical hat sat atop her dark curls. "Welcome, everyone." She waved a wand over the crowd. "We have a very special program for you—fairy tales from around the world told by our wonderful Story Mates."

First presented was the tale of *Cinderella*, told using stick puppets. Then came a musical version of *The Three Bears*, with the storytellers wearing finger puppets. Two more acts followed and, finally, Katie's turn arrived. The pig hand puppets Nina helped make illustrated the story perfectly, and Katie's voice changes for each character brought squeals and laughter from the audience.

When the story was over, Katie popped up behind the stage, a puppet on each hand, to take a bow.

The audience cheered and clapped.

Nina felt as proud as if Katie were her own child.

A reception featuring punch and cookies followed. Nina and Cora found a moment to chat.

"I'm so glad we got acquainted." Cora sipped her punch. "I wish we had more time to get to know each other."

Nina selected a chocolate chip cookie from the refreshment table. "Will you be attending the librarians' conference in Oregon next spring?"

"Why, yes, I'd planned to go." Cora bit into her cookie.

"Me, too. How about sharing a room?"

"I'd like that, Nina."

Nina smiled, always glad to connect with a colleague. Even in the short time she'd known Cora, she felt a strong bond. Despite the distance that separated them, she had no doubt the friendship would continue to grow and flourish.

****

Later that afternoon, still mindful of her injured hands, Nina folded and tucked a blouse into her suitcase and shut the lid. She was all packed and ready to go. Tomorrow, she and Stephen headed back to Richmond. Feeling a tug of anticipation, she picked up her cell phone and called Jessica, happy when her grandmother's smiling face filled the screen.

"I can hardly wait to see you." Jessica clasped her hands together. "Is the mystery all solved?"

"Most of the questions have been answered. I'll fill you in when I return." Nina was reluctant to tell Jessica all the details of her ordeal, but in the end, she knew she would. She wasn't one for keeping things from her grandmother, even though she knew Jessica would be distressed to learn that while solving the mystery of Mark's death she almost met her own.

Nina and Jessica chatted a few minutes longer before saying goodbye. "See you soon," Nina promised.

She then joined the Barlows in the dining room for the evening meal.

David was present, too.

Once they all were seated, Judy tapped a spoon against her water glass. "Tonight is a special occasion to honor our two new family members." She gestured toward David, sitting on one side of Stephen, and then toward Nina, on his other side. "David and Nina, we are so happy to welcome you into our family. May this visit be the first of many."

"Hear! Hear!" The others cheered and clapped.

Touched by Judy's words and the family's enthusiastic agreement, Nina felt the tears well up. "Thank you all for welcoming me and for—for putting up with me and my—my—" She searched for the right word.

Stephen grinned. "Meddling?"

George held up a hand. "Not meddling, Stephen. Nina's actions are better defined as her determination to right a wrong."

"Thank you, George." Nina sent him a grateful smile.

"Well said." Stephen nodded toward his brother-in-law and then turned to Nina. "You know I was only teasing, don't you, honey? I'm very proud of you." He leaned to plant a kiss on her cheek.

Warmth filled Nina, and, yes, she knew he only teased. From the very beginning of their relationship, he'd supported her sleuthing.

David looked around the table. "I've had a great time with Stephen and all of you. You're the best."

"Thank you both for the tributes." George raised his water glass. "Here's to family."

The others raised their glasses. "To family," they chorused.

A family composed of many people was not part of Nina's experience. Could she be a member of this one? Of course, the answer depended on her and Stephen's future. For the present, she believed their relationship would continue and so accepted the Barlows' invitation to be considered family.

Later, she and Stephen enjoyed their coffee on the porch, sitting together in the swing. "Our last night." Nina leaned her head against Stephen's shoulder.

"For now, but not forever." He squeezed her hand. "We'll be back. You'll see."

"I hope so."

After awhile, the door opened, and Katie appeared.

"Come sit with us." Stephen patted the seat beside him.

Katie climbed up, and Stephen put an arm around her shoulders. Nina settled back, too, listening to the crickets and the distant sounds of an occasional passing car. From the garage came the voices of Rick, Blaine, and David, who inspected Rick's motorcycle. From the house's open front door drifted the low drone of the TV. All familiar sounds, and all comforting.

After a while, Katie leaned around Stephen and looked at Nina. "Can I ask you something, Nina?"

Nina turned her attention to the child. In the dim porch light, her eyes reflected anticipation as well as uncertainty. "Sure. What's on your mind?"

"Is it okay if I call you *Aunt* Nina?"

"Aunt." Nina let the word roll over her tongue as warmth and affection for Katie filled her. "Of course, you can, Katie. I'm honored to be your aunt."

"Goody." Katie clapped her hands. "Next time you come, can we make more puppets?"

"Definitely. I'll look forward to that occasion." She hoped Stephen was right and that there would be a next time. The Barlows and the town of Parkers Landing were firmly embedded in her heart.

****

At eight o'clock the following morning, after eating breakfast and then bidding the family a final goodbye, Nina sat beside Stephen in his car as he drove them from Parkers Landing.

"Leaving early will allow us to make good time. The traffic's not peaked yet." Stephen pointed toward the four-lane highway ahead where only a few cars traveled in either direction.

Nina stifled a yawn. "Better have more coffee, though." She pulled the flask from the insulated pack and refilled their cups anchored in the cup holder. With the flask stashed away, she sipped her hazelnut coffee while gazing at the passing scenery. Farmlands in full summer bloom filled either side of the road. In one, a farmer steered a tractor through a field of hay, while in another, cows grazed under a stand of birch trees. Still another farm included an apple orchard with fruit ripening in the sun. Mountains framed the scene, stretching their snow-capped peaks into a bright blue sky.

A couple hours later, Nina spotted the sign that

read *Welcome to Washington State*. She cast Stephen a glance. "Are you sorry to leave Idaho?"

"I'll always be fond of my original home, but remember the old saying 'home is where the heart is'? Now, my heart's in Richmond, with you." He took a hand from the steering wheel and patted her arm.

She laid a hand over his. "I'm glad, Stephen. Thank you." With Stephen's words of reassurance, she turned her thoughts to the days ahead. "The weekend's coming up. Are we staying at your place or mine? I've lost track of our schedule."

"I have, too, but let's stay at my place. Except for Sunday dinner at Jessica's."

Sundays spent with her grandmother had become traditional. Nina always looked forward to their time together. She was eager to return to work at the library, too. She missed her colleagues and the interaction with the patrons, which she always enjoyed.

The future would not be without challenges, however. David would visit at Christmastime. Plus, the question of whether or not she and Stephen would take their relationship to a more permanent level hovered in the background. What if another mystery to solve came her way? Would she accept the challenge?

For now, though, she savored the moment and being with the man she loved. She settled back to enjoy the rest of the trip home.

A word about the author...

A resident of the Pacific Northwest, Linda Hope Lee writes contemporary romance, romantic suspense, and mystery novels. She also enjoys watercolor painting, photography, collecting children's books and anything to do with wire-haired fox terriers.

Visit her at:

www.lindahopelee.com

Also by the author

Standalones

Dark Memories

Under Gemini

Nina Foster Mysteries

Murder Between the Pages

Secrets to Die for

Red Rock, Colorado series

Finding Sara

Loving Rose

Marrying Molly

Thank you for purchasing
this publication of The Wild Rose Press, Inc.

For questions or more information
contact us at
info@thewildrosepress.com.

The Wild Rose Press, Inc.
www.thewildrosepress.com

www.ingramcontent.com/pod-product-compliance
Lightning Source LLC
Chambersburg PA
CBHW051533260626
47170CB00003B/909